COMRAICH

ALSO BY SHANI STRUTHERS

JESSA*MINE*

EVE: A CHRISTMAS GHOST STORY
(PSYCHIC SURVEYS PREQUEL)

PSYCHIC SURVEYS BOOK ONE:
THE HAUNTING OF HIGHDOWN HALL

PSYCHIC SURVEYS BOOK TWO:
RISE TO ME

PSYCHIC SURVEYS BOOK THREE:
44 GILMORE STREET

PSYCHIC SURVEYS BOOK FOUR:
OLD CROSS COTTAGE

PSYCHIC SURVEYS BOOK FIVE:
DESCENSION

BLAKEMORT
(A PSYCHIC SURVEYS COMPANION NOVEL BOOK ONE)

THIRTEEN
(A PSYCHIC SURVEYS COMPANION NOVEL BOOK TWO)

THIS HAUNTED WORLD BOOK ONE:
THE VENETIAN

THIS HAUNTED WORLD BOOK TWO:
THE ELEVENTH FLOOR

COMRAICH

SHANI STRUTHERS

Comraich

Authors Reach
www.authorsreach.co.uk

ISBN: 978-0-9957883-3-6

For Julia Tugwell – a wonderful sister-in-law.

Acknowledgements

Writing a book is a far from lonely profession. So many people help me craft my books, from beta readers to editors and proofreaders. Thank you in particular to Robert Struthers, Louisa Taylor, Sarah Savery, Lesley Hughes, Julia Tugwell and mother and daughter duo, Alicen and Millie Haire – your input is invaluable. Also thanks to my editor, V K McGivney and Gina Dickerson for yet another wonderful cover and formatting. Thanks also to Authors Reach, the publishing company owned by its authors – check us out online – www.authorsreach.com - and discover other books you might enjoy. Last but never least, thank you to the readers, many of whom have written to me to tell me how much they enjoyed Jessa*mine* and that they'd love to read a sequel. I wasn't planning on writing a follow-on, but because of you I did – I hope you like it.

Prologue

IT was snowing again. Beth watched as countless white flakes spiralled downwards, as graceful as ballerinas, as ethereal as angels, beautiful and pure. Extending a hand to touch the window, she registered how gnarled her hand had become rather than the icy cold that nipped at the tips of her fingers. How many years had passed since that day at the loch? So many. Decades in fact, and yet it felt like no time at all. The pain had never lessened, but grown, filling every crevice of her heart. Guilt, sorrow and anger. Oh, especially the anger! Back then it had been like a vice.

The same hand now covered her mouth. This cough was getting worse. She knew it and Stan knew it. 'Beth,' he'd say if he were to come into the room and catch her sitting by the window, 'come away, it's too cold for you there. Och, come on, lass," he'd insist. "I'll tell you what, I'll make us a cup of tea. I'll bring some shortbread up as well. We can have a natter.'

A natter? What about? These days, only one thing dominated her mind and neither of them wanted to talk about that.

Finally the coughing subsided, although she was left short of breath because of it. No matter. Stan wasn't in the room to fuss and she wasn't going to move. Instead, she inclined her head and continued to peer through the frosted pane; her faded blue eyes searching the white landscape beyond.

Was he out there? Was she? The two of them together as they always were, as they should have been? She hoped so. In life she might have torn asunder, but she prayed, night after night, that death had put right what had gone so wrong. Because he was dead too: Mally. Stan had found out about their former friend, had confirmed it, but nonetheless she'd felt it in her bones. He'd gone to join her sister, Flo, at last, hence the reason she sat here, day after day, as soon as Stan had left the room, because she wanted so desperately to see them reunited. *Please be together, please.* So often those words would repeat in her mind. That and '*sorry*'.

Why had she lived so long when they hadn't? It was unfair. An injustice. She hadn't wanted to live, but she'd been too afraid to end her misery and meet the fate that surely awaited her. And so she'd lived, *half-lived*, and Stan had half-lived alongside her, another life ruined. There'd only been one burst of happiness – when Kristin was born – she was such a bonny wee thing, with such an abundance of hair. And then she was taken too, her body ravaged by cancer, and so young. Without her, Beth went careering into old age – a death of sorts she supposed, one so slow as to be torturous.

I'll die soon, though. The final reckoning is almost here.

Flo and Mally, were they lying in wait, but creeping closer, year by year, month by month? Soon they'd re-enter the walls of Comraich to stand over her bed, no longer just shadows, but as they used to be. Not quite as they used to be, maybe not at all, fury having twisted their souls.

At that thought, that vision, Beth screwed her eyes shut. She was the reason for their fury. Stan had stood by her all these years, had kept her secret. But there was so much he didn't know. If he did, would he have continued to stand by her?

Her eyes flitted towards the bureau in the far corner of the room. That's where her secrets were, her life – such as it was – laid bare. Only recently had she started to write it all down. Perhaps that was unwise and it should stay locked within, but the burden she carried, it weighed so heavy sometimes. So she'd sat and the words had formed, they'd poured from her, to be locked away again each night, hidden once more. Maybe Stan would find what she'd written when she was gone, maybe not.

It wasn't just her hand that was cold now from where she'd touched the window, her entire body was shivering. She'd have to rise soon and return to bed or Stan would indeed catch her. Once a meeting place, this house had become a self-imposed prison. In Stan's room, which she no longer shared, wanting as much solitude as possible in latter years, she, Flo and Mally used to gather; here they'd laugh and rib each other, making plans for the future.

At that memory, a brief smile chased away at least some of her weariness. Oh, the things that they were going to do! What they were bound to achieve! The four of them best friends since their first days at the village school. She and Flo more than that; twins. On the surface identical, but underneath, what a difference! Rarely had the darkness found Flo. Not whilst she'd been breathing at least.

A sob replaced her smile as she rose, stiff joints screaming with the effort. Flo and Mally weren't outside, not yet, but they would be.

Comraich was Gaelic for Sanctuary, but soon there'd be sanctuary no more.

Chapter One

"DEAR God, Jessamin, you weren't joking when you said you were busy!"

"Do you like it, the colour I mean? *Winter Willow* is the name on the tin, it's supposed to be a sort of sage green. It suits the house, don't you think? It's meant to be …" Jessamin took a step back and focused on the wall in front of her, "…*soothing*."

Maggie also pondered. She stood next to Jessamin in the living room of Comraich – a *pregnant* Jessamin, five months of her term having passed already – and rubbed at her chin. "Aye, it is, it's very soothing. But if Finn comes in and catches you on top of a ladder just as I did, he'll be furious. Can you not get Rory to help? He's a dab hand at decorating, he did the shop for me a couple of years ago."

"Rory?" Jessamin's green eyes sparkled as she laughed. "As happy as he is with Shona, he'll still insist on staring at me all doe-eyed, so no, I think I'll give Rory a miss. I am taking it easy though, honestly. Besides, I'm pregnant, not incapable."

Maggie laughed too. "Och, lass, I meant nothing by it. But you know what Finn's like. I'm surprised he's letting you climb ladders at the moment, that's all."

"Actually," Jessamin winced as she confessed, "he doesn't

know. He got up early this morning to go to Inverness to sort out some lease details on one of the estate cottages, and I got up early too, to do this. Oh Christ, Maggie, I hope he likes it. It's just… it needed doing. I love this room but if you looked, really looked, it was a little bit on the dingy side. I wanted to make it warmer, cosier, you know?"

"It's that nesting instinct," Maggie replied. "It's kicking in good and proper."

She was right – it was. This house Jessamin lived in – Comraich – with the soon-to-be father of her child, Fionnlagh Maccaillin, historically the Laird of this land hereabouts, was home, truly home. She adored it and had done from the day she'd first set foot in it almost four years earlier when she'd come looking for Finn, then her landlord, concerning a temperamental boiler, and had found his grandfather, Stan, instead. She'd adored him too, the pair of them striking up a ready friendship. Not so much with his grandson, not initially. Finn had been offhand, brusque even. But there'd been reason for that, and reason why her actions had mirrored his. But with Stan it had been easy from the start and in this living room their friendship had blossomed. It was here she'd listen to him talk about Comraich, and his life within it.

The walls that she was trying to brighten – there'd been so much loss experienced within them, in this once formidable hunting lodge that stood on the edge of an equally formidable moor in the remote Highland village of Glenelk. But now new life was about to be born into it. The day she'd found out she was pregnant she'd barely been able to breathe with the surprise of it. Finn had been the same.

"How did that happen?" he'd asked.

"I'll give you three guesses," had been her somewhat wry

reply.

Along with the pregnancy had come the urge to push aside something of what lingered still; not the memories, but a melancholy that at times was like a shroud.

Maggie, who'd once confessed to Jessamin she had a talent for sometimes being able to catch thoughts, clearly caught the gist of what was careering through Jessamin's mind. Gently, she laid a hand on her arm and smiled.

"It's amazing what a lick of paint can do, but hand me a brush, because no way am I allowing you to climb that ladder again. You can leave the high tops to me."

"Maggie, no, I couldn't ask—"

"Och, I'll not be dissuaded. And no more shifting furniture either, leave that to me too. It's a surprise we want to give Finn, not the shock of his life."

Gratefully conceding, Jessamin handed Maggie a brush, and watched as she discarded the coat she'd been wearing and rolled up the sleeves of her blue checked shirt to get stuck in. She was such a dear friend, someone who'd welcomed her to the village with open arms when she'd arrived; who had over the course of time helped her to let go of the loss that had driven her here in the first place, every bit as much as Finn had helped her. How she'd wanted to stop the world from turning back then, step off the ride – an impossible thing to do in a busy city such as Brighton – but here, in the vast wilderness of the Highlands, *anything* was possible. Looking down at her burgeoning stomach, she was still learning that.

The hours passed, both of them working attentively, stopping every now and again for a fortifying mug of tea and a sandwich at lunchtime. As they toiled at the room where Stan used to sit by the fire, where she would sit with him, admiring the artwork on the walls, pictures painted by Stan who was a revered artist in his day, Maggie did the lion's share of chattering.

"Lenny's due home from the rigs in a few days. Och, be still my beating heart!"

"How long's he back for?"

"Near enough three months instead of the usual twenty-one days. Some of it's unpaid, but most of it isn't actually, it's an accumulation of all the holiday he's accrued that he never used to take." She sighed a little guiltily before adding, "You know, that he said he had no *reason* to take."

Lenny and Maggie had been together years before, but Maggie had ended the relationship, her love for him diminished by the love she felt for Finn, whom she'd known since childhood – a love Finn claimed he was unaware of. Not that it would have been reciprocated. Maggie, a motherly figure despite having no children of her own, was a friend in his eyes – his *best* friend, someone who'd taken him under her wing when he was at school; the shy, bewildered boy from the big house who'd lost both his mother and his father when he was still so young. Her love and the love of his grandfather had got Finn through his formative years, but as soon as he could, he'd left the village, joined the army, and broken Maggie's heart; broken a fair few of the girls' hearts around here, according to Maggie. However, his experience in the army had changed him and he was no longer the Lothario he might have been in his youth. He had returned a mellowed and wiser man, a one-woman man, and that woman was now Jessamin. Maggie declared that she was over Finn and had since rekindled her love affair with Lenny. From the excited way she talked about him, Jessamin believed she was telling the truth.

"Do you know what?" Maggie continued, a blob of green paint flicking off the brush to land on her nose. "I think there's another reason Lenny wants extended shore leave."

A roller in hand now, Jessamin paused. "Oh? Why?"

"C'mon, Jess, *think*."

"Erm... Okay, hang on; give me a minute, could it be... Is it? Oh Christ, Maggie, he wants you to marry him, doesn't he?"

Maggie didn't seem to care that she was hugging the paint-brush to her. "I think he does!"

Jessamin bridged the gap between them to hug her, getting paint over them both. "Oh, Maggie! I'm thrilled for you."

As both women were squealing, they hadn't realised some-one else had entered the room – someone staring at them in a mystified fashion.

"Is this a private party or can anyone join in?"

It was Finn, tall, broad and dressed in what Jessamin always thought of as his 'Highland uniform' – a green waxed jacket, khaki trousers and Timberland boots. Although his right eye was covered by an eye patch, hiding damage sustained in the army, she could tell how aghast he was, not just because she and Maggie were hugging and squealing, but at the state of the room too. "Well, well, well," he muttered, "this is somewhat different to how I left it."

"Maggie's getting married!" Jessamin declared, unable to stop herself.

Maggie at once admonished her. "I said I *think* I might be getting married. Lenny's yet to propose."

"Oh he will, you know he will. Isn't it great, Finn?"

Finn ran a hand through dark hair that had been slightly dishevelled by the wind. "It is," he enthused. "It's the best news I've heard all day."

Striding across the room, he in turn hugged Maggie, whose eyes glistened slightly when they eventually parted. "Och, look at you," she said, waving a hand in his general direction, "you've gone and got paint on your coat."

He had, but it was so small as to be microscopic – as per usual, his old friend was fussing over him. Accepting this in good grace, Finn walked over to Jessamin, and put his arms around her. "So you've taken to decorating in my absence?"

Her uncertainty increased. "Is that okay? I thought I'd surprise you."

"*Another* surprise? You're getting good at that."

"Finn," she said, impatient for his response.

"I like it, I do. Who's climbing the ladder?"

"It's me, Finn," Maggie informed him. "Although neither of us are touching the ceiling, we've both decided that can stay as it is."

Jessamin bestowed a quick grateful smile on Maggie for saving her. "I just want to get things spruced up a bit, you know, before the baby. I love this house, but—"

"It needs cheering," Finn interrupted. "It always has."

"So you're not angry?" Jessamin double-checked. After all, this was his home, hers now too of course, but only for the past year – Finn's heritage was here.

"Jess," he murmured, that gaze of his always so intent, "I don't mind you redecorating, what I do mind is you being the one to do it. You've been up that ladder, I know you have." Briefly he addressed Maggie. "Just so you're aware, your left eye twitches when you're lying." Ignoring Maggie's gaping mouth, he went on to suggest, as Maggie had, that Jessamin hired the local handyman, Rory, to help her, or that he himself would help in between running the estate, ceilings included. "I don't want anything happening to you." Touching her stomach, he added, "Either of you."

Maggie made a show of being affronted. "And why am I not being considered for the job? Have I not proved my painting prowess enough today?"

"But what about the shop?" Jessamin replied, referring to the village shop which Maggie owned and ran with brisk efficiency.

"Aye, true," she sighed, "that does rather tend to take up all my time. Still, I've enjoyed this, it's made a nice change." She glanced at her watch. "I'm going to have to run I'm afraid. I've a call due from Lenny soon, on the home phone."

"No problem," replied Jessamin. "I was going to suggest we call it a day anyway."

"Are you coming to The Stag tomorrow evening, either of you? Maidie's having a bit of a knees-up."

"What's she celebrating?" enquired Finn.

"Her divorce from Ewan. It was finalised today."

Both Jessamin and Finn burst out laughing.

"She doesn't waste any time, does she?" declared Finn.

Maggie agreed. "But God bless her she's happy, the best I've seen her in a long while, that's for sure." Her eyes widened. "It seems to be fresh starts all round in Glenelk, doesn't it? For Maidie; for you two with your bairn on the way – I'm still betting it's a boy by the way, Jess, even though you think it's a girl; for me too hopefully and, of course," she gestured to the room around her, "for Comraich."

"Aye, aye, it is," said Finn and his voice held a wistful quality as his gaze lingered on the fireplace, where he once stoked the fire to warm his grandfather's bones.

Jessamin noted his wistfulness and felt a lump in her throat as she also stared at what was now an empty space. The wind that had ruffled Finn's hair was whistling down the chimney. Not a whistle, when she thought about it; more like a low moan.

Fresh starts all round, that's what Maggie had said.

Not easy, not always. And for Comraich, a fresh start might be hardest of all.

Chapter Two

JESSAMIN had spent a lot of the time in the house recently – 'nesting', as Maggie called it, as half the medical profession called it – a very real phenomenon and often described as *'an overwhelming desire'*. Certainly it was true in her case. She, Finn and Rory had finished off the living room between them over a couple of days and it looked lovely, just as she'd hoped it would, so much fresher. It was September, and the summer – what little there'd been of it here – was well and truly over. The baby was due mid January. Not the ideal time, not when you lived in a remote Highland village. There was no midwife in Glenelk; the nearest was at the Kyle of Lochalsh, which meant you had to travel over the mountain pass that separated the Glenelk peninsula from the rest of civilisation, and if the weather was bad, if it happened to be snowing, then you had a task ahead of you. The village had its own snowplough, driven by the gregarious Winn Greer, the proprietor of The Stag pub, but using it wouldn't get you anywhere in a hurry, as he was fond of telling anyone who'd listen. If you wanted to tackle the mountain pass in harsh weather, you'd need to exercise patience – plenty of it, something she didn't think was possible when your belly was full with a baby demanding to catch its first glimpse of daylight. With this in mind, Finn had struck a deal. Around Jessamin's due date, if there was even a hint of snow, Winn would be there; he'd clear the route if needed and keep on clearing it, so they could hit the main roads easily enough and reach Inverness, seventy miles away. 'We'll see your bairn's delivered safely, don't you worry,' he'd assured Jessamin, words that Finn had echoed. And she took comfort from that – the team effort – whilst reminding herself that women had had babies in this part of the world for centuries, *healthy* babies. She was by no means the first and she wouldn't be the last. There was no need to panic so many months in advance. Yet, standing in the bedroom she shared with Finn, looking out across the unending moor, at the hard rain that slashed down, she felt a definite sense of unease. Here, the rain was bad enough, but when combined with a Highland mist, it was treacherous. Beyond view, a couple of miles up a track that led from the house into the moorland proper, was a loch – Stan's Loch she used to call it, still did to be honest – as much a focal point of his stories as Comraich, where he and his friends, Mally, Flo and Beth would gather on warm days to swim and just be with each other, soaking up the glory of their surroundings as well as their youth. When he'd first started talking about the loch, Jessamin had been desperate to visit it, especially as it had been the subject of a painting that had cemented her decision to come to Scotland in the first place; a painting owned by her mother, that an S McCabe had supposedly painted – Stan in other words. Only later it transpired that Mally had been the artist – Jessamin's grandfather – hence the reason it was in her family's possession. He'd painted it under Stan's tuition when they were boys. That fate had guided her towards the same place he'd come from, had stunned her, but not the locals when they'd found out. They called it serendipity.

The loch was within walking distance, but reaching it had been another matter – the weather determined to drive her back time and time again. When finally she'd set eyes on it, her heart had leapt. It wasn't just beautiful, it was *magnificent*, boasting a series of pools over which presided natural arches and bridges; faerie pools as Stan used to call them, their green and blue-tinged waters brighter than jewels. In the distance were mountains, tall and brooding, the age-old guardians of all they surveyed. It was the site of so much happiness, but so much tragedy too. Not that she'd known of the tragedy when she'd first visited, and so, for her, for a while at least, the loch had been unsullied.

With her hand on her belly, she turned from the window. Finn was out again, busy with estate matters. Soon after she'd arrived in Glenelk, she'd set up a soup business from her cottage: Skye Croft, one that had, surprisingly, taken off, Finn finally offering her the vast kitchen at Comraich to continue making and supplying businesses hereabouts. She'd long since handed over the small enterprise to her assistants, Shona and Gracie, local girls who still ran it, but from the village rather than Comraich, expanding it to include other goods too. Jessamin didn't miss work as such and it wasn't as if she needed the money as she still had plenty left over from the house she'd sold to come here, but she did miss doing something useful with her time, although, she mused, she'd be busy soon enough with a baby to look after. And, looking at the walls, at the jagged cracks that punctuated them, at the paint peeling in several dark corners, she was aware that Comraich too would keep her busy for a while to come. Redecorating had to be done carefully, considerately. Just like a person who'd lived a very long time, it needed to be treated with respect. Next on the agenda was the nursery. She needed to make her mind up which room that was going to be. A kick in her abdomen signalled the baby agreed.

"Okay, okay," Jessamin said, grinning – she *loved* it when it did that, when it made its presence known – "let's get the ball rolling."

Upstairs at Comraich there were five bedrooms, all of them generous in size. Of course she'd want the baby in with her and Finn for the first three months or so, but after that it could have a room of its own. She ruled out Stan's room straightaway, the room he'd died in. Not because she was afraid of his ghost lingering – who could be afraid of Stan? He was the very definition of a gentleman – but because she missed him so much it made her sad every time she went in there. Even so, as she left her room and passed his, she couldn't resist opening the door.

She always thought of Finn's room as predominantly masculine and Stan's room was much the same. There was very little colour on the walls, they were off-white and it was sparsely furnished with just a bed, a chest of drawers and a wardrobe. It had been Stan's room since birth and the room he'd shared with Beth too, until she'd moved into a room of her own after the death of their daughter, Kristin.

The rain still battering the windowpanes and making them rattle, she sat down on Stan's bed, running her hand over the counterpane that adorned it.

The last time Stan had been to the loch, it was she who'd taken him. He was ill, dying in fact, but he'd insisted, wanting to face the ghosts of his past who he believed were still there – his former friends, waiting for him. She'd taken him and he'd staggered, fallen and broken his ankle, there in the wilderness, with no one else around. Thank God for Maggie and her intuition. She'd guessed where they'd gone, had fetched Finn and come after them. Back at Comraich, laid on this very bed, he'd taken Jessamin's hand in his and asked her, *beseeched* her, to look after his grandson in his stead. Finn had been furious with her for taking Stan to the loch when he was in such ill health. There was no way he wanted her near him afterwards. But Stan had known better. He'd realised how they'd felt about each other even before they had.

I miss you, Stan.

Sometimes, when she sat like this, alone in this big, ancient house, she fancied she could still hear him – his voice – over and above the more general sounds that Comraich tended to make, the wheezing and the sighing; but not just *his* voice, others too. Low murmurs, laughter, and at other times a sharp intake of breath, or a sob.

When she'd told Finn this, he'd laughed.

"If there's one thing I love about you, it's your wild imagination."

"I'm not imagining it. I do hear things."

"Jess, there are no ghosts here."

"Maybe not, but there are definitely echoes."

Rising from Stan's bed, she returned to the landing. There were three more bedrooms to choose from – which one would be perfect for their child? Even though she trod lightly in bare feet, one or two floorboards still managed to creak in protest. Opening the door to another bedroom, she remembered this one had belonged to Stan's parents, Mr and Mrs McCabe and, after them, Finn's two sisters, who'd left the melancholy of this house as soon as they could for faraway places and never returned, not even for their grandparents' funerals. There was a musty smell and in the air, dust motes performed a frenzied dance. Once the room had contained a double bed, but now there were two singles, at opposite ends of the room, and in between them a bay window that overlooked the woodland at the back of the house. Because of this the light was obscured. *Not this room.* And not Kristin's either, which was next to it – in there no amount of redecoration could erase the tragedy of a life cut short from such a terrible disease. Which left the fifth bedroom; the room, according to Finn, that Beth had imprisoned herself in; his own grandmother, the woman who'd lived under the same roof as him during his formative years, and yet he'd barely known her.

Beth.

Was it her that the sobs belonged to, the pain of what had happened at the loch remaining forever potent, followed years later by the anguish caused by the loss of Kristin, Finn's mother, causing her to retreat not just inside this room but deep inside herself too? How Stan had loved her; how loyal he'd been, asking nothing more than to just be with her, his Beth; the girl he'd fallen in love with, at the loch of all places, the very first time they'd gone swimming. Although Jessamin had seen photographs of her before – one on her wedding day, with Beth staring beyond the camera rather than at it; another with her holding a tiny Kristin in her arms, a happier Beth in that one, with a more genuine smile on her face, she wondered what Finn's grandmother was truly like. Stan had also painted a portrait of her, one that hung in the living room – Beth in her middle years sitting by a window, that faraway look in her eyes perfectly captured. Had Stan deliberately painted her sadness, or were Beth and that disposition inseparable?

As her hand reached out to turn the slightly tarnished doorknob to Beth's room, Jessamin was suddenly nervous. She'd often been in this room before, as she'd often been in all the rooms at Comraich, but this one only for a minute or two at a time. She'd briefly visited, nothing more, feeling it disrespectful to do anything else. This was Beth's room, her sanctuary within a sanctuary. It was private. Beth had wanted it to be private after Kristin, only allowing Stan entry and no one else. Finn said he barely knew the room either and, like Jessamin, hadn't been in there for a long while. But change was coming. This room couldn't be left to fester any longer. In all honesty, none of them could. If she had her way, she'd inject them all with new life, a rogue thought that made her smile. *Steady on, Jess; see what it's like having one baby first!*

It'd be wonderful; she knew that. She and Finn would bubble over with excitement at the prospect of a child, *their* child, adding to the mix. It was like being handed a miracle, something further to drive out the darkness.

Opening the door, she did as Finn tended to do and strode into the room, purposeful rather than timid, not stopping until she was dead centre. There she released the breath she hadn't realised she'd been holding; a sigh that only temporarily blocked out the drumming of the rain at the window. It was a beautiful room. Not quite as large as the other rooms, but a little more compact, and, if anything, in a greater state of disrepair, but somehow that didn't matter. It was another room caught in time. The bed was made of the finest walnut, the furniture too, including a dressing table matching the one that had been in Kristin's room, a wardrobe and a bureau. Like all the beds in this house it was covered with a counterpane, pale pink in colour, damask rose – gentle, delicate – a reflection of the one who'd inhabited it? That was the impression she always got when anyone talked of Beth, and from standing in this room too; an impression that she was delicate both physically and mentally. Where had she sat and what had she done all the hours she'd spent in here? Jessamin crossed over to the window, another large bay with a chair standing close by that she dragged over so she could sit looking out. The view was of the moor, as it was from her and Finn's bedroom. Pressing the palm of her hand against the windowpane, she found it was as cold as the room.

"Oh, Beth," she whispered, exhaling. "I'm so sorry you suffered."

She felt helpless – unable to do anything to ease the pain of what this woman had endured – this *shadow* woman, because that's what she'd been, even to those closest to her. Maybe even to Stan.

"I wish I'd known you."

Beth had died in her eighties, a short while before Jessamin had arrived in Glenelk. Even if she'd still been alive, Jessamin probably wouldn't have been granted an audience. What Finn had said once came back to her. *'In my teens I don't ever remember Gran stepping outside of Comraich. Sometimes she never even left her bedroom and I'm not talking weeks, Jess, I'm talking months, many, many months.'*

Because of her twin and what she'd done to her? Killed her, essentially. Jessamin shook her head. No, she hadn't killed her; it had been an accident. They were eighteen; that age when passions run higher than the mountains hereabouts; when tempers explode and rain down nothing but angst. Accidents happened. Jessamin knew that herself from the circumstances that had eventually changed the course of her life and brought her here; from what had happened to her husband, James.

Could she be called a murderer because of it? It was she who'd insisted he leave work that night and drive home from London to Brighton, knowing he was tired, that he wanted instead to grab a hotel room and come home in the morning refreshed. There'd been no one else on the road when he'd crashed, no obvious reason why. The subsequent knock on the door, the police in uniform breaking the news…

And Connor, young, idealistic Connor, had died because of Finn; at least that's what Finn thought. When they'd been in the army together, Connor had been under Finn's care, and Finn had given his trainee the go-ahead to perform a sweep of a building that had already been checked. It *had* been checked, but something had been missed, something buried deep. In the ensuing explosion Finn had rushed into the flames and tried to save Connor but had failed at that too – his words, not hers. The guilt that had dogged him ever since, like that which dogged Jessamin, was horrendous. Daily they had to chip away at it and remind themselves that none of it was intended. An accident. They were all accidents. And it was working – slowly.

Not for Beth, though. It had never worked for her.

A loud clap of thunder startled Jessamin. Jumping up she clutched at her belly, the baby startled as well and beginning to kick furiously.

"Okay, okay," she soothed. "Everything's going to be all right."

The thunder rumbled on, but soon died out, the baby eventually settling. In the silence that followed, her words seemed to echo as she repeated them.

"It's all going to be all right."

Chapter Three

THE Stag was packed. Maidie's divorce celebration had been at the beginning of the week and now, at the end of the week, it appeared to be Ewan's turn! As it had stopped raining at last and the evening could be considered a pleasant one, not too cold and with no gale about to rise up and sweep them off their feet, Finn and Jessamin had decided to walk to the pub. If they cut through the woodland at the back of Comraich, they'd emerge close to Skye Croft, now a holiday let, and from there it was only ten or fifteen minutes to the pub. They'd taken torches with them but mainly for the return journey; en route to the pub it was still light enough to see the well-trodden track that lay in front of them.

"Maggie will be there with Lenny tonight, too," Jessamin informed Finn as they walked, her arm linked with his, relishing the comfort of being so close.

"Oh aye?"

"Yep, today's the day he's back from the rigs."

"Is it the day he asks her to marry him, though?"

Jessamin smiled. "We'll just have to wait and see."

"I wonder what he's like, this Lenny?" There was a slight frown on Finn's face.

"Maggie likes him, that's what counts."

"Aye, well, Maggie's special. I hope he's good enough for her."

"He's in love with her, he has been for a long time. I think that's special enough."

Finn only shrugged in reply and again Jessamin smiled. She liked that he was protective of his best friend. And actually, heaven help Lenny if he wasn't up to scratch! If he hurt Maggie in any way he'd have her to deal with, as well as Finn.

As they passed Skye Croft, Jessamin cast a nostalgic eye over the little white cottage with the red door and magnificent views of another loch, Loch Hourn, which separated Glenelk from the Isle of Skye. From here they exchanged the track for a tarmacked road, one that led to the hub of village life – the pub. In the main this was where the locals gathered, with no excuse needed much of the time. Maggie's house was another gathering place, her 'Girl's Only' nights every Thursday the stuff of local legend. Would they continue with Lenny on the scene? Jessamin hoped so.

As they continued walking, the clouds were rolling in over Skye, the shape of the island reminding Jessamin of a slumbering whale. She sighed with contentedness. She loved it here and didn't miss Brighton at all, although occasionally those that resided there still, particularly her other best friend, Sarah. She'd been up to visit a few months ago but still considered Glenelk and thereabouts the 'arse end of nowhere'; somewhere no sane person would willingly choose to ensconce themselves.

"So, you're calling me insane?" Jessamin had asked her.

"Yep," Sarah had replied amidst fits of giggles.

"Sarah!"

"Okay, come on, tell me what the weather's like up there, right now I mean, this very minute." It had been May at the time, prior to her visit.

"Well… erm…"

"It's raining, isn't it?"

"Yes, okay," Jessamin had mumbled. "It's raining."

"Yet down here the sun's shining, it's blazing in fact, we're in the middle of a heatwave. You see what I mean?"

Jessamin had nodded, "I see what you mean."

"You're insane."

"I am," agreed Jessamin and then burst out laughing too.

Even now the memory caused her to chuckle.

"Jess?" Finn enquired.

She looked up at him. "Oh, it's nothing. I'm just happy, that's all."

He smiled at her and when he did, it lit something inside him and subsequently inside her. How was it possible to have found another love so complete? She'd been lucky when she'd met James and lucky with Finn too, a thought that caused another old friend to step forward: guilt. A second chance was a double-edged sword.

"Jess, what is it?"

"I…" Despite feeling happy, or perhaps because of it, water began to pool in her eyes. "Oh, Finn," she said, giving in to her rogue emotions.

Immediately he wrapped his arms round her. "You just said you were happy!"

"I did, I am," she replied, her voice muffled against his chest. "That's the problem."

He pulled an inch or two apart. "Jess, you're confusing me."

"It's Beth."

"Beth? What about her?"

"I was in her room yesterday. I was trying to decide about the nursery. Anyway, I pulled a chair over to the bay window, sat down and thought about her, *really* thought about her. She incarcerated herself in that room, Finn. She barely left it."

"Gran was depressed, you know that. My mother's death finished her off."

"But she had people to live for. Her husband, you, your two older sisters."

"My sisters didn't know her either, not really."

"Just like I didn't know my grandfather." Jessamin's brown hair swayed as she shook her head. "I was only seven when Mally died. But I do know that what he did, it wasn't so different. He married, had children, but he hid himself away too. Not to the extent Beth did, I don't mean that. He went to work, in a supermarket of all places, but when he came home, he'd go to his room, his office we used to call it, and no one would see him, least of all his wife. He existed, nothing more than that."

Concern still creased Finn's face. "All this is old news. Why are you getting so upset about it now?"

"Because… life is so unfair sometimes. And because…" she rubbed at her eyes with the back of her hand. "I wish everyone could have a second chance."

"I do too," Finn replied and his voice had softened. "But, Jess, we have and we mustn't squander it, okay?"

Nodding, she stood on tiptoes so that she could brush her lips against his. What he'd said, that was something they'd both agreed the first time they'd kissed – that they'd live every day that was granted to them, they'd make the most of it, together. And, aside from when work dictated, they hadn't spent one day apart, grabbing their second chance by the jugular, not letting it go; refusing to. And now they'd been further blessed – a child was on the way. There were one or two in the village that frowned at this, the older inhabitants. A child out of wedlock was still considered sinful to some, but marriage was what she'd shared with James, and so it remained sacrosanct, something that had been theirs and theirs alone. She'd tried to explain this to Finn once when tentatively he'd broached the subject. Quickly he'd gone quiet, understanding what she meant, or at least she hoped so.

"Jess," Finn murmured, "as much as I'd love to stand here all night kissing you, people are expecting us."

"Sorry," she said, placing her feet flat on the ground.

"Och, don't apologise. Later, when we're back home, I'm at your mercy."

Home – she loved the way he said that: *their* home.

"I'll look forward to it," she replied, holding his gaze.

"Jess, Jess!" A voice behind them broke the spell.

It was Rory shouting, hurrying towards them with Shona by his side.

When they caught up, Rory embraced Jessamin, as did Shona, the two men shaking hands afterwards. Shona smiled shyly at Finn, whom she found somewhat formidable. It amused Jessamin that this was the case, but then she'd found him formidable too in the beginning – a man mountain whose obvious scars, his damaged eye, the burn marks to his hands and those that lay beneath his clothing as evident as deeper scars, at least to her. He was far more relaxed now, but the likes of Rory and Shona insisted on treating him with deference – the man from the big house, the descendent of Lairds – but in truth, he was just a normal man and humble with it. He might run the remnants of an estate but never 'lorded' it over anyone.

As the four of them approached the pub, Jessamin could hear the night was in full swing – a chorus of male voices, Ewan's probably the loudest. They were singing a song she'd never heard before but one that frequently included 'freedom' in its lyrics.

Rory noticed her puzzled look. "It's an old Scots song," he explained, "*Freedom Come All Ye.*"

"Aye," Shona added, smirking, "it's about the winds of change."

"Oh poor Maidie," Jessamin replied, immediately feeling sorry for her.

Quickly Shona put her right. "Don't even! You weren't at her celebration, were you? You didn't hear what she was singing?"

"What was it?" asked Jessamin, noting Finn's intrigued expression too.

Glancing at Finn, Shona shook her head. "I can't say, it's far too rude." It only took a moment to reconsider. "Och, to hell with it. It was *Fuck You* by Cee Lo. Her mother and some of her mother's friends were there, they'd come from all over the peninsula, and I can tell you, the looks on their faces, it was priceless!"

All four of them laughing, they finally entered the pub. It was wild inside, a real shindig. In amongst the crowds there was Maidie and, right beside her, Maidie's mother. Although she and the friends that surrounded Maidie sported scowls on their faces, Jessamin could tell they were hiding amusement too. This was a celebration, as Shona had said; a gale blowing after all in Glenelk, metaphorically speaking.

As Finn was ordering their drinks, Jessamin spotted

Maggie. Lifting her hand, she started waving. "Maggie, Maggie!" Not waiting for a reply, she pushed her way through the crowds to reach her. "Maggie!" she said, arriving by her side. "How are you?" Looking either side, she could see there was no man in tow. "Where's Lenny?"

There appeared to be no Lenny and there was no excited smile on Maggie's face either. If anything, she was downcast. Not just that but agitated too.

"Maggie, is everything okay?"

Another loud burst of song drowned out any reply. Jessamin shook her head to indicate she hadn't heard. Maggie simply stood there, looking helpless, prompting Jessamin to come to a decision. She mouthed the words '*follow me*', turned her back on Maggie and led her past a bemused-looking Finn and out into the night air.

When they were alone together with nothing but the stars above them for company, she asked Maggie again if everything was okay.

"He didn't turn up," Maggie said, looking really quite shell-shocked about it. "I phoned his work place, they said he'd left the rig earlier today, and I've been trying to get through to his parents, they live over in Larnside, a few miles away, but they're not answering. Oh, Jess, I've even rung all the hospitals hereabouts, you know, just in case, but nothing."

"The friends that he flew back with, what about them?"

"I don't know any of them."

"The crew transport department?"

"Aye, I've checked with them too, the helicopter landed, and he was on it. But where he's gone since, I've no clue."

Jessamin was as perplexed as Maggie.

"Jess," Maggie said suddenly, "do you think… I mean… Is

it possible he's reconsidered his plans? He's taken fright?"

"If he has, he's a fool." She shook her head. "Let's not get carried away. You've said his parents aren't answering the phone, perhaps one of them's been taken ill and he's rushed straight there. In his panic, he may have forgotten to let you know."

"I should get over to Larnside."

"If you do, I'm coming with you."

"Oh God, I'm worried now. What if…? What if…?" Her panic visibly rising, she gripped Jessamin's arms. "We have to go. We have to find out what's happened."

"Maggie! Hey, Maggie!"

Both their heads turned in the direction of the voice that had shouted.

It was a man, tall, some might even say lanky, as slim as Maggie was wide, longish hair tied back in a ponytail, and wearing jeans, boots and a heavy jacket. Slung across his shoulders was a rucksack which looked liked it was filled to bursting.

"Lenny?" Maggie whispered. "It is! It's you. Oh, Lenny!"

Finally letting go of Jessamin, she hurled herself forwards. As she did, Lenny started to pick up pace too. Their bodies collided as they embraced.

"Lenny," Jessamin heard Maggie say. "Where've you been? I was so worried. You were meant to be here hours ago!"

"Och, don't fret, girl. I had a little shopping to do on the way, that's all."

"A little shopping?" Maggie pulled away from him. "You could have phoned!"

"Aye, I could, if I'd thought to charge my battery this morning. Which I didn't."

"So what did you go shopping for?" Maggie's voice held a sly curiosity.

"Ach, that'd be telling," Lenny replied, giving nothing away.

As he pulled Maggie back into his arms, Jessamin decided that three was a crowd and returned inside. Nothing had happened to Lenny, he was safe; they were all safe, in this tiny little village that teetered at the edge of the world. She elaborated on that thought as more singing permeated the air – safe *and* happy, and privileged too.

* * *

Later that night, Jessamin lay entwined in Finn's arms, listening to the silence that encapsulated them. *This* was peace – she, him and the baby – this was sanctuary.

Neither one of them was sleeping, both of them simply enjoying the aftermath of coming together, the memory of his hands, his lips all over her still vivid in her mind. As her body relaxed, her mind started wandering again, leaving the comfort of their bedroom to slink along a landing that was drenched in darkness. Further still she ventured, her shadow-self in search of another; opening the door to that particular shadow's room which was also in darkness except for a single shaft of moonlight that pierced the gloom. Would she encounter Beth, sitting by the window, staring outwards, ever outwards? In search of what? Just before Stan had died he'd said his three friends were waiting for him – Beth, Flo and Mally. She had no doubt they were. Even so, when you left, was it possible to leave something of yourself behind? Beth's angst, sorrow and guilt were still evident in this room – her emotions saturating the walls, the floorboards, and everything in between. Part of Finn's grandmother *was* still present, she was certain of it. A woman who'd lost so much, including her mind. Perhaps now was the time to give something back.

Finn inclined his head. "So, have you decided?"

For a moment she was confused. "Decided what?"

"Which room you want for the baby?"

"Oh." He was so in tune with her sometimes. "Yes. I've just made up my mind, this very minute in fact."

"And?"

"Beth's room. I want that to be the nursery."

Chapter Four

IF she was going to transform Beth's room as she'd done with the living room, it would have to wait. The very next day after making her decision, Jessamin came down with a cold – a heavy cold, one that floored her for the best part of two weeks. Finn was wonderful, seeing to her every need, settling her in front of the fire if he had to go off for the day and keeping it stoked, just as he had for Stan. Maggie too had made regular visits, a twinkle in her eyes all the while.

"Has he asked you yet?" Jessamin probed one afternoon, in between bouts of coughing and sneezing.

Maggie duly handed her tissues, but from arm's length. "No. He's a tease that's what he is, keeping me hanging on like this."

"He's just waiting for the perfect moment," Jessamin replied.

As impatient as she was, Maggie agreed. "Aye, there's a time for everything."

When she wasn't having visitors, including the midwife who'd come over from Kyle to make several checks on her, as well as Rory, Shona and Gracie, who'd all brought bunches of flowers, which unfortunately only added to her misery, the asters amongst them making her sneeze even more, Jessamin spent the time reading or dozing – predominantly dozing. Whilst doing so she entered some sort of half-world, or at least that's how she'd come to think of it, once again hearing whispers, a burst of laughter or a low murmur. After they'd painted the living room, they'd reinstated all the original pieces of artwork, including the portrait of Beth in her middle years. When hearing such noises, Jessamin would turn her head in its direction. *Is it you, Beth, making that noise? Is it all of you?* This was an old house, centuries old, and there'd been other people who'd lived in it or frequented it, but somehow Jessamin thought it was Beth responsible for the noises, Flo, Mally and Stan too. The four of them were not just a unit but also a force of nature, as wild, as beautiful, as dangerous even, as the land they'd grown up in, their presence, their very spiritedness, ingrained. *What's your story, Beth? Your real story?* She knew Stan's version of events, he'd sat by the fire and told her, drawing her into his world, word by word – into the sheer joy of it, and the sadness too. Regarding the other three, she'd only ever seen them through his eyes. Beth in particular intrigued her, a lost soul. Whenever she slid into her half-lucid state she hoped, if she listened hard enough, that she might hear exactly what the whispers were saying, but she never could – it was only ever an impression of speech, tantalising and frustrating. She didn't tell Finn anything about this. Not because she was worried about his reaction, but because he always held true to their pact of living in the present. She did too, but she couldn't deny it; her fascination with Beth was growing.

As soon as she was back on her feet she asked Finn to help prepare Beth's room for painting.

"No need to move all the furniture out, what there is of it," she said to him as they stood in her room gazing about them, "it's probably enough just to shove it into the centre and cover it in dust sheets whilst we see to the walls and paintwork."

"We'll have to move it out at some point, though," he countered.

"Not the wardrobe or the bureau." They were quality pieces of furniture, no doubt antiques. "But the bed, yes, I agree that can go. But just the bed, Finn, I mean it."

"I hear you," he said, holding his hands up in a gesture of surrender before getting to work.

With the walls fully revealed, it was clear to see how grubby they were. Mould flowered in several corners, which Finn informed her they were going to have to get treated before any painting could go ahead. With work coming to a temporary halt, he'd left the room to tend to other matters, but she'd lingered still, deciding to spend the afternoon trying out paint testers she'd hoarded from a previous trip to Inverness. An hour or so later, various shades of yellow, blue and lavender adorned the walls in neat rectangles and yet still she was having difficulty choosing the right one. Perhaps if she'd found out whether the child was a boy or a girl, it might have helped in the decision-making. *Pink for a girl, blue for a boy.* Although blue, she conceded, would suit either gender. Standing amidst the furniture, she looked over at the window and sighed. The morning had been bright enough, but now it was grey again, the air becoming thick with drizzle and a mist hovering precariously above the treeline. The weather helped her to make up her mind. She'd opt for yellow, the colour of sunshine, not a garish shade, but something soft and lemony. Happy with that choice, she was about to turn and leave the room, venture down to the kitchen, when a sharp kick from the baby stopped her in her tracks.

"Ow!" she cried, one hand clutching her stomach, the other extended so she could lean against something, the bureau in this case. For a kick, that was fearsome.

"Perhaps you are a boy," she muttered. "A footballer in the making."

If so, he was lying still now. Grateful for that, she reached out and held onto the bureau with both hands, trying not just to calm her breathing but also, if she were honest, her runaway mind. The pain had been slightly different to anything she'd experienced before. If anything should happen to this baby…

Everything's going to be fine. She'd stood in this room before and said that. All she had to do was believe it.

Tea, that's what she needed, a good strong cup, with two sugars instead of one.

Straightening up, she made her way to the door. As she reached it there was an almighty bang. Instinctively, her hands went back to her stomach, protecting the precious cargo inside, but this was something external. Thunder perhaps?

Turning once more towards the window, it certainly looked miserable outside but not stormy, and there were no accompanying forks of lightning.

Rather than leave the room, she retraced her footsteps to the bureau. That's what had been responsible for the noise – the lid had fallen open. Her curiosity piqued, she peered inside. There were two main drawers across the middle, and two small side drawers placed either side of them, little brass knobs on each and every one. It really was a lovely piece of furniture, rich in colour, although mellowed in some places, with a green leather inlay on the inside upon which to write.

Unable to resist, she ran her fingers across the inlay, feeling the various indentations where a pen had once pressed hard.

Her fingers travelling upwards, she pulled at the tiny drawers first, they were empty of everything except dust, each one of them. Disappointment flooded through her. She'd expected them to contain something, anything: a pen perhaps that Beth had used; some old receipts – titbits, trivia, but nonetheless a clue to an inhabitant long gone. There were just the two main drawers to go. *Eeny meeny miny moe.* Which one should she try first? Tugging on the bottom one, it finally yielded – but again nothing was inside. The top drawer was all that was left. After several yanks, she realised it wasn't stuck, it was locked. *Damn!* There must be a key, lying behind a hidden panel perhaps. Bending, she re-opened the drawers she'd previously explored and pushed and prodded their interiors, coming away empty handed each time. She might need to take an axe to it at this rate, the image of herself wielding such a weapon temporarily making her laugh. Why was it locked, what was inside it? Further prodding and pulling only added to her frustration. *Double damn!* Perhaps she should wait until Finn got home, he might know more about this confounded piece of furniture than she did. Deciding to do just that, she turned around and as she did, a glint of something caught her eye. On the carpet, in front of her, was a key, a tiny key, the kind that would fit a bureau drawer.

For a moment all Jessamin could do was stare at it. She hadn't noticed anything on the floor before. But it was possible, just possible, that shifting the furniture earlier had dislodged a key that perhaps wasn't hidden in the bureau but elsewhere.

Rather than stand and contemplate this enigma further, she bent down to retrieve the previously elusive object. It really was tiny, intricate even, made from bronze. Her heart fluttered as much as the child in her belly when she inserted it in the lock. It released with such a satisfying click. Straightaway she opened the drawer, surprised at how much her hands were trembling. Unlike the others, it wasn't empty; it was stuffed with notepaper, reams of it. Her hand closing around the thick bundle, she released it from where it had lain hidden. Hardly able to believe it, she feasted her eyes on the letters. With Beth's bed not yet dismantled, she sat on it, laid the bundle to one side and picked up the top sheet. Holding it in her hands, she noted the date – November 2014. That it was so recent was another surprise. If Beth was the scribe, she'd died not long after. The handwriting appeared feminine, letters beautifully rounded with sweeping tails and graceful arches.

As she gazed at the notepaper, she heard a sigh – not hers, so whose was it? One of the four's? Beth's even? It had begun to rain harder, pelting the windowpanes, drumming against them. Ominous perhaps? Jessamin didn't think so. Like the sigh, it seemed to be a gesture of relief, a letting go, a release.

When she'd been ill, resting on the couch downstairs, she'd asked Beth a question: *what's your story?* Could it be that Beth was now ready to tell her?

She scanned the top sheet, the text was easy enough to decipher.

I don't know if these words will be read, or by whom. Stan, if it's you, know this, I loved you. I came to love you so very much. I'm sorry for being so undeserving. I can imagine your reaction if I said that to your face. You'd shake your head and deny it. You'd lay your hands on my shoulders, stare into my eyes and tell me over and over just how worthy I was, and I would want more than anything to believe you. I almost did once, after the birth of Kristin. How could I be a bad person if I'd helped to create something so beautiful? And then she was snatched from me and I knew...

without doubt. I'm not worthy. I'm wretched. I'm also a coward. You think you know me, but you don't. You think I'm better than I am, but I'm not.

It might not be Stan reading this of course, it might be a stranger, someone who doesn't know me at all. Think twice before you carry on. There's another possibility. These papers may never be discovered and my secrets will remain unknown, buried, as my body will soon be buried, although not my spirit. That will remain in limbo, a place neither here nor there, but which nonetheless exists. Is that where you are, Mally? Flo? In limbo because of me? I detest that thought. It tears me apart. I've so much to be sorry for and I am, I truly am, I conduct my life in sorrow, I've strived to do that. But that's the end of the story, not the beginning. Our beginning – mine and Flo's, Mally and Stan's – it was glorious, it was innocent. And it remained that way until love reared its head and made demons of us all.

Jessamin's eyes widened.

Demons?

Is that how Beth really regarded herself, and the others too?

She quickly laid the first sheet down and picked up another. This one also had a date on it – 1936 and a subtitle scrawled beneath it: *The first day of school.*

She inhaled and then slowly let the breath out.

Think twice before you carry on.

There was no question about it. Beth was going back to the beginning and so Jessamin would go with her. She'd journey alongside this shadow woman, this *tortured* woman. She'd read her words, her thoughts, and would never falter.

Only then would she decide if Beth was right; if love could make a monster of you.

Chapter Five

Beth

"BETH, Florence, come on now, will you stop chasing each other around? We've school to get to. It's your very first day. Och! It's so exciting."

Our mother, Nancy, was trying to extract her two errant children from the tiny cottage we occupied, in order to accompany us the three quarter mile to the school on the edge of our village, in Glenelk. There'd be other mothers doing the same with their children but with one difference, they didn't have two the same age to contend with. Twins. I'd heard Mam say it was both a blessing *and* a curse – which one depending on the mood she was in at the time! Still, even as she frowned, there was pride in her eyes. We looked *brèagha* she said, wearing our best frocks and with our hair, the colour of wheat she described it as, hanging in ringlets.

"Now come on," she said again, her voice much sterner this time. "We don't want to be late, do we? What would Mrs McNeill say?"

"Who's Mrs McNeill?" I asked.

"I've told you, hinny, she's your teacher."

Her words sunk in. What *would* she say if we were late for school? Would she admonish us and not as gently as Mam either? Abruptly, I came to a standstill.

"Stop it, Flo," I said, "I don't want to play tag any more."

"It! You're it!" Flo yelled, taking no notice of me.

"No, Flo. I said stop it."

"It!" she said again.

"Flo, listen to me."

"What?"

"We have to go to school."

My sister screwed up her face as she stamped her feet. "I don't want to go to school, I want to play!"

"We can't."

"You're no fun anymore."

"And you're just silly," I retorted.

Ach, we were always arguing, Flo and me, it used to drive our mother mad. Our father too, whenever he was home, which wasn't often – he was a fisherman and would be away for days, sometimes weeks at a time. But Mam managed to put up with us – just.

Eventually we were out the door and skipping down the gravel path. The sun was blazing, but then whenever I remember my childhood, those early days, it always seemed that way. Perhaps that's just memory playing tricks on me; this is Scotland after all, the Highlands where the sun isn't known for putting in a regular appearance, or maybe, when you're happy, the world around you shines because of it.

The school in Glenelk was a far from grand building, it was three cottages joined together that had been given over for the purpose of educating the youngsters hereabouts. It was held in high regard though, and I know there were many who considered us lucky to have it. No, there was nothing fancy about it, but oh, what a spot it nestled in, set against a backdrop of mountains, the heather only recently in bloom and colouring the otherwise green landscape such vivid shades of pink and purple. Outside the building stood Mrs McNeill, wearing a tweed skirt suit, her wiry black hair secured in a bun and owl-like glasses perched on her nose. Flo ran happily up to her, whereas I held back, clutching my mother's hand. To my eyes at that moment she was austere, formidable even, but nothing could be further from the truth. As soon as Flo reached her, a smile lit up her face, one that carried over to me.

"Ah, the twins," she said. "And such bonny twins too."

The next thing I knew we were being ushered inside. Flo didn't even turn to say goodbye to Mam, she just flew into the gaping interior. I, on the other hand, had to be prised away from Mam, clinging, yelling, kicking and screaming. As I've said, we might be twins, but we were different. I recall the moment I calmed down, however, the *exact* moment. It was when another latecomer passed us by, his mother nowhere to be seen. It was a boy, no taller than me and thin with such pale skin, but his hair, it was as black as jet; his eyes were too – eyes that glanced in my direction and stole my breath away.

I entered the classroom meekly after that and took my seat beside my sister, but not before spying where the boy was sitting, at a desk to the far side of us, beside another boy, one I recognised; the boy from the house in the woods, the house that me and Flo used to think was haunted. Such a big house it was – imposing with thick grey walls and stone mullioned windows – it even had a small turret, like a castle would. We'd passed it with our parents several times when we were out walking, skirting the woods in which it sat, Mam and Da keeping their gaze averted all the while as if in reverential respect. It was on one of these occasions that I'd seen the boy, playing close to the house with a ball, bouncing it against one of those thick walls, although he was so involved in his game, I don't think he saw us. But perhaps I was wrong about that, because it was he who leaned forward while the boy with dark hair stared straight ahead; it was he who smiled at me, a tentative smile, shy – one that, strangely, echoed the reverence of my parents. I smiled back, but it was his companion's attention I really wanted. The teacher later introduced the boy from the big house as Stan McCabe, and beside him was Ben Murray. It took a few days to coax a smile from Ben, or Mally as he was known by then, thanks to Flo's perpetual slip-up in pronouncing his surname, and it was aimed at Flo, not me.

* * *

Mally wasn't from Glenelk, and maybe that accounted for why we'd never seen him before. In a village such as Glenelk, everyone knew each other, except for the McCabes of course, who kept themselves slightly apart, but then that was to be expected; they were higher in station, not common working folk like the rest of us, although certainly their son was friendly enough. No, Mally lived closer to Larnside than Glenelk, the next village along, a good three or four mile walk from ours. He was from farming stock, and apparently had had an older brother who'd got ill and died. Perhaps that was the reason he hardly smiled, although Flo, she could coax a smile from anyone. Not for the first time something twisted inside me, something sharp – that she had the power to do that and I didn't. It seems she'd taken a liking to Mally too and Mally had taken a liking to Stan, who was thin like him, but with sandy hair and a smattering of pale orange freckles across his nose. Soon the four of us were spending all our time together at school, playing outside when the weather permitted, and, in the classroom, exchanging glances and giggles when Mrs McNeill's back was turned. Mally used to look at us in wonder sometimes, at Flo and me – 'I can't tell who's who,' he'd say and Flo would giggle some more. But he *could* tell, even if he didn't realise it, because his eyes sparkled whenever they fell on Flo – from being dark and sombre they'd change in an instant. But children are children, and back then that sparkle was innocent enough. We were friends, soon best friends, and as our bodies grew taller and began to fill out, we remained that way, allowed to roam together after school, whilst our parents toiled at home or at work. Children were freer in those days and here, in the Highlands, I think it's fair to say we were wild too. But who could blame us for that – glance around, look at the landscape that inspired us! It's the very essence of wild. Of course I've never been out of Scotland, so you could say I've nothing to compare it to, but truth be told, I've never *wanted* to leave. In my life, the furthest I've been from Glenelk was a cottage in Aberdeenshire; it was for a week, no more than a few days, but all the time I was itching to return. For better or for worse, Glenelk is my home, this peninsula in the far northwest; my land, and I wasn't just living in it, I was a part of it. Flo, on the other hand, talked about visiting other countries. Often she'd do that and Stan would too, but Mally didn't and I didn't. As we'd traipse through the high grass around here, beating it back with a stick, Flo would tell us how she'd love to cross the water one day – 'to places like America, or Canada, or even… even… Africa. Doesn't Africa sound exciting, Mally, don't you think it does?' Stan would nod in enthusiastic agreement, but Mally and me, we'd remain silent on the subject. He was as much a part of this land as I was. More than that, he was like the stag, the Monarch of the Glen, king of all he surveyed. I remember the time we ran under clouds that were struggling to keep the rain at bay for us, and he said words to that effect. We were ten, nearly eleven, and still to find the loch we'd spend the rest of our adolescent years by. It was just Mally and me, as Stan had a family event to attend and Flo was in bed with a head cold. It felt odd at first; we were so used to being a foursome rather than divided – at that stage anyway. Instead of glancing at each other, we'd kept our eyes trained ahead, barely even uttering a word. The day was as uncomfortable as our silence, not hot but humid, my ringlets becoming fuzz because of it. Mercifully, Mally broke the ice.

"Tag," he said, reaching out to push me.

My eyes – ice blue in colour – widened as I careered sideways. "Hey, that's not fair! I didn't know we were going to play tag."

"Life's not fair," he answered, "that's what my Da says," and with that he took off, running a hand through his hair, making it look more unruly than ever.

I ran too, of course I did, but I didn't have a hope of catching him. Like the Highlanders of old, who'd cross mountains carrying messages to each other in all manner of weather, he could run for miles and never falter. Realising I was nowhere near him, he stopped and turned to watch me, laughing at the fuss I was making; how red in the face I'd gone; how breathless I was. His hands were by his side and his head was thrown right back. A sight he looked, I can tell you, in trousers that barely fitted, that were too tight and too short; in shoes that I knew were too small, and a shirt that Mam would have said was 'hanging on by a thread'. His father farmed the land he owned, but they were poor, certainly poor in comparison to my family. As for Stan's family… well, there was no comparison. But he was rich in spirit, was Mally; he *blazed.*

Eventually I caught up with him and gave his arm a hefty punch.

"No more running," I spluttered.

"Och, it's good for ya." Thumping his chest, he added, "It builds your muscles, it makes you strong. Look at me, I'm the Monarch of the Glen."

"Mally," I continued, "let's just… walk. Please."

He shrugged but conceded and we continued onwards, picking our way through the wilderness, feeling as though we were the last two people on earth.

"Just imagine," I said, "if it was only you and me left."

"No Flo or Stan?"

"No Flo or Stan," I repeated.

He screwed his face up. "It'd be strange."

It would be, but somehow I craved it – no Flo matching Mally in laughter, no Stan, laughing too, but never in as raucous a manner. Stan, who loved the world we lived in; who'd regularly bring a sketchpad along with him on our jaunts; who'd sit while we frolicked, capturing the beauty of all he surveyed. There'd only be Beth and Mally.

Sometimes I wonder, is it possible to love another at first sight, as I did? Is it possible to know from such a young age – I was four when I first saw Mally – that there was something different about the way you were feeling; that it soared above normal love somehow? I have to believe it, because it's true. As I said, I *craved* this boy beside me – his ribbing; his grin that Mam described as cheeky; the stark contrast of his pale face against his dark hair. When I was without him, I lived and I breathed just to see him again, counting down the hours, the minutes, the seconds. His ill-fitting clothes didn't matter; I found them both endearing and heartbreaking. I asked Mam once if she could make something new for him to wear but she'd looked horrified.

"And what would his Mam say if I did such a thing?"

"She'd be happy, wouldn't she?"

"Let me tell you, Beth, she would not! I don't know Mrs Murray; his parents obviously prefer to keep their own company, but I'll nae go courting trouble."

As much as I didn't understand her attitude, I didn't ask again – when Mam made her mind up about something she stuck to it, I knew that from experience.

"He's a raggle-taggle gypsy boy," Flo used to say in her sing-song voice, and I'd shrug. He was and it was fine. Why try and change what was already perfect?

After an hour or so of wandering and idly chatting about various inane subjects, school mainly and Mrs McNeill whom I'd grown to love but Mally had gripes with – 'She sets way too much reading,' being one of his familiar complaints, 'what use are books when it's a farmer you want to be? A farmer has no time to read!' – we eventually came to a stop, flopping down on a hillside where the heather was yet to bloom. Our view was Loch Hourn and Skye. We sat and we stared at such natural majesty. Above us the clouds had gathered, but a shaft of sunlight had managed to break through, creating a ring of bright water that sparkled like a diamond.

"I love it here." Mally's breath caught in his throat as he said it.

"I do too," I answered.

"I wonder what lies beyond that mountain ridge," he was

pointing towards Skye.

I shrugged. "I don't care. I've got everything I need here."

Briefly considering this, he nodded. "Aye."

As the shaft of sunlight faded, I lay back on the grass and so did Mally.

"Mally, even if the others leave, we don't have to, you know."

He laughed. "They won't leave."

I turned my head towards him. "They might. Stan said he overheard his parents talking about sending him to boarding school."

"Boarding school?" Mally gave a derisory snort. "Stan's parents are soft on him, they'll do what he wants and what he wants is to stay."

"But you never know, one day..."

"Nah. We'll be together forever."

Did he mean all of us or just him and Flo?

"You only care about her," I said. The words were out of my mouth before I could stop them. In shock, I simply lay there, unable to believe how bold I'd been.

"What?"

When I refused to answer, Mally pushed himself up onto one elbow to stare down at me. "What did you just say?"

His eyes felt like they were boring into me. "All you care about is Flo," I said again, my voice weaker this time. Desperate even.

"I don't!"

I pushed myself up too. "You do, you love Flo."

"Love?" He screwed his face up again, his expression bewildered.

"Yes," I said with sudden determination. "You love her, not

me."

"But… but…"

When I look back on this I cringe. We were so young.

"Do you love me? Do you, Mally?"

"Well… You know… I…"

"Prove it."

"Prove it? How?"

"Kiss me."

"But…" again he stuttered.

"Mally, please, I want you to kiss me."

His eyes held uncertainty, but more than that, there was fear – fear of the unknown. Nonetheless he did as I wanted and leaned towards me. Our lips met, and not just briefly, they lingered, mutual pressure becoming fiercer as he reached out to pull me closer. We were two ten-year-olds, sitting in the long grass on a muggy, cloudy afternoon, feeling something stir within, deep within. If I close my eyes, I'm there again, experiencing every split second of wonder, every single emotion, including triumph.

It was my first kiss, but more importantly, it was also Mally's.

Chapter Six

"JESSAMIN, Jessamin… There you are! I've been calling you."

As though emerging from a deep sleep, Jessamin roused herself, staring at Finn as he stood in the doorway of Beth's room. "You've been calling? I never heard you."

"I was yelling at the top of my voice!"

"What is it, what's the matter?"

"Well… nothing's the matter, I was just wondering where you were. What are you doing by the way; reading something?"

Just as he stepped closer, as she began to rise from the bed, about to answer him, to tell him what she'd found in the drawers of Beth's old bureau, the baby delivered another almighty kick.

"What the…!" she said, doubling over and letting what was in her hand flutter to the floor.

Finn was by her side in an instant. "What's happening? Are you all right?"

"I… Aargh…"

Her hands clutching at Finn, she could hardly draw breath.

"Jess," Finn's voice reduced to a whisper as all colour drained from his face. The ensuing silence was leaden, until

Jessamin yelled again as another pain – not just a kick this time, it was more than that, it was searing – seized her.

Galvanised into action, Finn swept her up in his arms as though she was weightless and strode out of Beth's room, heading back to their bedroom. Laying her gently down on the bed, he retrieved his mobile phone and immediately scrolled to a contact, speaking urgently as soon as his call was answered.

"I need to speak to Doctor Buchanan."

Jessamin called out to him. "Finn… the pain seems to have passed."

Finn shook his head. "I'm not taking any chances." Speaking into the phone again, he frowned. "Well for God's sake, can you contact him and ask him to include us in his rounds? My… My … partner…" he seemed to stumble over that word, as if somehow it wasn't quite fitting, "…is pregnant, and she's having pains, a few minutes ago she was doubled over with pain. We need to see the doctor! Get him to come to Comraich. Please."

Ending the call, he started to wring his hands. "Perhaps we should just get you in the car and drive you to the hospital in Inverness. Christ, perhaps we should *move* to Inverness, you know, until the baby's here."

"Finn, please, calm down. Look at me, I'm fine now; it was cramp probably, nothing more than that. With a bit of luck the doctor will be here soon, he can check me over and put it down to cramp too. There's no need to overreact."

In an instant he was on the bed beside her, his hands on her shoulders, his expression beseeching. "Where we are, it's too isolated for someone in your condition. I meant what I said. I can rent us a flat in Inverness, one overlooking the river. It'll only be until the baby is born, just a matter of weeks."

"My condition? Finn, don't be so old fashioned! Women have been giving birth in Glenelk, in Larnside and in Amberley, the next village along, since time immemorial, and that includes your mother. I remember Stan telling me, all three of you were home births." She tilted her head. "Actually, I think Stan was born at Comraich too."

"Aye, he was, but it's not a given that it'll go smoothly."

"But that's true no matter where you are!"

His voice rose. "If we're closer to a hospital it's safer."

"Finn, we'll get to the hospital, we've made plans, remember?"

At her words, his shoulders sagged – the man mountain crumbling.

"I'm going to see the doctor soon," she continued. "We'll find out what's happening and then we'll take a deep breath, the pair of us, okay?"

Still he was sombre. "Do you know how precious both of you are to me?"

"I do." She also knew that once you'd experienced grief, you feared it. "Look, nothing's going to happen to me and the baby, we're going nowhere."

As it turned out, Jessamin's words were prophetic. Doctor Buchanan did indeed include her in his rounds; she was his last patient of the day. He took her temperature, checked her heartbeat, felt her stomach and picked up the baby's heartbeat too via his stethoscope. Despite finding nothing untoward, he ordered bed rest for the next week at least, Finn nodding his head in enthusiastic agreement. Jessamin, however, protested.

"Doctor Buchanan, I've got too many things to do, a nursery to prepare, more decorating downstairs. I want this house perfect for when the baby arrives!"

"Jess," the doctor accompanied his reply with an exaggerated sigh. "What you want is typical of all pregnant women at your stage, but the trouble is you've been overdoing it. Now look here, I've checked with your midwife, and you're due for another appointment in a week and so I'm afraid it's bed rest until then. There's only one thing you should be doing right now and that's growing this baby." He addressed Finn. "I take it you're with me on this?"

"She won't move from that bed, David, I'll see to it."

Jessamin continued to fume. "I can't believe you two. I'm pregnant, not ill!"

"Aye," Doctor Buchanan replied, "and that's exactly how we want it to stay. Having said that, your blood pressure is erring towards the high side of normal, but it's little wonder if you've been climbing ladders."

"I haven't—"

"I'll not change my mind, I want you to rest."

"If you're afraid of being bored, I'll bring the TV up," Finn offered.

Jessamin shook her head. "No, no, it's not that, as I've said there's so much to do."

"Jess," Finn answered, his exasperation evident, "the baby will be in with us for the first three months at least, so what's the rush? Besides, it'll take a week or two to get the mildew in Beth's old room sorted. I've just made an appointment with a friend of Rory's and he's coming over to sort everything out, check for any leaks, that sort of thing. Only when he's finished can the decorating begin and, Jess, no matter what you say, we're getting Rory in. You're not doing it by yourself any more."

The sigh that left Jessamin's mouth was as heavy as Doctor

Buchanan's – there was nothing wrong with her or the baby, the doctor had said as much, yet still these two would have her bed-bound. Then again, if she did ignore doctor's orders and something happened… Ah, to hell with it, she'd do what they wanted and rest this week, and read too, the notes that Beth had written. She could hardly believe she'd found them, and the way she'd found them, that had been odd too. She'd thought there was something of Beth still in that room, but she'd meant it purely in an ethereal sense. To be able to read about the woman's life in her own words was phenomenal. In her head, it was Mally and Flo who'd been the great love match, but it was Beth who'd extracted from him his first kiss. What else had happened between these children that only they knew about?

Finn was showing the doctor out, and she resolved to tell him at last about her discovery when he returned. As he entered the room, she sat up straighter.

"Finn," she began, just as his mobile started ringing.

"Hang on, Jess," he said, answering it.

There ensued swathes of silence, the person on the other end of the phone clearly jabbering away, punctuated only by a few nods of Finn's head and the odd 'uh-huh' and 'aye, of course.' He ended the call, promising to be over straight away.

Jessamin's heart sank. "You're going out again? It's almost seven o clock, Finn!"

Finn looked none too pleased either. "It's old Mrs McConnell from Kyle, she's got a problem with her heating apparently."

"Can't you send Rory, you usually do when it's odd jobs like that?"

"I could, but she's fussy and she doesn't like Rory, she

thinks he talks too much, and eats too many biscuits whilst chain-drinking tea."

Jessamin didn't know whether to be amused or bemused. "Well, perhaps the solution lies in *not* offering him tea and biscuits?"

Finn laughed. "You dare not refuse old Mrs McConnell when she's pressing her homemade shortbread on you, although it's worth knowing you're damned if you take more than one or two!"

"You keep saying 'old' Mrs McConnell; how old is she?"

Finn shrugged. "That's just what everyone calls her, what she *likes* being called. I think she sees it as a sign of respect. She's ninety-four, Jess."

"Ninety-four!"

"Aye, and she's been our tenant all her life. She brought up six children in that cottage, she and Mr McConnell, who never got so old. He died thirty years ago."

"Oh, that's sad," replied Jessamin.

"It is, but she copes well enough. Her children are scattered far and wide but she has people close by that look out for her."

"Including you?"

"She has asked me to go over rather a lot lately. And most of the problems, well, they've not been problems at all. I think it just gives her comfort knowing there are people on hand, who'll come when she wants them to."

"At the drop of a hat?"

Finn smiled and Jessamin did too. She loved the kindness beneath his gruff exterior; that he was willing to indulge any complaints Mrs McConnell might have, no matter what the hour and if they were trivial or if they didn't even exist. "When I've had the baby, when everything's more settled, I'd like to help you run the estate."

"I'd like that too, but there's a while to go before we reach that stage. All I want you to do now is rest."

Again her good mood crumbled. "I feel like an incubator!"

He took a few moments to settle himself beside her on the bed. "That's because, technically, you are," he said, cupping her face with his hands, "keeping what we've created safe and warm."

Any resistance she might have had melted as he drew her face closer, as his lips met hers, as their kiss deepened.

"I thought you had to be somewhere," she said, when finally they parted.

"Aye, I do, but hold that memory, we'll revisit it later."

Memory...

"Finn, guess what I was read—"

The bedroom window burst open.

Both of them turned their heads to stare at it.

"Didn't you put it back on the latch?" Finn said, getting up and going over to it.

"Me? I didn't take it off the latch. Why would I? It's not exactly warm out there."

"It's not that windy either," he muttered, a frown on his face. Once the latch was back in place, he declared he really did have to go. "I'll be home as soon as I can though, I promise. You'll be okay until then?"

"Of course I will."

"Are you hungry? Can I bring you something to eat?"

"No, I'm not hungry."

"You've got to eat, Jess."

"Okay, just some soup or a sandwich will be fine."

"Coming right up." Turning from her, he hesitated.

"Perhaps you're right, perhaps I should see if Rory's free..."

"Finn, I'm fine – *we're* fine. Go on, hurry, the sooner you go, the sooner you'll be back."

"After I've got you some soup."

"After you've got me some soup," she repeated, smiling.

Once she had a bowl of vegetable broth in front of her and he'd left the house, she remembered the pain that had doubled her over when he'd found her in Beth's room, preventing her from answering his question – *what are you doing, reading something?* The phone call had stopped her from telling him too, as had the window suddenly bursting open.

As steam gently rose from the plate, realisation dawned.

You don't want me to tell him, do you?

In a house characterised by grief, Beth had perhaps carried the greatest burden. That she was now relieving herself of that burden took courage; she didn't want it broadcast. What did she want? Simply to test the waters, or someone who wouldn't judge, even though she clearly judged herself? But Finn had to know – one day. This was his family's history. Until then, however, she'd do as Beth seemed to want. When Finn was out of the house or asleep, she'd read, let Beth's story unravel.

Finn would most likely be gone for a couple of hours. She'd finish her food and then she'd rest, but not on her bed, on Beth's, keeping an eye on the time and creeping back to her room well in advance of his return. Surreptitious behaviour? Perhaps. But if the dead were confiding in her, the least she could do was listen.

Chapter Seven

Beth

THERE was a war on.

Not between the four of us. Not yet. It was World War II, the year 1941. It had been raging for two years but at ten going on eleven, we were far too young to realise the gravity of it. As summer dipped into autumn what concerned us as we spent afternoons lounging in Stan's bedroom, was the weather and how harsh it was. There were days and days of constant rain, pelting down from the heavens; storms too, and thunder as loud as the bombs we imagined were falling elsewhere. On the rug that covered the floorboards in Stan's bedroom we'd lie and complain, Mally idly flicking the tin soldiers that Stan had spent an age lining up.

"I'm bored," he'd spit, and in his eyes there wasn't the laughter we were used to, but something else – anger perhaps?

Flo just shrugged and pointed at the window. "We can't go out in this, Mally, our Mam would tar us. She only allowed us to go to your house, Stan, because it had eased off slightly. Should have known it wouldn't last."

Mally sat up and looked at Stan who was eyeing his scattered soldiers, no doubt itching to undo the damage Mally had caused.

"Shall we go out, Stan? Leave the namby-pamby girls to it?"

Flo sat upright too. "Hey, who are you calling names? We're no' like that."

"I don't want to be stuck in all the time, that's all. I *hate* being stuck in."

"Even here?" Stan asked and I turned my head to look at him instead of Mally. What did he mean by 'even here?'

Back then I didn't know about Mally's home life and Flo gave no hint that she did either. Why would we? We never went to his house; we'd never been invited. The boys *had* been to our house, Mam had given them scones and homemade raspberry jam, which the pair of them devoured, licking their fingers afterwards and laughing at a dollop that had landed on Stan's lap. Mam had smiled at that; I'd smiled too, Flo, on the other hand, had done the same as the boys and just dove in, getting as messy as them. Our cottage though, as I've said before, was tiny, there was no room for anyone other than those that resided there, not on a regular basis, and so it was Stan's house in the woods – Comraich – that became the place for the gathering of the 'Glenelk clan' as we sometimes called ourselves. Mally's house and his parents intrigued me, however. I wondered what they were like; which one he took after in looks and mannerisms. What was his bedroom like too? Not like Stan's, I'd bet. Stan's was warm and comfortable with drapes at the windows, a sturdy bed and so many toys. As well as soldiers, he loved making models, of cars, and aeroplanes, and ships, and these he'd paint as meticulously as he sketched the world around him. Stan's was a privileged life compared to so many. His room was full of books too, actual books, by authors Mrs McNeill spoke of sometimes, Dickens, Thackeray and Chaucer. Even so, I'd never met a more humble person than this sandy-haired boy in front of me. Not once did he make any of us feel less because he had so much more. As much as we loved being at Comraich, however, I think the contrast was sometimes too much for Mally. In this room, I could always sense his agitation, and as I said before, his anger. So yes, in a way, 'even here' was no haven.

He was sitting now with his legs drawn up tight against his body, staring out of the window. Flo either wouldn't countenance his moods or genuinely didn't notice them. Instead, she got up, picked one of the books off the shelf – a heavy tome it looked like – and started to read from it, her eyes growing wider and wider, probably at the use of words she'd never encountered before. Stan meanwhile took the opportunity to reassemble his men, whilst I edged closer to Mally, my eyes trained on him, willing him to turn his head and acknowledge my advance.

That moment on the hillside overlooking Loch Hourn – that kiss – neither one of us had mentioned it again. Had he forgotten? I certainly hadn't. A light had sparked inside me the day I first set eyes on Mally and that kiss had caused it to burn.

Mally didn't turn his head, but instead started muttering.

"I wish I could go with them, I *want* to go with them."

"Mally—"

Flo interrupted me. "What does this say?" she asked. "It's an odd word, I'll spell it out – M o n s e i g n e u r?"

"It's French," Stan piped up. "I think it means mister. Is that *A Tale of Two Cities*? That's got French in it. Father reads it to me sometimes."

Stan finally left his soldiers to go to Flo's side. He took the book and began reading the passage, which delighted Flo as she always found words more difficult than the rest of us. "*For scores of years gone by, Monseigneur had squeezed and wrung it, and had seldom graced it with his presence…*"

As his staccato voice continued, as Flo giggled on hearing what for her was akin to a foreign language, I whispered to Mally, "Where is it you want to go?" I was desperate to know.

"To war, of course."

"War? But you're too young!"

"I can fight!"

I didn't deny it. There'd been a time in school when a much bigger lad had been bothering Flo, pushing her in the playground, making fun of her because she hadn't been able to solve a sum that the teacher had posed – a relatively simple sum admitted. Mally noticed, shot over to her side and felled the lad with one blow. As well as Mrs McNeill giving him a tongue-lashing, he'd got a tanning at home too, from his father I presumed, although he never actually said. I noticed the next day in school a bruise that bloomed beneath his eye and how he winced when he sat. I think the teacher noticed too, because she kept glancing over at him and biting her lip. I was dying to ask what had happened, to find out if it *was* his da who had inflicted such damage, but one look at Mally and I refrained.

Making sure Flo and Stan were still engrossed in what they were doing, I reminded Mally of what he'd said to me in the summer, that he never wanted to leave here. "They send the soldiers to places like France," I continued, trying to remember snatches of conversation between my parents, "that's a long way from here. And some…" I swallowed. "Some don't come home. They *die* in France."

He turned to me then, his dark eyes practically black. "I'll take my chances," he declared, such venom in his voice.

"There's nothing for me here."

I was at a loss. How could I respond to that? There was *everything* for him here. This is where he belonged. He'd said as much himself. Had something further happened at home? Had he got into more trouble with his da? I had so many questions but I couldn't ask any of them, not with the others in the room. They were private questions, the answers to which I'd have to wheedle out of him. If only I could get him on his own again. I'd ask then. And I'd *make* him answer me. Because I knew he burned too, but with a fire that was different to mine.

The door burst open.

"Ah, children, I..." It was Stan's mother, Mrs McCabe, a slight woman but very elegant, her blonde hair swept up in a neat chignon and wearing a skirt, jacket and sensible flat shoes. Flo, Mally and I were in awe of her but I don't remember her as anything but kind, if a little remote. She offered us hot milk and biscuits whenever we visited, which we always accepted. I was presuming this is what she'd come to fetch us for, until she spoke further. "More men are leaving the village this afternoon, heading for the continent." She stopped, seemingly upset at the prospect, although for the life of me I couldn't figure why. It wasn't as if Stan was going. "I wasn't sure if you knew or... whether you'd want to join the rest of the village in seeing them off."

I was about to shake my head but Mally jumped to his feet. "My da said something about more men enlisting. He said they'll clear the villages of all their working folk at this rate. There won't be enough left to work the land or sea and we'll starve."

As Flo's mouth opened in alarm, Mrs McCabe's hand flew to her neck. "That won't happen," she assured everyone, "but when this blasted war will end, I don't know."

Her eyes were shining as she said it and still I couldn't understand why. It was only years later I found out she'd had two brothers who'd died on the battlefields – another reason why Stan had never been sent to boarding school. She couldn't bear to lose him as well. Heroic deaths they were, medals awarded posthumously, but, to my mind, death is death. You can't take medals with you.

"Are… any of your family going?" Mrs McCabe asked us.

Flo shook her head and so did I. Our father's occupation prevented him from going, as did Mally's. As Mrs McCabe had said, starvation wouldn't happen, certain people needed to stay behind, farmers and fishermen included, their women toiling beside them in the absence of younger hands. Besides, our da was forty-four. He and Mam had had us later in life than most. As for Mally's da, I had no idea how old he was. I had no idea about him at all.

Mally told Mrs McCabe that he had no family going either but then he shot to his feet and ran from the room.

"Where you going?" Stan called after him.

"To see, to wave them goodbye of course," Mally answered, already halfway across the landing.

And he was right. That's exactly what we had to do. I made to follow him, as did Flo, Stan looked briefly at his mother who nodded and then he too joined us, all of us flying down Comraich's grand staircase, across the hallway with its mounted stagheads staring blindly at us, through the old oak door and out into the cold, hard rain.

We continued onwards, tearing through the woods at the back of Comraich, emerging the other side in green fields; four sets of mud-splattered feet, eventually reaching the track that led to the heart of the village. And there they were, those who'd just come of age; those who could no longer turn a blind eye; those who were angry and those who were filled to the brim with excitement. Men from Glenelk, from Larnside, Amberley, and the hills all around, leaving everything they'd ever known to fight for the lives of others; for freedom; for liberty. They stood proud, they stood like Scotsmen, shoulder to shoulder, surrounded by fathers, mothers, brothers, sisters, children, aunts and uncles. No one was weeping, rather there were hearty pats on backs and the firm shaking of hands; fierce hugs too.

We'd taken shelter under a willow tree and were observing from there, but on seeing the gathering of people Mally stepped forward, back into the rain.

"What are you doing?"

Flo asked the question but she didn't move. Only I moved, to stand by Mally's side, both of us not only soaking wet but shivering from the cold, watching as the men were driven away to a designated meeting point; as the last truck left the village; as the tears started to flow at last, the wailing, and the sobs. The women were falling apart, knowing the reality of it, that they might never see their kith and kin again.

"I don't want to go," a wide-eyed Mally said on witnessing this, "not anymore."

He'd realised this just as I realised something too; that Mally could blow hot or cold. He could swear blind he wanted one thing and the next minute be after something else entirely. That was Mally. That was him all over.

Chapter Eight

Beth

I'VE mentioned that we knew nothing of the home Mally came from, except he'd had an older brother who'd died. That was it, the sum total. Mally had met the McCabes, he'd met my Mam and Da, but his parents were an enigma, just as their son was. I wanted to get the measure of at least one of them, however.

Flo, Stan and I were out walking one fine day. The village was quiet in the absence of those who'd recently left and melancholy hung in the air, as heavy as a Scottish raincloud. Wanting to escape it, I suggested we leave Glenelk behind us, taking the road that led westwards towards Larnside, which in all truth was a hamlet rather than a village, a cluster of thatched cottages overlooking fishing boats that bobbed on the water. Mally wasn't with us, he was working, helping his father in the fields. Sometimes he wouldn't even make it to school because he had to work. Every time he was absent, I'd see Mrs McNeill raise an eyebrow as she called out the register, muttering to herself something like *I see he's too busy to grace us with his presence… again.* I used to think she was angry with him because of it, but now I tend to think it was more concern in her voice, and upset too, because he was bright was Mally;

educationally he could have gone far. But working in the fields wasn't a chore to him. Nothing was a chore when it came to the land he loved.

As I said it was a bright day. We'd endured for so long the harshness of winter with its rain, snow and plummeting temperatures. Spring was in the air, at least the verdant promise of it. Soon the trees would be in full leaf and the bluebells would lend a splash of colour – *Brog na Cubhaigor*, Mam told us they were known as, which translated as cuckoo's shoe as it bloomed when the cuckoos called to each other. Another name for bluebells was *Fuath-mhuc*, or 'hated by pigs', as they apparently suffered digestive problems after eating them. Mally enlightened us regarding that one, but I always stuck with Mam's version. It really was an ideal day for walking, but Stan and Flo had started to flag.

"Let's just go back to Stan's house," Flo suggested, "see if we can persuade Mrs McCabe to give us some tea and cake."

"She'd be happy to," Stan replied, smiling.

Even I suffered a moment of temptation; after all her scones were every bit as good as Mam's. But my other desire won out.

"I'm going to carry on," I said.

Stan screwed up his freckle-splattered nose. "Why? You usually hate walking."

"I do not!"

"You do. You're the first to start moaning."

"Moaning?" I came to a standstill, my cheeks growing hot with anger. "For your information, Stan McCabe, I like walking, I *love* walking and I do not moan. If I do it's not because of the walk I can assure you, but the company I'm forced to keep."

Stan burst out laughing.

"Och, Beth, your eyes fire sparks when you're angry, I swear it."

"What—?"

"Oh come on," Flo said, making a huge show of being bored by my outburst, "let's just do what she wants and carry on. Best we don't upset her anymore."

The two of them strode on, leaving me staring after them open-mouthed and yes, there probably were sparks flying from my eyes, but those two, honestly, they were like peas in a pod at times – not me and Flo, not Flo and Mally, but Flo and Stan. Nothing seemed to touch them, certainly not one of my moods. This walk had been my idea and now they'd ganged up on me. I wasn't having it. I stormed onwards, overtook them and made them follow *me* – after all, I knew where we were going.

I'd worked out where Mally lived, having made him tell me once the farm's rough whereabouts, how far inland it was from Loch Hourn, on the shores of which Larnside lay.

The others never seemed as curious as I was about Mally's home, but I was desperate to see it, thinking it would help to flesh out the boy.

His was a lone white house, as many were and still are around here. All we had to do was turn inland at the second house in the village, and walk in a direct line for about a mile or so. As we passed the turn-off, I was full of enthusiasm. Flo, however, decided she was thirsty.

"I can't go much further without a drink. I'll die if I don't get some water soon."

"You're not going to die, Flo," I said, irritated with her dramatics.

"She's right, though," Stan defended. "She's thirsty and I'm hungry. Perhaps it's time to head home."

I stood my ground. "We have to keep going. It's not far now."

"*What's* not far?" Flo said and her face was a picture of confusion.

Stan scratched his head as he gazed around him, squinting slightly. "Isn't this the way—?"

"Yes, yes, it is," I answered before he could finish. "It's the way to Mally's house."

Now Flo simply looked stunned. "How do you know?"

"Because I asked him, that's how." I couldn't keep the sharpness out of my voice. "Haven't you ever asked him?"

She shrugged. "Why should I? We either see him at school or at Stan's."

And there it was, she was happy with that, with such *simplicity*.

I noticed Stan was shaking his head.

"What's wrong?" I said.

"I'm not sure about this…"

"Why?"

Stan's grey-green eyes were not as clear as usual. "He's never invited us to come over, has he?"

"No, but—"

"Maybe for good reason."

"We're here now."

"Not yet," he pointed out.

I was growing ever more frustrated.

"We are!" I insisted. "Just over this hill, that's where his house will be."

Stan was still obviously unsure but Flo's eyes had widened. "We might as well I suppose, as we're so close. Yes, let's do it!

We can surprise him. He'd love that."

"It's just… It's because…"

Stan couldn't quite get the words out. More to the point, we didn't let him. Flo looked at me and I looked back at her, noted the consent in her eyes as together we turned and continued onwards – united suddenly. I was right. On the brow of the hill we saw it in the valley below, a white house – his house. The first word that came to mind was one we'd learnt courtesy of Mrs McNeill – Spartan. There was nothing that drew me to it. Except Mally. And so, turning sideways to cope with a descent that was sharper than I expected, I made my way down the steep hillside to the Murray place.

As you approach a house in the Highlands, there are usually signs of activity; a dog might come racing out, wagging its tail in greeting. Often there are chickens or hens in a coop, clucking away. But here, there was nothing – only silence.

Clearly I wasn't the only one unnerved by this. Flo stuck to my side and even reached out to hold my hand. Stan had drawn closer too, although he kept his hands to himself. At just a few yards distant, I could see how shabby the house was – whitewashed it might be in theory, but actually it was more grey than anything. Someone was in because smoke was billowing out of the chimney – his mother perhaps? Around the house, in the grounds, lay various bits of farming equipment that had rusted their way into disuse. The windows – four of them – had no nets on the inside and one or two frames looked rotted. I raised my hand to knock at a door that was worn by the elements. As I did, my heart sank. Mally's house was unloved. Did that reflect upon those who dwelt here?

We all scarcely breathed as we waited for the door to open.

It took a while, more than a minute, possibly two or three,

and at one point I wondered if it would ever be answered. Eventually, however, it opened slowly, so slowly, to reveal a woman with the look of Mally about her. She had dark hair, although it was wiry and speckled with grey. She had dark eyes too, but they were dull somehow, with none of his fierceness. It *had* to be Mally's mother, as he'd told me it was only he who lived here with his parents, his grandparents having gone the way of his brother and dying years before. But still it was confusing because this woman looked old, far older than Mam or Mrs McCabe. Her back was stooped as if a series of rocks lay across it.

A heavy silence hung in the air as the three of us stared up at her. Thank goodness she broke it, because I don't think I'd have had the courage to.

"Can I help you?" She craned her neck as she asked, looking over our heads rather than at us.

"Hello, Mrs Murray," I ventured. "We're–"

"I know who you are," she continued, still with her eyes on the horizon. "You're Ben's friends, from the school. Why've you come?"

"We wanted to see him," Flo spoke next, adopting a wide and hopeful smile.

"He's no' here," was Mrs Murray's curt response.

"Is he working, Mrs Murray?" Stan asked, standing ramrod straight.

"Aye, that's it, he's with his da. Now go on, away with you," she said, finally with her eyes on us, one hand shooing as if we were nuisance flies buzzing around her. "And you'd do better to wait for an invite next time rather than come calling outta the blue."

Whilst she was speaking, I was trying to look beyond her,

into the house that Mally lived in – but it was dark, so dark, and I could see nothing at all.

"Go on," Mrs Murray continued, stepping forward now in order to force us backwards. "He's back at school next week, wait to see him then."

She might have been determined, but she was anxious too, gnawing at her lip in between demanding we leave. I hadn't known what to expect, not really, but I'd hoped for something better than this.

"Would you… could you tell Ben we came to visit?" I asked. I wanted him to know that we were thinking of him, or rather that I was. "It's just he loves school and he hasn't been, not for a few days. I think Mrs McNeill gets cross…"

Mrs Murray's eyes widened as her hand flew to her mouth.

"What's this about Mrs McNeill?" a voice roared behind me.

Although fear seized every bone in my body, I managed to swing round, as did Flo and Stan, all three of us coming face to face with Mally, who was not alone unfortunately. He stood beside his father, a look of complete horror on his face.

I was dumbstruck – completely unable to speak.

"I said," Mr Murray growled, "what's all this about Mrs McNeill?"

He was tall and his shoulders were broad, the texture of his skin not pale or smooth, but leathery. He had on breeches and a grubby linen shirt, the shirtsleeves rolled up to reveal powerful arms and hands that were capable of bruising.

Silently I cursed myself. Why had I said what I did, about Mrs McNeill? My mouth had run away with me. It sounded like I'd come here blaming them and that hadn't been my intention. Not in the slightest.

Stan did his utmost to save me.

"Hello, Mr Murray," he greeted, only the merest hint of a waiver in his voice. "All we wanted was to say hello to Ben. We've missed him, you see."

Oh the look on Mally's face, I could hardly bear to see it! It was as if he was silently pleading with us to pipe down, to not say another word. But we were kids and, well... kids don't always do the right thing, the *sensible* thing.

When Mr Murray asked again about Mrs McNeill, and what 'bother' there'd been, I attempted to answer. I had to.

"Mrs McNeill, I think she likes Ben. I mean, of course she likes him. But sometimes he doesn't go to school because he has to work..."

"He works because there's a war on." Spittle flew from Mr Murray's mouth as he yelled back at me. "Did that little fact happen to pass you by, lassie?"

"N... no," I stammered, "of course not. It's just... he's very clever is Ben, and well... we're *supposed* to go to school."

There'd I'd said it when really I should have obeyed Mally's silent pleading. How I wished I had. Even Flo and Stan were looking at me in an appalled manner. I closed my eyes, but the respite was only brief. I had to open them again when Mr Murray drew near. His face had turned crimson, as if he were about to explode. Mally meanwhile was whiter than white and his mother was visibly trembling.

Mr Murray's voice when he spoke was low and steady but all the more frightening because of it, and his eyes, far more intense than his wife's, than Mally's, held so much anger, anger that if it boiled over... I knew by proxy how powerful his fists were.

"If Mrs McNeill has a problem, then she can come and see

me about it. Actually, I'll go one better; I'll go and see her, find out what all this fuss is about. *I* decide what my son does and does not do, not wee chits, not the school and certainly not bloody Mrs McNeill."

All the while he was speaking I was nodding avidly, desperate for that anger, that *fierceness*, to remain contained. Flo had started to breathe heavily and I could see Mally's worried gaze was on her, rather than me. When he happened to look at me there was only fury in his eyes – more than enough to rival his father's. And that's what felled me. That's what really caused my own terror. I'd insisted we come to Mally's house and because of that, I'd got him into trouble, Mrs McNeill into trouble and ourselves into trouble too. And not only was his father enraged by that, so was Mally; he was angry with me, and he'd be angrier still if his father beat him later because of it. And he *would* beat him, I had no doubt of it, because this man standing in front of me, who was shaking like his wife, but with an emotion that was quite different from hers, wanted to hit *me* – I could feel that longing in him, the *desire* – but he couldn't, he daren't, and so he'd hit someone he could; who wouldn't tell; who'd take it – his son.

I'm sorry.

I sent that thought over to Mally, even as tears sprung to my eyes; prayed he could see how much I meant it.

Mr Murray was still staring at me. Worse – he'd taken another step forward.

"Da," Mally finally spoke, his tone nothing less than beseeching.

"Jack," Mrs Murray seemed to be pleading too.

I stiffened. Stan was also rigid, and as for Flo, she was openly crying.

Although his hands by his side were bunched, it was just words Mally's father threw at me. "Get off my land and don't come back. This is private land, *my* land. If you dare to set foot on it again, if you try and interfere, I won't be responsible for my actions, do you ken?" When I made no response, he bellowed once more. "DO YOU KEN?"

"Aye… Aye, Mr Murray," I managed eventually. "I do."

Flo started tugging at my sleeve. I backed away, as did she and Stan. They turned much quicker than I and started running. I couldn't, for two reasons. First, I had to make sure my legs would carry me for they felt so weak; second I had to try again to make Mally understand that I hadn't meant any ill by our visit.

My eyes held his, but only briefly, a second or two, no more than that.

Mally, forgive me.

But like his da, there was no forgiveness in him that day.

Chapter Nine

AS she read to the end of Beth's sentence, Jessamin was crying too. How awful to know that Mally had suffered hurt at the hands of his father. Why had he suffered, though? What was the reason behind the anger that seemed to infuse Jack, her own great grandfather? The death of his eldest son perhaps? She'd experienced her own fair share of anger over the loss of James – she'd railed and she'd screamed; she'd wanted to hit out, but at herself, not another person. Mentally, she'd beaten herself up over and over again. But everyone was different, as were their reactions.

She eyed the bundle of papers in front of her, the sheets as yet unread, knowing that this was a story that would drain her if she let it; that couldn't be rushed. She had to take her time over it, give it the attention it deserved. It was a *confession*, one that might drag her too deep into darkness if she didn't get the balance correct.

Her sigh somewhat ragged, she gathered Beth's notes, carefully marking her place before putting them back into the bureau. Finn would be home soon, but not only that, earlier in the day she'd invited Maggie and Lenny over to dinner. There was food to prepare and wine to chill – the latter not for her unfortunately, though she could do with a big glass of cold wine after what she'd just read. Still, an evening of lively conversation was something she was looking forward to. It wasn't exactly the bed rest the doctor had prescribed, but it wasn't anything heavy duty either, it would be relaxed, enjoyable, a contrast to how she'd spent the day, in solitude, with only the ghosts of Comraich for company. But these ghosts, they'd hover in her mind, just as they'd done from the moment she'd first learnt about them via Stan. This was a time for change, strange then that the past seemed more real than ever – *they* seemed more real, Stan's friends, including her grandfather, Mally, thanks to Beth. No longer just shadows, but growing in substance. Mally's house in the valley over by Larnside, should she go in search of it one day? She already knew that after what happened at the loch, Mally's parents had moved away. She had no clue where they'd gone – she'd never met her great grandparents, never even heard them being spoken of – they'd simply *disappeared*, taking their shame at their son's supposed actions with them. Cutting ties must have been a mutual decision, she imagined. Not an easy one, though, no matter what had gone before.

Jessamin thought for a moment. It might be that she could trace her great grandparents via the online archives. She didn't know Mally's mother's name, but his father was called Jack. If he'd been born in Larnside, it'd make the search easier.

Why'd you want to trace someone who hit his own child?

It was a valid question she'd asked herself, but things were different then, she had to remember that, brutality perhaps more commonplace, regarded by most as discipline, or simply the 'way of it'. Then again, Mally had been frightened of his father, truly frightened. Beth had seen that in him. Had Flo and Stan seen it to the same extent?

This was exactly the reason she had to take it slowly. Her mind was on fire with question after question demanding an answer. Like Beth, she burned, but with curiosity about a history that was, incredibly, not just Finn's, but linked with her history too. Being only seven when Mally died, all Jessamin remembered was that he was a solemn man; 'gruff' she'd described him as once.

More tears fell. If she'd known *why* he was gruff, if she'd even had an inkling as a child… Instead, just as his father had engendered fear in him, he'd done the same to her. Privately, he'd been christened 'Grandpa Grumps' – a nickname that had made her and her brother, Dane, laugh, but which right now, didn't seem funny, not at all.

Jess, you weren't to blame. You didn't know.

No, she wasn't to blame, not for that anyway. She had to leave Beth's bedroom and the past behind for now and focus on something else: the forthcoming dinner party. Wiping at her eyes with one hand, she sniffed, even managed a smile as she made her way downstairs. Finn didn't yet know that Maggie and Lenny were joining them this evening. As pleased as he'd be to see them, he'd be cross too that she was 'exerting' herself. In which case, he'd insist on taking over the cooking, whilst she sat with her feet up. And she'd do as he said, of course, whilst enjoying the spectacle. Her smile became wider. This pregnancy lark, it certainly had its perks.

* * *

"So Lenny thinks I've too many cherubs about the house. What do you think of that?"

Finn and Jessamin glanced tentatively at each other.

"Erm..." Finn ventured.

Maggie shot him a warning glance. "Don't say it, don't you dare. There's no way I've too many. In fact, I've been thinking of adding to my collection."

"Adding?" Lenny looked horrified. "There'll be no room for me at this rate!"

Maggie leant into him, gave his arm a squeeze. "Och, there'll always be a spare corner for you, Lenny, rest assured of that."

"A corner?"

"Aye, and be grateful for it."

Jessamin laughed to hear the banter between the pair of them. Comraich felt more at ease too; it suited so much chatter. Having said that, it suited the quiet too. Just like a person, it was a house of many moods. But tonight, after what she'd read – what she'd *discovered* – the laughter was especially welcome. She needed this lightness of being; she *craved* it, understanding suddenly how Mally had craved the lightness of Flo. Too much darkness was never a good thing.

Finn was in fine form. As she'd suspected, he'd been worried about her overreaching herself, but she'd soon put him right about that. As she'd also predicted, he'd taken over the execution of everything, producing a simple but tasty meal of local smoked salmon to start and then venison with roast potatoes. There was no pudding; rather they'd gone on to nibble at cheese and biscuits, Jessamin sticking mainly to the cheddar, as soft cheese, like wine, was a no-go.

"I love being pregnant, but honestly, white wine, red wine, Brie, Camembert, I can't wait to taste them all again."

Finn snorted. "Don't get too excited, Jess. As soon as this baby arrives, we need to be working on the next. It's a brood we said we wanted, didn't we?"

Jessamin's mouth fell open as Maggie and Lenny did their utmost to stifle bursts of laughter.

"Finn Maccaillin, we'll see how you go on night duty before we start planning anymore!"

"Night duty, me?" Finn looked aghast at the idea.

"That's right, a new mother needs to keep her strength for the days."

"But..." He really was quite ashen-faced.

"Relax!" Jessamin declared, bursting into laughter. "It'll be a joint effort."

"This baby business," he reached for his glass of red and took a gulp, "it might be a little more taxing than I first gave it credit for."

"Och, stop your mithering," Maggie replied, polishing off the last of the cheese and crackers, "it'll be fabulous – a wee bairn in this house again, a *happy* wee bairn."

Although smiling, Finn lowered his gaze. His mother had died when he was still so young, and, despite his youth, he must have felt that loss; the happiness that had ensued following his arrival dying along with her, never to return, until now. Comraich *would* be graced with a happy wee bairn, as Maggie had said, Jessamin would do everything in her power to ensure that. Life was slowly edging its way back in through the door. With the arrival of this baby it'd burst into full bloom.

Although she hadn't touched a drop of wine, she felt a rush of excitement – both sudden and all encompassing. Quickly, she turned to Finn. "I want a home birth."

She hadn't meant to say those words, they'd barely even formed in her mind – but now they were out there; they were spoken; she wasn't taking them back.

It wasn't just Finn who gaped at her; so did Maggie and Lenny.

"We'd agreed on Inverness, Jess," Finn finally responded.

Maggie also closed ranks. "It's your first baby, love, it might be safer. You know… if there were complications."

Jessamin shook her head. "The midwife in Kyle…" Jenny her name was, Jenny Campbell, "…she'd agree to it I'm sure." Her hands cupped her stomach. "Besides, why should there be complications?"

Finn nodded towards her stomach. "Because of what's happened just lately."

"Everything's fine now!" Noting the concern on his face, she forced herself to relent. "Okay, look, if I have to go into hospital, I'll go, I'm not about to put the baby in danger, but if all goes well from now on, if what happened is nothing more than a blip, then I want a home birth. I'll speak to Jenny about it tomorrow."

"But David…"

"Finn," again the words were out before she could properly process them, "Doctor Buchanan's a doctor not a god!"

"Aye, Jess, I know that," Finn was quick to retort, annoyance replacing concern, "but surely I have a say in the matter too!"

"I want to have the baby here. It… seems right, fitting."

"What do you mean fitting? *Why* is it fitting, Jess?"

"You were born here, Stan, your sisters, *safely* born, I mean."

"That doesn't mean we should tempt fate."

"Tempt fate? Oh, Finn, come on—"

Maggie butted in. "We've got something to tell you."

Both Finn and Jessamin, their expressions as tight as the

situation, turned towards her.

"Oh?" Finn said, his nostrils still flaring.

"What is it?" Jessamin enquired, making an effort to regulate her breathing.

There was a brief silence, during which Maggie cast a tentative glance at Lenny, and Lenny's mouth stretched into a wide grin.

"Oh God," Jessamin's mouth fell open. "Are you…?"

"Aye!" Maggie burst out. "We are, we're getting married! Finally, he got round to asking."

"Och, Maggie," Lenny quickly defended himself, "it's the devil's own job trying to pick the right moment with you, there's always someone knocking at your door."

"Not in the quiet reaches of the night, there isn't!"

"Well, I did it, didn't I?" Lenny countered. "I asked." His grin faded and in its place was a look of such longing, such devotion, that Jessamin almost swooned. "I've wanted to marry you since the first time I laid eyes on you, Maggie. You know that."

Maggie's eyes became somewhat misty. "Aye, I do, Lenny, I do."

After taking in such a tender exchange, Jessamin rose to her feet, her arms spread out as she rushed round to the other side of the table to hug them both. "I'm so happy for you," she declared, breathing in Maggie's familiar musky scent.

Finn was right behind her, shaking Lenny's hand then enfolding Maggie in his arms. The two of them shared a wealth of history, and so much love, felt on many different levels. Maggie loved Lenny as well, maybe not with the passion she had loved Finn, but it was there, it was solid and it would continue to grow.

When Finn broke away from Maggie, declaring he'd best crack open his finest bottle of Talisker – bottled on Skye thirty years before – the bittersweet mood continued.

It was wonderful that Maggie and Lenny were getting married at last. Jessamin couldn't be happier for them, but marriage was a subject she and Finn had never properly addressed. *Their* marriage. Even with a baby on the way, she tended to avoid the subject, only discussing it once with Finn in the past, but not properly. Catching a quick glimpse of sadness in his expression as he released Maggie and ushered them all into the living room where the whisky bottle resided in the drinks cabinet – the same vessel that would have been used to toast so many similar announcements for Comraich's generations – she realised just how brief that discussion had been.

Chapter Ten

Beth

DA was dead.

The moment I found out will stay with me forever, the brittle starkness of it. How dare the sun still shine that day, when it shone so little anyway? Why did the birds continue to sing? How could lives simply carry on when ours had fallen apart?

He was dead. And Mam, poor Mam, I'd never witnessed a person so broken.

Flo and me were with her in our kitchen, preparing vegetables recently dug from our garden to include in a broth for supper when someone started to thump at our door. I remember how Mam froze – her hands, previously busy chopping carrots, became stock-still, her eyes, ice blue like ours, widened as her back became rigid. It was as if she knew already. The Scots are a fey lot, I've lost count of how many times I've heard that said, and certainly Mam could be intuitive at times. As another thump resounded, she dropped the knife and flew to the door, yanking it open. There stood Georgie McBride, a fisherman just like Da, and the look on his face was fearful.

"Georgie," Mam exclaimed. "What's happened? Are you all right?"

"Aye, aye, I am, but… Ronnie…"

"Ronnie? What's wrong with him?"

Wrong?

Cold fear clutched at my heart. I looked at Flo as Mam uttered those words but Flo kept her eyes on Mam, one small fist stuffed into her mouth.

Georgie hadn't answered straightaway; instead there'd been a heartbeat of silence between the two adults, giving them both time to brace themselves.

"Can I come away in?" he said at last.

Mam stood aside. She seemed so small suddenly.

Coming to a standstill in the centre of the room, Georgie removed his cap and held it between his hands, wringing it as he swallowed. He was a young man, somewhere in his early to mid twenties, with springy red hair and freckled skin. Having lost his da when he was young, we knew he looked up to ours and our da made no secret he was fond of the lad too. This was hard news to break.

"There was an accident at sea. One of the lads, wee Davey, got into trouble on the nets and started panicking. Your Ronnie got him back inside the cabin – there was a storm, see, high winds and white horses. But something happened, I don't know what, I didn't see. None of us did. Ronnie went out on deck again… he disappeared… he went over…"

As my mother's legs buckled, Georgie rushed to her side, just preventing her from crashing to the floor. Beside me, Flo, who'd stood so silently throughout all this, was silent no more; she started wailing, a terrible sound, dredged up from the depths.

"I'm sorry, so sorry," Georgie was muttering, over and over, tears pouring down his own face as he half dragged Mam to a chair, where she sat weeping, her chest heaving, her eyes not on us but on some distant point, as though she were searching, praying, beseeching. *You're not dead, Ronnie, you can't be!*

As for me, I could hardly breathe let alone cry. My da, my loving, funny, kind da, if what Georgie was saying was true, was simply no more. His body was lying at the bottom of the sea, cold and alone, with no graveside marker, entombed by water.

How could it be that I would never feel his arms around me again, holding me close, tickling me, or hear his gruff voice relating a seafaring adventure at night as we all sat rapt around the fireside? It didn't seem real. It *wasn't* real! Was it?

Unlike Mam, unlike Flo, I didn't scream or cry; I didn't do anything, except stand and watch helplessly as such a visceral outpouring of grief continued to flow from the others. If it were Mally's da, perhaps he'd rejoice if this news was brought to his door, but we were born lucky with our parents, and now that luck had run out.

The days, the weeks, the months that followed, I can't write about them; they're too much of a blur. Mostly. One thing stood out, however, scarring me further.

I've said that Flo was the light and that I was the darkness; that we were like different sides of the same coin. But losing Da brought out the darkness in my sister. She became moody, withdrawn, and silent too, sometimes refusing to speak to anyone for days on end, me, Mam, Stan and Mally included.

Mam was also different, although she was doing her best to remain stoical and to ensure the daily routine in our household continued. But she would lapse into long periods of silence, her mind not with us, but continuing to reach outwards perhaps, searching for the man she'd loved, married, and borne children with. And so, ironically, it fell to me to inject a little lightness at times; to lift the weight that seemed so settled upon our shoulders.

The year was 1943, we were aged twelve, nearly thirteen; war was raging still, and other hearts, not just ours, were also full of sorrow. Such a sombre year; there was no sign of blue skies, just day after day of lashing rain. On one such day, the four of us were seeking shelter at Comraich again. Flo, her blonde hair scraped into a ponytail, was staring out of the window, as I would spend so much time doing in later years. She was searching too, just like Mam, her eyes on the horizon.

"Let's play a game," I declared, causing three pairs of eyes to widen in surprise such was my enthusiasm. "Hide and Seek, we'll play that. This house is perfect for that game, there are so many places to hide."

Mally glanced at Flo. "I'm not sure…" he began, his dark eyes aching with concern.

"Flo," I called, "you want to play, don't you? Come on, it'll do you good. It'll be fun."

When Flo ignored me, I shifted my gaze to Stan. "Stan?" I cajoled.

He ran a hand through his sandy hair and shrugged. "I don't mind counting down," he said. "Just stay out of my parents' room, that's all. But everywhere else… well, Mother and Father are out anyway, so everywhere else is fine."

"That's settled then. Flo?" my voice held more of a command this time.

Mally crossed over to her, gently took hold of her hand and started tugging.

A flash of annoyance rose in me, but I tried to keep my voice lighthearted all the same. After all, that's what he liked, didn't he? Lightheartedness. And right now Flo was exhibiting little of that. She was darker than I was. "We can't follow each other," I instructed, still striving for authority, "it'll be more fun if we go our separate ways. Flo, come on, let's just... hide."

Finally, she started to move, her hand still in Mally's, although I willed him to let it go. He did, gradually, reluctantly, their fingertips touching right until we reached the door. I flew through it and now again my will was strong. *Don't follow her. Don't!*

He did of course, he always did, and yet, I couldn't fathom it. It was the light he craved and in Flo that had been extinguished. Couldn't he see what I was now? What I was *trying* to be? The effort I was making – not just for Flo, but also for him? It was always for him! So why was it he still wanted her above everyone? She and I, we looked the same. In terms of build, height and our features, there was hardly any difference between us. So why couldn't it be me he wanted? When we kissed, he'd kissed me back, just as hard. He'd wanted me then, I know he did. I'd felt it.

When I was sure we were out of Stan's earshot, I turned to them. "I'm going downstairs. Where are you going, Flo?"

"I'm staying upstairs," she replied, with no hint of enthusiasm in her voice.

"I'll stay upstairs too," Mally declared.

On hearing that, I wanted to scream at them; to shout, to fly at Mally, at them both; claw to shreds the invisible thread that bound them so tightly. Instead, I forced another smile, bright and eager. *I can be what you need me to be, Mally.*

"Just remember it's different rooms we need to hide in. We mustn't make this easy for Stan." There was a warning in my words, a plea, but one that washed right over them as, in perfect synchronicity, they turned and ran down the hallway, as far from me as possible.

My smile faded as I descended the stairs alone, hearing Stan's voice ringing out loud and clear as he eagerly counted backwards from one hundred, never missing a number. Mally wouldn't have been so diligent, he'd have skipped plenty.

There's a lean-to on the ground floor at Comraich, and an old rickety door opens onto it. It houses a long trestle table that's covered with plants, their green fronds trailing to form a natural curtain. It was that which I hid under, hugging my knees to my chest and finally letting the tears flow. Da was dead. Mam and Flo were not who they used to be. I was trying to be different, but failing. And Mally, he stayed the same – my friend, my *best* friend – but nonetheless distant, belonging to another when I needed him to be mine. If he *were* mine, this hollow feeling inside me, this torture that as a twelve-year old I couldn't fully comprehend, surely it would ease? Flo never needed him as much as I did. Flo could have coped without him. I couldn't.

I wanted to die, as I've wanted so often since; to join Da at the bottom of that treacherous sea; reach for his hand and just lay there beside him. To feel nothing would be blissful. I wanted that, I *desired* that. And that was the trouble. I desired things I couldn't have. Always. I wasn't going to die, not then, not for a long time. And yet I even practised holding my breath, under that table, in the lean-to by the side of Comraich. It'd be a relief, a miracle. What was the point of carrying on?

The tears wouldn't stop; perhaps I'd even begun to howl, I don't know. If I was howling, it didn't stop me from hearing the click of the door as it opened and footsteps drawing closer. The fronds gently parted and a face appeared – Stan's.

"Beth?" His voice was gentle, his expression as stricken as mine.

He reached out a hand, but I shrank back. I didn't want to be found. Not by him. And he knew it. He knew it, but he never blamed me. Not then. Not ever.

He withdrew his hand. "Come and find me, when you're ready," he said, his voice sombre but filled with so much kindness. "I'll be upstairs, searching for the other two."

"Beth," he reiterated, just before he rose to his feet and left me, "you know I'll be waiting."

Chapter Eleven

MAGGIE and Lenny had gone and Jessamin and Finn were lying in bed, neither of them sleeping. Finn lay on one side, and she on the other, gazing into the hazy dark and listening to the silence as it settled like a blanket. Even the ghosts were quiet tonight.

"Finn," her voice was barely above a whisper. "I love you."

There was a moment of silence, perhaps even confusion, before he replied. "I know you do. I love you too."

"It's great about Maggie and Lenny, isn't it?"

"I'm very pleased for them."

"A wedding. That's something to look forward to."

"Almost as much as the divorces around here."

She laughed. "Hmm… well, hopefully a bit more than that."

"Aye. Lenny seems like a good man."

"There's so much happening right now."

"Plenty of change."

"Plenty of change," she repeated, placing one hand on her stomach. As she did, Finn moved position to lie on his back, both of them with eyes wide open in the darkness. This was it. She should seize the opportunity, talk about the elephant in the room, properly talk about it, not just refer to it, but nerves seemed to paralyse her. Why should that be? She was having this man's baby, for God's sake, and yet… marriage. It was a pledge, a promise to forsake all others. *Forsake James?*

"Jessamin, are you all right?"

"Me?" Her voice was somewhat strangled. "I'm fine."

His hand joined her own over her stomach. "All quiet in there?"

"Oh yeah, he or she's fast asleep."

"Maggie thinks it's a boy."

"I know she does."

"We still haven't decided on names."

"It's hard, isn't it, trying to pick one from the millions out there."

"Millions?" There was a tease in his voice.

"It seems like it!"

"So, what's wrong with Murdoch Archibald Aonghas Maccaillin?"

Jessamin giggled. "Quite a lot actually!"

"It's a fine Scottish name!"

"I'm not denying it, but… it's also a bit in your face."

Finn laughed too. "I can see I'm going to have my work cut out convincing you."

"Oh, Finn, please tell me you're not serious."

"Aye, I'm serious!" His hands began to gently tickle her, making her writhe and squeal. "Honest I am! It's a noble name my son will have."

She batted away his hands. "Finn, Finn, stop, you'll wake the baby! And before you get too carried away, keep in mind we could be having a girl."

"But Maggie—"

"Is intuitive, I know, but give me credit, perhaps I am too."

He rolled onto his back again. "So you think it's a girl?"

She sighed again. "I've actually got no clue. Perhaps we should have found out at our last scan. It would have made decorating the nursery easier, that's for sure."

"No, we agreed, a surprise is best. God, I can't wait to meet whoever it is."

"Nor me," she replied gently. "As to where to have the baby, Finn, I really am keen on a home birth."

"Let's see how it goes, shall we? Keep our options open."

"Fair enough," she conceded.

"Come here."

She snuggled in as close as she could to him. "Do you ever get the feeling," she said, giggling again, "that something's come between us?"

"Surely if you shift yourself, you can get closer than that."

"'Fraid not, this is as good as it gets."

"My arms don't reach that far!"

"If they don't, you've only yourself to blame."

He inclined his head. "I'm pretty sure you had something to do with it as well."

She fluttered her eyelashes. "Mr Maccaillin, I was taken advantage of."

"And now you're pregnant."

"Indeed, I've been left in a sorry state."

A sorry state. Unwed. Now was the time to go in for the kill. *The reason I'm reluctant isn't because I don't love you, Finn, I do. I adore you.*

"Finn…"

"Hmm."

Go on, Jess, just say it – he'll understand.

She'd even rehearsed what she was going to say, something along the lines of: *Marriage is something that James and I shared, whereas with us it's the baby – it's something that's unique to both of you. It's what sets you apart.*

Did that explain it enough? Would he accept that? *Why am I getting so het up? It's not as if he's even asked me to marry him!*

But he wanted to, she knew that; he'd marry her in a flash.

Get on with it. Stop procrastinating.

Taking a deep breath, she tried again. "Finn…"

When she got no answer this time, she raised her head slightly.

The only sound that punctuated the quiet was the light sound of his snoring.

* * *

It was the kind of day Jessamin loved – the cold air brittle but so fresh that when you breathed it in it not only cleansed your lungs, but every cell, every sinew in your body. Today was a good day to explore – principally Larnside, or the land that lay towards the back of it. Mally's house – was it still lived in or was it a ruin? Quickly she did the maths. If he'd been eighteen when he left, that would have been around 1949/1950, nearly sixty years ago. His parents vacated it soon after; they'd run away, from him and from everything they'd ever known, eradicating their existence entirely. Parking her car close to the village, she proceeded to walk inland, just as Beth, Flo and Stan had in another era, a small bag containing some more of Beth's notes slung across her shoulder. Her week of supposed bed rest was long since over, and it felt good to be out and about, to be free. Finn was as busy as ever, paying a visit to old Mrs McConnell again, as well as to another tenant slightly further afield. Around her the hills were a heady mix of colours, although more pastel in shade than vivid, the heather having passed the height of its glory.

Trudging onwards, she took another deep breath. How far could it be? Not too far she hoped. She knew that the three had climbed upwards and stood looking down at Mally's house, nestling in the valley below. If it was too long a trek, she'd have to abandon it, but she wouldn't give up just yet, she had water with her, a sandwich and a chocolate bar – enough fuel to last her a while longer.

Half an hour later and she was beginning to admit defeat. She'd climbed not one hillside, but two, and there was yet another to negotiate. Her legs were tired and the extra weight she was carrying was becoming more and more obvious with each step. This wasn't a pleasant stroll in a park somewhere; this was land as harsh as the weather, and she daren't venture too far from Larnside. Finn had warned her before about the dangers of exploring deep countryside in Scotland; how easy it was to lose your bearings; how the storm clouds could rush in and cover up a clear blue sky. Just one last hill, that's all she'd tackle. *Before they turn into mountains.*

Her breath was short in her throat and the baby had issued several kicks by the time she reached the ridge. *This is it. It has to be.*

She gazed downwards with anticipation, glad that the sun was bright; that it illuminated all that lay in front of her. Where was it, the house Mally had grown up in? The house he'd been forced from. All that greeted her was acres of emptiness, some cattle grazing in the distance and birds swooping overhead. No house. No history.

"Damn," she muttered. "All this effort for nothing."

How disappointed she was surprised her. She was on the verge of tears. Maybe it was hormones, or simply plain old tiredness. Or maybe she'd just wanted something more solid than words on a sheet. Getting to know her grandfather was as important as getting to know Beth, even though she *had* known him. An enigma, that's how Beth had described him, and stubbornly he remained that way, even in death.

She was about to call it a day and return home to Comraich when something caught her eye; something in the valley, but off to the left, in amongst a clump of trees. What was it, a person? *Is someone down there?*

She craned her neck and took several steps forward. Before she knew it, she was all but flying down the hillside, no longer heavy but lighter than air, feeling young again, invincible; a child, full of excitement. If Finn could see her he'd have a fit!

At the bottom she stopped to catch her breath, which was once more coming in short bursts. There *had* been someone, in amongst the trees, which were now just a few yards away. Not feeling nervous at all, she ventured in their direction. After a few yards she half stumbled over something on the ground; some kind of obstruction. She gasped. It appeared to be bricks and mortar; a low wall of some description, somewhat hidden by tall grass and bracken. Bricks that used to belong to a house – a whitewashed house no doubt – now in ruins, as she'd feared.

A sound from behind her, a rustle, made her swing round.

"Hello? Is anybody there?"

Deep down she realised she hadn't been expecting a reply. The figure she'd seen had been no more than a shadow; a hint of something; a wisp.

"Mally," she whispered. "Was it you?" It could even have been Beth.

These ruins that she stood in where once a warm fire had

glowed, she was meant to find them, just as she was meant to find the notes that were safe in the bag she'd brought with her, a section of them anyway – the next section.

Before settling herself on one of the low brick walls to continue reading, she took a minute to soak up her surroundings, imagining the rusted items of farming equipment that Beth had described; the smoke that had billowed out of the chimney; the walls that were already battered and in need of repair; that had finally surrendered to gravity and the encroaching forest. A sad state of affairs, but had it always been that way? Or, when four had lived here instead of three, had there been happiness? Had Mally's father been a mild man, even-tempered before his eldest son had passed? Had Mally's mother smiled and welcomed visitors to the house rather than shooing them away? These were questions that even Beth didn't know the answers to. The archives, if any existed, might prove invaluable in tracing the Murrays, but it would be even better if there were someone alive who still remembered them. Maybe she could knock on every door in Larnside and ask.

She laughed. What an idea! Perhaps she was getting too involved. Then again… The dead were restless. What she'd experienced lately told her that. Beth especially.

Taking a swig of water from her bottle, she took out the notes, positioning herself as comfortably as she could on the bricks beneath her, and began to read.

Chapter Twelve

Beth

I had no more tears to shed. Not after that day when we'd played hide and seek at Stan's. It seemed the well had run dry for me, but Flo continued to cry. For weeks after Da died, for months, she'd cry herself to sleep. Mam cried too, I'd hear her as I lay awake, long after Flo had exhausted herself and drifted off to sleep. They were quiet sobs but that didn't make them any easier to hear. In the daytime, however, it was different; she 'got on with things', taking care of her daughters, trying to maintain some semblance of normality when all normality had flown.

We may have struggled emotionally but financially we did indeed get by. When tragedy strikes in the Highlands, people pull together. Those that lived in the village ensured we had enough to eat, and when Mam started taking in mending, she was practically deluged. But then Mam was artful with the needle, and those that gave her clothes and sheets to mend and socks to darn were always thrilled with the results.

In those days, leading up to our thirteenth birthday, I was so glad of Stan and Mally; they were as solid as rocks, always there, Mally more so for Flo than for me, but I'd come to accept that, or rather I was growing numb to it. I look back on that with wonder, and also with regret. If only my emotions could have stayed that way: numb. But the heart is a strange thing; it won't be tamed, or permanently subdued. Put simply: it wants what it wants. It lies, it plots, and it can blind you. But for a while I was in charge, everything in me contained and a lid placed upon it. And during that time I was, if not happy, grateful for what remained of my family and my friends.

Stan's art had also started to come on. He'd not only sketch the surrounding landscape, but he'd sketch us, sometimes individually, at other times together. And just as he captured the wildness of the country, he did the same with his friends, Mally in particular – the jet of his hair and the depth of his eyes caught in thick strokes of charcoal. Mally's expressions could change like the weather, but on paper Stan captured each and every mood; his grin, the fire within him and sometimes his sadness too. With Flo it was different. He portrayed her giggling, with her blonde hair tumbling around her face, or wistful, perhaps when she was thinking of Da.

Mally sometimes ribbed Stan for spending so much of his time drawing and painting. Perhaps he thought doing so made him seem more of a man. Art wasn't a typical male pursuit, like farming, fighting and climbing the scree slopes. That was what the men of the Highlands did. Stan always took it in good spirit, which amazed me, but he told me once that Mally wasn't quite so scathing in private. In private, he'd asked Stan for lessons.

"He can draw, can Mally," Stan told me, and there was pride in his voice. "He shows a good understanding of colour. Do you want to see what he painted?"

Of course I did, I was desperate to see it.

"Hang on," Stan replied. We were in his bedroom, just the two of us. I don't recall where the other two were, Flo was probably sick again, she was always less robust than me, given to head colds, and Mally was probably needed in the fields. Stan got up, opened his wardrobe doors and pulled out a canvas, one that was far bigger than I was expecting. "Don't tell Mally you've seen it," he said, "you know what he's like."

Not fully I didn't, that was the problem. I was hoping this would tell me more.

"Here it is," continued Stan, holding it up, "it's not bad, is it?"

The first thing I noticed was Stan's signature. "Why's your name on it?"

Stan laughed – it wasn't the deep belly laugh Mally was capable of, but it was always pleasant to hear. "That's Mally's joke. He says I'm going to be famous one day, that if it's got my name on it instead of his, he can sell it for vast sums of money."

He lowered his eyes, talk of fame clearly embarrassing him.

I reached out. "Stan, I think Mally's right, I think you will be famous."

"Och, I paint because I love it, that's all."

"And it shows, in your work, I mean. It shines through."

We were kids, just kids, but I recall this as a very adult moment between us, one filled with honesty and belief, the latter not just in his work, but also in each other.

Stan hurried on. "So come on, tell me what you think of it."

I stepped back a few paces and studied it properly. It had none of Stan's finesse, his gentle strokes, his perfect shading. It was crude. There's no other way to describe it. As though a child much younger than Mally had done it and yet... As I continued to gaze at it, I realised it had something. It definitely had something. Whereas Stan captured the almost surreal beauty of all he surveyed, Mally had managed to portray its darker side. The picture, of a loch with mountains in the distance reaching up towards a storm-ridden sky, was brutal almost; certainly it was brooding, with no light at all. But then, if you peered closer, if you *examined* it, you noticed there *was* a light; it was shining on a patch of water – a dazzling contrast to all that surrounded it.

That patch of light gave me hope. It did so because it reminded me of the patch of light that had shone on Loch Hourn when Mally and I had kissed. We might not have spoken of it since, but had it imprinted itself on his soul somehow as it had done on mine? In this painting, had it pushed its way up from his subconscious?

This, however, wasn't Loch Hourn.

"Where is it?" I asked.

Stan's brow furrowed somewhat. "It's near Comraich, apparently, further out on the moor, a couple of miles up the track, maybe a bit more. Mally found it only recently. One day, when he left here, he went walking instead of going straight home. He says it's a secret loch and no one in the world knows about it but him. He'll take us there one day, though. I made him promise. You haven't said; do you like it?"

"Yes. Yes I do." I loved it.

"It's a raw talent he has, but talent is talent."

"You giving him any more lessons?"

"If he wants. Can't force him, though."

"No, I know that."

Stan looked at me peculiarly, a frown marring his features.

Confused, I checked if he was okay.

"Aye, I'm fine. Anyway," he said, taking the picture back to his wardrobe to stow it away again, "there you are, that's Mally and his hidden talent."

"A hidden painting too by the looks of it. Why do you have it, instead of him?"

As Stan closed the wardrobe doors he turned towards me. "It's his father, he wouldn't approve. I think that's the real reason he put my name on it instead of his, so he'll never find out."

The hairs on the back of my neck bristled. "His da's a brute!"

"It's none of our business."

"But he's our friend!" I protested.

Stan appeared hurt at what I was intimating. "Aye, I know, but interfering won't do us any good."

Not just hurt, I was angry too. "Are you accusing me of interfering?"

"Beth—"

"Because I happen to care about our friend."

"I care too."

"His father hits him!"

"Mally can take care of himself."

"Stan, are you serious? He gets beaten, sometimes black and blue."

Stan averted his gaze. "It's complicated, Beth."

I leapt forward and grabbed him by the arm. "What's complicated? Has he told you?"

Stan nodded. "Aye, of course, we talk Mally and I."

"All I know is he had a brother who died."

"Duncan? That's right, it was cancer that ate away at him."

Stan paused before amending that revelation. "It ate away at them all."

"Cancer?" I know more than my fair share about that hateful disease now but back then it was just a word. "How old was he when he died?"

"Eleven and Mally was four."

Four? I remembered the first day of school and Mally walking into the schoolyard alone, as young as he was, his mother having come no further than the gates. I strove to see if I could remember her face, I couldn't, but I can imagine it well enough now – the sadness on it, the shock, the inability to face other people as she tried to keep her grief from spilling over. I judged her then, for not doing what all the other mothers were doing, handing us over to Mrs McNeill, one by one. I'd thought her uncaring. Of course now, knowing what she'd been through, identifying with it, all I have in my heart is sympathy. Years later, when we went knocking on her door, that grief was still evident; time hadn't erased it at all. It promises to, but then it renegades, plunging you right back into the depths. I don't condemn Mally's father as much as I used to either. When it comes to it, who am I to condemn anyone?

Tears started to fall from my eyes that day Stan and I stood together in his room, discussing subjects that were simply too big for us at that age. That painting of Mally's was a reflection of his soul I was sure of it – filled with darkness but a light ever present that was trying to burst through. I wished I could run to Stan's wardrobe, grab it with both hands and take it to his father and his mother and thrust it under their noses. I wanted to scream at them '*See? This is what you've done to him. Your eldest son is dead but it's not your youngest son's fault!*'

Those tears became a torrent – the well not dry after all.

Stan put his arms around me. "Ach, Beth, what's the matter? What's wrong?"

"It's... It's..."

How could I even begin to tell him? I had no words. Not then.

I pulled away from him, sniffing and wiping at my eyes with the backs of my hands. "I have to go home," I said.

Stan didn't disagree but he asked me to wait a minute.

"Why?"

"Because there's something else I want to show you."

I was intrigued and a little scared. I'd been shown enough for one afternoon.

"Stan—"

"Please, Beth. Just a minute, that's all I'm asking."

He crossed over to his wardrobe and this time withdrew something from behind it, another canvas.

I steeled myself as he brought it over to me, turning the canvas in his hands, revealing what was on it. It was me! Just me! A close-up of my face.

Looking at it, I was breathless. It was the best painting of his I'd ever seen; every brush stroke, every contour executed with such precision that it seemed more like a photograph than something created with oils this time, rather than charcoal.

I looked at Stan and he looked at me. I truly couldn't speak. Not a word.

That painting – it was so much darker than Mally's.

Chapter Thirteen

"FINN, Finn, I know my great uncle's name!"

Amazingly, given that she was in a valley in the middle of nowhere, Jessamin's phone boasted a good signal. Desperate to share this news, she phoned Finn straightaway. It felt momentous somehow; she had a great uncle called Duncan, who'd died aged eleven, in Larnside. As she thought of it, one hand cradled her stomach. What a young age to die! Despite this, she held onto the excitement of his identity being revealed rather than dwell on the tragedy.

"Your great uncle?" Finn's voice was slightly tinny on the other end of the line. "Mally's brother I presume?"

"That's right, Mally's brother Duncan."

"How'd you find out?"

"How'd I find out?" Her excitement faded and she faltered. It had temporarily slipped her mind that Finn didn't know she was reading Beth's notes, or indeed that Beth had left anything of the sort behind. *What do I do? Do I come clean?*

Quickly, she made her mind up. "I accessed the online archives, that's how."

"Why the sudden interest?"

"Oh… erm…" Her mind was whirring. "I suppose because we're starting a family, it's made me interested in those who've gone before, you know…"

"Your ancestors?"

"Exactly."

It was feasible. The future and the past were colliding, not just in mind, but in body too.

Finn seemed to accept her explanation. "Where are you? At home?"

"No... well, I was. I'm out walking."

"I see. So your great uncle's name was Duncan, another fine Scottish name."

He laughed and she did too, but actually, concealing the truth didn't sit well with her. Although tempted to come clean, she couldn't shake the feeling that Beth didn't want that. *There's a time for everything,* Maggie had said – a recollection that pushed its way to sit at the forefront of her mind.

"Jess, are you still there?"

"What? Oh yes, sorry, I'm still here."

"Don't walk too far, will you? Remember you're supposed to be taking it easy."

"I will... I am." Again she was lying, and she winced because of it. "Look, I have to go, the signal's beginning to dip. I'll see you at home soon."

"Aye, you will."

Finn rang off and Jessamin found herself alone once more amidst the ruins. Standing up, she hugged her phone to her as she closed her eyes. She had no idea which room she would be occupying if the walls had been standing; perhaps it had been the parlour or the kitchen. Nonetheless her mind started to furnish it, placing a chair here, the fireplace there, and a long wooden table with sturdy legs where her great grandmother would stand and chop vegetables, just as Beth's mam had done. She went one further – pictured her great grandmother as pregnant as she was, not with Mally but with Duncan; her excitement at starting a family, her great grandfather's excitement too, coming in from the fields after a hard day's work to gaze upon his wife's glowing face.

A baby's cry – she could hear it; the image in her mind's eye of a toddler running around the place becoming almost real to the touch; she could hear the adults' laughter as they watched him take his first tentative steps. Not just one child, now there were two, playing games together, running faster than the wind, the pair of them; brothers.

So happy. You must have been so happy. Until… until…

Opening her eyes, she swung round. Was that a sob she'd heard? More than that, a howl, coming from just behind her and filled with so much anguish.

Once again she called out. "Is anyone there?"

Once again she was met with silence.

It was an echo, merely that, sadness vying with anger for dominance. To be given a gift with one hand then to have it snatched back with another, she'd be angry too; she'd be filled with fury. Even so, the happiness she'd sensed, it had felt so real. She was certain that before Duncan's untimely death, rage had had no place here at all.

She shook her head. How quickly life could change, and how awful that it could.

According to Beth, the picture Mally had painted showed only a glimmer of hope – who was that hope aimed at? Beth, Flo, his parents? Or was it just a child's youthful optimism that had gradually been eroded?

"Another foursome torn apart."

Her family.

If only she could find a way to bring them all back together again.

* * *

Arriving back at Comraich, Jessamin made her way through the hallway, the stagheads on high watching her intently. As always, she shuddered slightly at the sight of them but not once had she asked Finn to replace them. Although nothing to do with him, they were ancestral trophies, part of Comraich's fabric; to remove them would remove something of the essence of the house – its heart and soul and in that respect she'd only go so far. Despite being tired, she vetoed the living room and went straight to another room at the back of the house; a room in which Stan used to paint. His easel was still in place and on it, a painting in progress – one of Finn's, for he had inherited some of his grandfather's artistic skill, although he regarded it as a hobby rather than a profession. Currently, the running of the estate took enough of his time.

It wasn't his painting she'd come to see, but nonetheless she was drawn to it. He was good, really good, and, like Stan, favoured landscapes – where he lived providing an endless source of inspiration. She'd love him to spend more time painting – it soothed him, deflected, for a time anyway, any memories of Connor, of his time in the army and all that he'd seen whilst in the army. When he stood in the exact same spot as Stan had, his palette in one hand, his paintbrush in the other, his expression was almost beatific. She'd never seen Stan paint, but she could imagine Stan wearing the same expression. History was repeating itself. *History.* Mally's was the painting she'd come to see, hung on the far wall, flanking two other pictures, and outshining them despite being so dark.

Jessamin walked over to it, reached out a hand and gently touched the edge of the frame, noticing the glimmer of light that sparkled on the water, *truly* noticing it. Beth was right, it was dazzling, a stroke of genius.

The loch, Stan's Loch she'd called it in the past, but now she knew it had been Mally who'd discovered it; who'd taken his three friends there when they'd all turned thirteen to share the beauty of it with them. Jessamin remembered Stan telling her about their first visit. Every word he'd uttered was imprinted on her heart as well as her brain. It was the summer of '44 and the world was still at war, but in Scotland, four children were on the brink of adolescence, and the sun was shining. And as everyone around here knew, when the sun shines, you don't waste a minute of it.

She glanced at her watch. It was too late to go to the loch today, but she'd go soon, choosing a day when the skies were clear. She'd *have* to go, because Beth would have written about it – the loch and everything that had happened there, the good times, the magic, and the unthinkable.

There was a thump. Nothing to do with the baby in her stomach, it came from the room directly above her, Beth's room; and such an impatient sound.

Jessamin tilted her head. "I'm getting there," she assured her. "I'm getting there."

Chapter Fourteen

Beth

I wanted to see the loch Mally had painted so much and so, I'm afraid to say, I let it slip I'd seen his painting, the one he'd put Stan's name to.

"He showed you?" Mally's face was as dark as a raincloud and I winced, annoyed with myself for not being more loyal to Stan.

"Aye. It's good, really good. Have you done any more?"

"A few," he mumbled, torn between anger and embarrassment.

"I thought you didn't like painting, you're always ribbing Stan about it."

He just grunted at that, messing with some pebbles on the floor.

School was finished for the day and we were sitting on the shores of Loch Hourn, Flo and Stan were playing a game of chase and were some distance away, although every now and then their laughter carried over to us on a gentle breeze. It was good to hear Flo laugh again, to see something of a return to her former self. Mally kept glancing up and looking towards them, but he was in no mood for joining in.

"Is everything okay at home?" I asked.

Again he grunted.

"It's good you've been in school so much lately."

His snort was derisive. "What good is school? Da's right about one thing, learning's not going to get me anywhere."

I shook my head. "That's not what Mam says, she says it'll get you everywhere."

"Did she go to school?"

"Aye, she did," I said, somewhat indignantly.

"A lot of good it did her."

If anyone else had said that to me, they'd be in trouble. But with Mally, it was different. As young as I was, I knew where that remark had come from – a place of hurt, one I could identify with, and so I refused to rise to it. Without Da, we might be forced to rely on the kindness of others sometimes, but Mam was always willing to work and she *did* work. She brought Flo and me up and she'd sew sometimes 'til her fingers bled, shifting her chair closer and closer to the candle before it burnt to a stub. We weren't like those who lived at Comraich; we had no electricity – hardly any of us in the village and the surrounding hills did; that would come years later.

Again laughter punctuated the air – Stan had caught Flo and she was squealing in protest. Their happiness – their *youthfulness* – it was so different to that which engulfed Mally and me – even I was feeling the weight of it that day, desiring something lighter; wanting Flo and Stan to join us perhaps, but they were too embroiled in their game.

I pressed onwards with my plan. His hand was just a few inches from mine and I was longing to take it, to soothe him somehow. In the spirit of friendship, that's something that can be easily done. When there are other emotions involved, however...

I kept my hands to myself. "Mally, we always sit here, in front of this loch; take us to the other one."

I was met with silence.

"Mally…"

"I could I suppose."

Wasting no time, I jumped to my feet. "Really? That's great. Shall we go now?"

He looked up at me, shielding his dark eyes. "Now? Are you serious?"

"Aye, I'm serious. I want to see it." This place with the pools and the mountains and a glimmer of light.

He shrugged, as though resigned. "Come on then, let's get the others. I warn you though, it's a fair trek."

He was right, it was; all the way back to Comraich and then a right turn just in front of the house and onwards down a road that Stan had correctly described as a track, disappearing deep into the countryside. It was breathtaking land, the sheer enormity of it never ceasing to amaze me, the big skies and the mountains colluding to form a barrier to the outside world, keeping us enclosed, us four in particular; herding us.

We chatted as we walked, Stan sometimes breaking into a run – his energy was boundless in those days – Mally with his hands thrust deep into his pockets, his pace more dogged. Flo was as excited as I was.

"Can we swim when we get there?" she asked.

"We've not got our costumes," I pointed out.

"Oh, Beth, we've our pants and vests, that'll preserve our modesty."

I pretended to be shocked by her words, but a swim did sound delicious; after all this walking it'd help to cool us down.

"Not long now," Mally informed us, his head not as low as before, his voice containing more enthusiasm. "It's such a special place. Flo, Flo, come here."

"Why?"

Yes, I thought. *Why?*

"Just come here." He was grinning at her, any former melancholy erased.

When she was close to him he swung her round and put his hands around her eyes. "What are you doing?" she yelled, but she was laughing too.

"I want to choose the moment you see it, the *perfect* moment."

I can still feel the pain of those words today; the jab to my heart.

Stan, meanwhile, had drawn closer to me. "You all right?"

"Why shouldn't I be?"

"No reason," he replied with a slight sigh.

I looked up, gazed ahead, and there it was – the loch, the secret loch, worth every step that we'd taken. There wasn't just a glimmer of light upon it, it was *bathed* in light; it was glittering. My steps faltered so I could take in its full majesty – the divided pools, the natural yet graceful stone archways, the colour of the water, crystal clear close up I'd bet, pure, although from here the green and blue of it was so vivid it was breathtaking. Nestled below slightly elevated ground, a series of waterfalls tumbled into it and the mountains on the horizon, which seemed to encircle it although they were a good distance away, were as black as the fabled Cuillins on Skye. Mally hadn't been exaggerating, it was magical. And, because his hands were still around Flo's eyes, it was me who'd seen it first; who yet again fell in love before she did.

"Ta dah! There you go, Flo, what do you think?" As my breath continued to remain lodged in my throat, she gasped.

"It's beautiful!"

"You like it?"

"I love it!"

"I love it too," I mumbled, but only Stan heard me. He nodded in agreement as Mally took Flo's hand and dragged her forward.

It took me some time to realise Stan had hold of my hand too and was pulling me along with equal enthusiasm. When we got to the loch's edge, he let go of me and bent to swirl his hands in the water. "It's lovely and fresh, Beth. You want to go in?"

I looked over at Mally and Flo; they were undressing, right down to their underwear. I hesitated. If Mam knew what we were doing, the tanning we'd get! It was a hot day though, and our clothes would soon dry in the sun.

Flo had taken to squealing again, Mally was roaring with pleasure too. As both of them entered the water, I gazed at him, at the breadth of his shoulders, the muscles beginning to develop and the smoothness of his skin. He was the second incredible sight I'd seen that day, Mally, who still had hold of my sister's hand, who only had eyes for her.

Trying to ignore that fact, at least for now, to steady my hands so that I could undress too, I let the shift dress I was wearing fall to the floor, neatly sidestepping it. Despite the warmth of the day, a shiver ran the length of my spine as I took several tentative steps forward. I remember that shiver so clearly and wonder at it still. It wasn't just jealousy I was feeling; it was something far deeper than that, far blacker.

Vehemently I shook my head, trying to rid myself of whatever had caused such sudden anxiety – a glimpse into the future I tend to think now – and as I did I sensed something else. Curious, I turned my head. Stan was standing there in his undershorts; his thin body still very much the frame of a boy rather than a man.

Gazing at me in my near naked state, with my blonde hair tumbling past my shoulders, he had the same look I wore whenever I stared at Mally.

Chapter Fifteen

"SO, you see, if Duncan died at Larnside, he's probably buried in Larnside. In those days, you were buried in your local parish and so I'm going over there again as soon as this infernal rain stops, to the church, to check each and every gravestone."

"Larnside, you say?" Maggie raised her eyebrows as she stood behind the counter of her shop, flicking through *You & Your Wedding* magazine. "Well, it's a small church, a small kirkyard too, so it shouldn't take you that long. Och, now look at this for an idea for a bouquet, just simple wild flowers, isn't it lovely?"

Jessamin leant over to look and oohed and ahhed too, but like Maggie, she was distracted, also dismayed, because the weather had been truly atrocious in the last few days. She'd got drenched just getting out of her car and hurrying the short distance to the shop, where she not only wanted to see Maggie but to pick up some everyday items that they were running out of. As soon as there was a break from the rain she'd have the graveyard at Larnside to explore and, of course, the loch. It'd been a long while since she'd been there, and her memories were mixed, but overall she was looking forward to going back, curious as to whether reading Beth's notes by the water's edge would conjure their ghosts again, though not in a real sense;

she didn't mean that, despite being absolutely sure she'd seen their ghosts there before. But as had happened when she'd visited Mally's cottage, when it reawakened them.

Earlier, when she'd first come into the shop, she'd debated whether to tell Maggie about the shadow she'd seen amidst the ruins of the Murray house and the howl she'd heard; the anguish in it. It'd be interesting to hear her take on it. But once more she had the feeling she'd betray Beth if she spoke up now and so was careful to keep even her thoughts cloaked, lest Maggie should pick up on them. Not that she had to try too hard; Maggie was too engrossed in her future plans.

"That's it, I've decided, a wild flower bouquet it is," Maggie declared.

"And the big meringue dress?"

"Jess, are you calling me a *Bridezilla*?"

Jessamin laughed. "No. You're far from it."

"The dress I have seen though, it's lovely, ivory in colour, such intricate lacework on the bodice. Sadly, I'm going to have to lose a few pounds before I can fit it."

Jessamin started to disagree but Maggie stopped her. "Don't you dare. You know full well I need to slim down. Still, how I'm going to do that over the next couple of months I've no clue. Lenny's a fantastic cook – he wasn't when we were first together, the man was useless, could barely fry an egg, but all those years on the rigs, and now it's his cooking the men prefer rather than the resident chef's!"

"A couple of months? So, you're going to have a December wedding?"

"Aye, we're aiming for Christmas Eve."

"Maggie, that's so romantic!"

"Well," Maggie looked bashful all of a sudden, "that's the

date I've had in mind ever since I was a wee girl. Just had to wait for someone to ask me, that's all."

And Lenny had, her second love as opposed to her first – a fact that hung in the air between them until once again Maggie waved her hand in a dismissive manner.

"Now, what's all this you were saying about Duncan? You've got a bee in your bonnet, have you, wanting to trace your Scottish heritage?"

"Something like that," Jessamin admitted. "I've been accessing the online archives and Duncan was registered as having died in Larnside, and his parents – my great grandparents – were both registered as having died in Glasgow. Their names were Jack and Margaret and he died in 1972 and she followed four years later. I'm assuming Duncan was buried locally, but as for them, I've no idea. If it was Glasgow, it'd be like looking for a needle in a haystack I should imagine."

Maggie's brow furrowed. "Where's Mally buried?"

"In Ealing in London."

"They're scattered to the winds then?"

"They are."

"Have you been to Mally's grave?"

"A couple of times, as a kid."

"And you want to go to the other graves because...?"

"I don't. I can't, at least not my great grandparents' graves." She glanced down at her ever expanding bump. "Not before this one makes an appearance anyway. But Duncan... well, if Duncan's is close by I'd like to pay my respects, take a bunch of flowers. He was a child, Maggie, just eleven." Recalling that, she closed her eyes briefly and took a deep breath.

Maggie reached out to squeeze her hand, but didn't say a word, allowing Jessamin to continue speaking. "It's just... I thought I knew pain, you know, when James died. And I did, I *do*, it still hurts to think of him, so much that it sometimes takes my breath away. But it didn't destroy me. That's the difference. It destroyed my great grandparents."

"Did it, Jess? How'd you know?"

"I… Because… It must have done. The prospect of anything happening to this baby, oh, Maggie, I can't bear it, I just can't."

Alarm registered on Maggie's face. "Jess, Jess, what's all this? Nothing's going to happen." Bustling round to the other side of the counter to give Jessamin a much-needed hug, she added, "You mustn't take on like this. It can't be good for the baby. Look, I'll tell you what, I'm going to close the shop, it's not busy anyway, let's sit for a wee while, you and me, take it easy."

Without further delay, Maggie turned the 'open' sign to 'closed'. As she did, Jessamin tried to get a grip on herself… and failed. Beth's words, the despair in them at times, how she'd described Mally and his home life, it had touched her. More than that, it had wounded her soul, or at least that's what it felt like, just as it had wounded them. Perhaps it was also the anticipation of what was to come that was getting to her; the full story as opposed to what Stan knew. To hear it from Beth, what she did and *why* she did it. Could she bear the heartache?

Maggie was back by her side. "You are happy, aren't you?"

Jessamin nodded.

"And this baby, I know it was a surprise—"

"A *wonderful* surprise."

"Aye," agreed Maggie. "But you're scared, aren't you?"

"God, it's stupid, isn't it? To be scared."

"Not at all, you've suffered loss. But it doesn't mean you're going to lose again."

"I hope not."

"Of course not!" Maggie insisted. "But this obsession with those that are gone, perhaps it's time to stop, for now anyway."

"Obsession?" She hadn't thought of it as such before.

"Aye," Maggie continued, undaunted. "And all this talk of traipsing around kirkyards, it's not what you should be doing. You should be focusing on *life*, not dwelling on the alternative."

There was so much sense in Maggie's words and yet... to shut Beth away again, ignore her. No. She had to see it through, share the load, but maybe she'd give herself more of a break in between readings, more than she was doing already. Dealing with someone else's extreme emotions on top of her own, was hard.

"Maggie, thank you," she answered, for a moment unable to say anything more. "And forgive me. You're so excited about your wedding and I rain on your parade."

"Not at all, but, Jess, take heed of my words will you?"

Smiling, Jessamin attempted to change the subject with a joke. "At your wedding, can I be a bridesmaid?"

"Once a bridesmaid..." Maggie quipped.

"Ah, but that's not true, is it? I have been married."

"And you'll no' consider it again?"

Jessamin faltered, her reply stuck in her throat.

"It's okay, you don't have to answer."

Maggie was right; she didn't, not to her anyway.

* * *

"I didn't know Rory was here."

In the kitchen of Comraich, Finn looked up from some letters he was reading. "What? Oh aye, Jess, he's here with his friend, *Mr Mould*, or at least that's what he calls himself. They're in the nursery, treating the walls."

"Oh right, Mr Mould," she mused. "It's apt I suppose. I saw the van outside."

Having composed herself fully before leaving Maggie's shop, she was feeling fine again, if still damp from her brief sojourn. As she crossed over to him, she asked what he was reading.

"Nothing exciting, it's just a bill that needs paying, some leasehold stuff… a couple of pamphlets."

"Pamphlets?" Her arms went round him as she queried what he was saying.

"Aye." Transferring the documents to one hand, he hugged her back. "The thing is, we're going to have get serious now we've a child on the way."

She reared back slightly. "Oh? You don't consider us serious enough?"

There was hesitancy in his voice. "I do, but, Jess, we need a will."

"A will?"

"Aye."

"A will," she repeated. "Yes… yes, of course we do. Is that what the pamphlets are about?"

"That and…" His voice tailed off again and he took a deep breath before continuing, "… we may have to draw up adoption papers too."

She couldn't help it, she burst out laughing as she stepped away from the circle of his arms to look into his face.

"Adoption? But you're the father!"

There was no smile on his face as he answered. "I've been looking into it. In a court of law I'd be responsible for the child, but I'd have no legal rights." He shrugged, a gesture that seemed forced. "Look, it seems a straightforward enough process. We can sort it out after the baby's born, of course. There's no hurry."

"Because it's not as if we're going to split up or anything," the sarcasm in her voice was evident.

"I don't mean it like that."

Of course he didn't. She knew that full well. And not being married did complicate matters. But was that a good enough reason to go ahead with it, to conform? *It's one reason, Jess.* But even as she thought it, her inner voice piped up again. *Wasn't killing James bad enough, that you'd betray him too?*

The voice, the thought – the brutality of it – shocked her. Refusing to have a second meltdown that day, she forced herself to look at Finn. Now would be a good time to talk about marriage and her issues concerning it, but she'd stunned herself into silence. Despite that, Finn looked hopeful, which planted a seed of hope in her too. *He'll understand,* she told herself, *he's certain to.*

"Mr Maccaillin… Ah, Jess, you're here too." It was Rory, entering the kitchen with his usual bluster and preventing any moment of honesty between them. "It's all done, and Greg's just tidying up. That's a lovely room for a nursery that is, the perfect size. What colour you painting it, Jess?"

"Erm… er… yellow, I've decided on yellow," Jessamin answered.

"Ideal for a boy or a girl," Rory replied, beaming.

"How much do we owe you both?" Finn had placed what

was in his hand on the table and held his wallet instead; opening it to reveal a bundle of cash he'd obviously taken out in anticipation.

Rory presented him with a bill and the deal was done – Beth's room was ready to be transformed, and yet… Jessamin had mixed feelings about it, as if somehow that was a form of betrayal too. She shook her head. Hormones, they had a lot to answer for.

It took a moment to realise Rory was speaking again. "Shona's told me not to say a word, as we've only just found out, but I can't help it, I'm fit to burst!"

Finn and Jessamin wore matching expressions of puzzlement. "What?" Finn asked.

"We're having a baby too!" Rory all but punched the air with glee. "Like you, we're expecting the pitter patter of tiny feet."

"Oh wow!" Jessamin responded, thrilled for him and for Shona. She and Shona got on very well; it was lovely to think they'd be rearing children at the same time.

Finn stepped forward and congratulated him.

"Thanks, Mr Maccaillin," Rory replied whilst shaking his hand avidly. "Good to know we're not firing blanks, isn't it?"

As Finn's mouth fell open, Jessamin laughed uproariously. Finally, Finn started laughing too. "Aye, well… I suppose it is."

"We shoot to score, eh?"

"We do our best," Finn muttered jovially enough.

"We didn't plan it, it was an accident, completely out of the blue. Was it the same for yourselves?"

"Erm… Yes. It was a surprise," Finn glanced at Jessamin as he added, "but one we're very pleased about."

Rory let go of Finn's hand at last, the biggest grin she'd ever seen adorning his face. Both he and Shona were in their mid to late twenties, a decade or so younger than she and Finn. After a bit of a bumpy start when Shona had to wait patiently for him to get over his somewhat puppy-dog affections for Jessamin, their relationship had gone from strength to strength. That they were taking it one step further seemed right. Jessamin checked herself. One step? It was more than that, it was a giant leap. There was more news to come, however.

Rory was fiddling about in his jeans pocket. As he did, Finn and Jessamin exchanged another puzzled look. What on earth was he doing?

Eventually he retrieved his hand and in it was a black velvet, heart-shaped box. Without further ado, he opened it to reveal a princess cut gold and diamond engagement ring – simple but beautiful.

"It's for Shona!" Rory declared, seeing fit to point out the obvious.

Jessamin swallowed. "You're going to ask her to marry you?"

"Of course I am! I love her; she's having my baby. I want us to be a family, a *proper* family I mean. I'm ready for this, the big commitment."

As he said it, Jessamin's heart sank further. She could hardly bear to bring herself to look at Finn. When she did, his expression, his *reaction* was hidden from her as he'd clasped hands with Rory again to congratulate him further.

"What with Maggie and Lenny, we're all getting hitched at the moment, aren't we?" Rory commented. "The baby's not due 'til the summer, but our wedding, I want it to happen as soon as possible."

"She hasn't said yes yet," Jessamin pointed out, striving to keep her tone playful.

"Aye, but she will. She's not subtle when it comes to hinting is Shona." Rory had taken to hugging himself such was his excitement.

"I'm thrilled for you," Jessamin managed. "*We're* thrilled, aren't we, Finn?"

"Aye," was Finn's somewhat plain reply.

"So, when are you two…"

Oh no, Rory, don't say it, thought Jessamin, *please don't say it.*

"… getting married?"

When he was met with silence, Rory's grin dissolved into a frown. "You *are* getting married, aren't you? What with…" he gestured towards Jessamin's stomach.

"Erm…" began Finn.

"We haven't…" Jessamin added.

"It's Christmas Eve that Maggie and Lenny are planning for, I could maybe persuade Shona that's a good idea too, and yourselves could join us; we could have a triple wedding. Imagine that! The shindig we'll have. It'll go down in village history!"

"Christmas Eve?" Jessamin croaked.

"She'll still be pregnant," Finn managed.

"So will Shona," Rory said, unperturbed. "A bit of a shotgun wedding, eh?"

"Oh no, no, no," Jessamin continued. "It's too close to my due date." She had to pause, take a breath. "Besides…"

Finn looked at her. "Besides?" he questioned.

When Greg, AKA Mr Mould, appeared, a stout, middle-aged man, clad in white overalls, Jessamin could have rushed over and kissed him. "You're all done," he said, rubbing his hands together. "The room's ready for ya now. Thanks for ya custom, Mr and Mrs Maccaillin, I appreciate it."

"Thank you," Jessamin returned, her voice strangled yet again.

As Mr Mould turned to go, Rory made to follow him. "Well, I'll be seeing you," he said, adding with a wink, "Mr and Mrs Maccaillin, it has a lovely ring to it."

With just the two of them left in the kitchen, they stood side by side, staring after those that had departed. The silence was agonising, at least to Jessamin.

"This… this will thing," she said, not knowing what else to say.

"Will?" he repeated, as if confused. "Oh aye, the will. I'll get onto my solicitor about it." Picking the bundle on the table back up, he added, "That and… other matters."

Whether he was reading what was in his hands or just making a show of it, he wandered from the room with nothing more said.

Chapter Sixteen

Beth

THAT first summer spent at the loch was idyllic. After we'd finished our respective chores, we girls would head out the door and meet Stan and Mally at Comraich. There we'd grab a glass of Mrs McCabe's homemade lemonade – she always kept a jug in the pantry – before heading off to the loch to spend the afternoon. The sun deigned to shine quite regularly, but even if it was overcast we hurried there. It had become our place, somewhere other than Stan's bedroom where we could relax and just be ourselves. We weren't supposed to swim without an adult present; well… Flo and I weren't, Mam had made that clear, but we did anyway, carefully drying off or concealing any wet clothes before returning home.

Oh those days! Whilst so many in Europe were being felled, we experienced freedom like never before. And solitude. No one ever came to that loch, not once. It was our shelter, our protection from a world that was still in the grip of madness. We'd swim and we'd talk, we'd laugh and we'd rib each other. The boys were terrible, they'd tease us mercilessly, but we would give as good as we got, or at least I like to think we did. And it wasn't so much Mally and Flo that summer, I'm sure of it; the four of us functioned as one. Not just a twin, I was part of a quartet.

When news that the war had ended reached us, our village as well as Larnside and Amberley took to the streets to celebrate, gathering in Glenelk as it was the largest of the three. Our family did too, what was left of it, as well as Stan's. Only the Murrays stayed away, although Mally came later. He must have snuck out or something, but as to where his parents were, he wouldn't say. I did ask but he ignored me.

Some of the women had made lemonade and were handing out cups; others had hung up bunting made from colourful clothes to welcome their men home. People had lost sons, fathers, husbands and uncles – Mary McCormack for one had lost her eldest son, and Mrs Dunbar her husband – but even they were there, cradled by others who knew their loss, just as we'd been cradled when Da died, both tears and laughter on their faces.

When the priest spoke, we all listened. "A great evil has been thwarted," he said, his chest puffed up as though trying to make himself bigger, his voice imperious, daring anyone to interrupt him, even the non-believers, "and in the battle, the men of Scotland have fought good and true, offering their lives so that we may live without fear. For those who won't be coming back, who've taken their place beside the Almighty God in the Kingdom of Heaven, we will mourn their loss, but we will also give thanks for their lives and their ultimate sacrifice. Evil must not be allowed to flourish. At any cost."

Strong words, wise words, words that caused more people to cry in the crowds around us, even those who hadn't lost anyone; words I should have taken more notice of, instead of craning my neck to see Flo and Mally who were standing together, side by side, just a few yards in front, their hands entwined. *Evil must not be allowed to flourish.* But evil has such a powerful grip.

The priest, his chest still puffed, duly bowed to the crowds and retreated back into his vestry, but not without accepting a glass of lemonade pressed on him by an awe-struck Jinny, a girl not much older than me. He took it with one hand and made the sign of the cross on her forehead with the other, thanking her with a blessing.

How envious I was of Jinny in that moment; *I* was the one who needed blessing.

Stan grabbed my hand. "Come on, there's a jig. Dance with me!"

He was right, it was a merry jig; several people were dancing already and more were joining in. Rather than looking for Mally, I searched for Mam; she was there in the crowds, and a man was talking to her, not a Glenelk man, maybe one from Larnside or Amberley. She was talking back to him, her head somewhat lowered. Despite that, I could see there was laughter on her lips and I felt both confused and relieved by it.

"Come on," Stan said again, his grip a little more determined as he twirled me round and then pulled me to him so that my chest was bumping against his.

I was about to admonish him, to tell him to stop his antics, but then I looked at him – *truly* looked at him and saw the hope that was in his eyes.

Stan was different to Mally in every way. Mally was dark, Stan was fair. Physically, he wasn't as strong, and his nature was calm, whereas Mally, like myself, was more like a winter storm. Aware that something was happening with Mam; that Flo was at Mally's side, as though stuck there with glue; that things were changing all around us, for good and for bad, I didn't feel like dancing. But Stan was one of my best friends and it would have been cruel indeed to deny him.

I took my first tentative steps of the jig, my hands on my hips as my feet moved. Stan stood still for a moment, watching me, not just hope in his eyes, there was something else; but like Mam I lowered my gaze as I continued to dance, Stan eventually matching me step for step, as the band – so hastily put together – continued to play, the sound of violin, drum, accordion and the harmonica filling the air that September day, while the sun valiantly did its utmost to keep the cold at bay.

How can you not smile when you're dancing? How can you not feel at least a degree or two lighter? As my feet grew more confident, as Stan continued to twirl me, to hold me, I forgot about everything and everyone. I threw my head back and laughed as the world around me faded, myself the only person left in it… and Stan.

It was just Stan and I.

Oh how simple that would have been.

Chapter Seventeen

THE decorating was underway in Beth's bedroom, Finn having called Rory back to do it, although Jessamin insisted on helping but doing more than that as it turned out, for Rory, too intent on chatting about weddings and babies, tended to stand there with his roller held aloft, not actually making contact with anything, let alone a wall. Deciding one day not to provide him with an excuse for distraction, she grabbed Finn and the two of them headed into Inverness, intending to make a day of it, buying all that they'd need for the baby. After filling Finn's Defender to the roof, they decided, before heading home to Comraich, to stop for dinner at one of the restaurants that overlooked the River Ness. Once seated, they sat staring out of the window as the rain pitter-pattered onto the waters, causing a series of perfect circles to overlap each other.

It was a pleasant day, an exciting day, not just for Jessamin but Finn also got quite emotional as they picked up various tiny outfits to show each other. As they'd walked arm in arm through the shopping centre, people had looked at them with smiles on their faces, some even nodding gently in their direction. The promise of new life seemed to lift everyone, lending a ray of light to an otherwise overcast day.

The waitress in the restaurant was equally as enchanted. A

young girl with brown hair the same shade as Jessamin's but whipped into a bun rather than hanging loose, she asked them the usual set of questions before taking their order: when's it due? Do you know if it's a boy or a girl? Have you chosen names yet? They answered these questions amicably enough, or rather Jessamin answered, as Finn seemed to be holding back, letting her take the lead. When the waitress had gone, Jessamin leaned forwards.

"Are you okay, Finn?"

"Aye. Are you?"

"I'm fine."

"And the bairn?"

"The bairn seems to be fast asleep." On finishing her sentence, Jessamin yawned.

"Looks like you could do with an early night as well."

"Probably. It's no mean task growing a baby."

"It's an admirable task. You look shattered."

"It doesn't matter, it's still lovely to be out with you, to be here. Inverness is great."

"We could rent a flat here, Jess, as I've said. Just until the baby's born."

Jessamin sat back in her chair and took a sip of sparkling water. "No, Finn," she said when she'd finished. "You know I want to have the baby at Comraich."

"*If* you can," he countered.

"Stop suggesting I can't, right now it's looking likely."

The meal arrived – fresh local fish for both of them – and they ate at a leisurely pace whilst outside the rain at last began to ease. It was warmer than she expected for this time of year – late October – something she remarked on.

"Well, you know how it can turn. We've got to be prepared

for all eventualities."

Having finished eating, Jessamin placed her knife and fork neatly on the plate. "You know something," she teased, "you're a bit doom and gloom at the moment, always anticipating the worst. We could have a mild winter, compared to last year anyway, and this baby, it could be the most straightforward birth in the world."

"You're going to sneeze it out, are you?"

"Well, I wouldn't go that far, but… you know what I'm saying."

Finn called for the bill. "Perhaps it's the Highland way, to be dour."

She thought of Rory, of Maggie, of others in the village. It wasn't. But occasionally it was *his* way, Finn Maccaillin's. Knowing this, *understanding* this, she reached out and took his hand in hers, felt the strength that had got him thus far in life.

"Finn," she began, feeling an urge, a need to let him know yet again how much she loved him, here in a packed restaurant, in the middle of Inverness. Taking a deep breath, she was about to continue when a voice interrupted her.

"Hen's teeth, it is, it's you, Finn Maccaillin!" The man accosting them, a stranger to Jessamin at least, pointed to a table at the far end of the restaurant. "I've been sitting over there, with my wife, wondering if it was you. I couldn't leave, not without making sure. Your eye…" His eyes travelled downwards to Finn's hand. "Your hand… Ach, Finn, I'm sorry, but it's good to see you again. So good."

Finn stood up and the stranger immediately clasped his friend to him, giving his back a hearty pat as he did. Upon release, the stranger turned to Jessamin.

"Is this your wife, is it?" He extended his hand and

Jessamin duly took it, inwardly wincing at the assumption.

"This is Jessamin," Finn said, neatly swerving the question. "Jessamin, this is Angus, we served some time together in the army."

Angus, as tall as Finn but a good deal stockier and with the reddest of hair, cropped short whereas Finn had let his grow, pulled a face. "I'm still in the army I'm afraid; no escape for me, not just yet." To Finn he said, "Are you rushing off?"

"Well… we've just paid the bill, and Jess, she gets tired…"

A broad smile graced Angus's face. "Aye, well I can see the reason why. You've been keeping yourself busy, Finn." He laughed, a booming sound. "Congratulations to you both! Look, it's been a while – what is it now? A good two or three years?" He shook his head. "What am I thinking? It's longer than that, isn't it; more like four or five? Time goes by so quickly. Let me call my wife over, perhaps we can just have a quick drink and a catch-up. We won't keep you long, I promise."

Rather than wait for an answer, Angus beckoned to his wife, who, as if she'd been waiting for the signal rose immediately and hurried over. Meanwhile, Finn caught Jessamin's eye, a silent apology in it. She shook her head, to let him know he needn't worry, that it was fine. More than that, it was good to meet people from his past – as with Beth and the notes she'd written, it helped to flesh him out.

Angus's wife was called Becky. The pair of them were slightly younger than her and Finn and had been married for ten years – tonight was their anniversary.

Becky, who was sitting beside Jessamin, looked admiringly at her stomach. "We've not been blessed with bairns. Well… to be honest, we've only just started to seriously try, but we're hoping the wait won't be too long. Is this your first?"

"Yes," answered Jessamin, "Finn and I have only known each other for a couple of years."

Both Angus and Becky's eyes widened. "Impatient then?" said Angus.

"It was a surprise," Finn patiently explained.

"Babies, marriage, they get us all in the end, don't they?" Becky lifted the glass she'd brought over with her to her mouth and took a sip.

"Let's hope so anyway," Angus replied, smiling indulgently at Becky.

"Yes," muttered Jessamin, not daring to shift her gaze towards Finn.

"So, Finn," Angus began as Jessamin prayed for a change of subject, "what else has been happening since you left us boys to it? You looking after that estate of yours? Becky, I remember him talking; he's got this great big house, over in the west, his family are the Lairds of… what's the name of your village, Finn?"

"Glenelk, and they *used* to be the Lairds."

"That's it, Glenelk. And that house of yours, it has a name, doesn't it?"

"Comraich."

"Comraich! I remember now." He patted Finn heartily on the back once more. "Aye, he's a posh boy this one, Becky, but for all that, he's a good 'un. You were always a good 'un, Finn, despite what happened. It wasn't your fault."

From looking slightly pained, Finn now visibly stiffened. As for Jessamin, her breath caught in her throat – Angus had done as she'd wished and changed the subject, but to go from marriage and babies to *this*?

Before Finn had a chance to form a response, Angus continued, his expression earnest as he nodded his head. "Aye, you were a good soldier, Finn, you're very much missed. Those bastards out there with their bombs and their hatred, they're relentless." He leaned towards Finn in a decidedly conspiratorial manner. "I know I wasn't there at the time, but I'm well aware of what happened. That building had been checked, plenty of people have confirmed that, but those bastards, they get cleverer each year, with every bloody month that passes."

Jessamin bit her lip. Finn lived with this every day, what had happened to Connor, and she was sure he replayed events over and over in his head, as she sometimes did, perhaps *too* often. He didn't need reminding. His face was pale and his hands were clenched together on top of the table, knuckles turning white with the pressure.

"Angus..." she began, wondering how she could try and explain this, but Angus was still speaking.

"I'm on extended leave at the moment, a few of us are, including Jamie and Davey. We're your *friends*, Finn, and we're always here for you, you know that. Don't be a stranger, what we've gone through makes us more than friends, we're a family."

At last Finn spoke, but his voice was different somehow, carefully neutral. "Aye, thanks. It'll be good to see you all again. Give me your number and I'll be in touch." Nodding at Jessamin, he said, "We really do need to get going."

He stood up, forcing Angus to do the same. They shook hands after which Angus scribbled down his number. "Give me yours too, Finn, just in case."

Finn hesitated.

"Ah c'mon, Finn, what is it?"

Reciting the numbers, he was still as pale as ever.

"Stay in touch." There was a plea in Angus's words.

"Aye," Finn replied, his voice barely above a whisper.

After saying their goodbyes, Jessamin and Finn left the restaurant to finally head home – Finn, she knew, was in desperate need of what it offered – sanctuary.

On the return journey she attempted to speak to him.

"Angus meant well you know."

"I know."

"Are you angry with him?"

"With him?" A harsh laugh echoed round the dark confines of the car. "No, I'm not angry with *him*."

After a second or two, she dared to say it. "Don't be angry with yourself."

"Jess…"

She heard the warning in his voice not to go any further.

Inside her, the baby kicked, another warning perhaps. Exhaling, she forced back the words that wanted to come tumbling out. Secrets. That's what her world seemed to be made up of at the moment – those written on paper and those held deep inside.

Later, when they'd unpacked the car and closed the door on the world, the house so silent around them, she laid a hand on his arm. "Come to bed."

"I will. I'll just… I want to catch up on the news first."

It stung that he'd turned her down. He knew damn well what she meant when she'd asked him to come to bed but after the encounter with Angus he remained distant. *It's not just because of Angus.* Her mind had started up again, was intent on goading her. It wasn't solely because of Connor either. It was because of her.

As she climbed the stairs alone, she hung her head. Why were words so difficult to say? Why were emotions so complex? Why did they dominate you? *Oh, Finn…*

She was awake when he finally joined her, although she continued to lie perfectly still. As he switched off his sidelight, the smell of whisky was pungent.

Chapter Eighteen

Beth

FINALLY, Flo and I turned sixteen, Mally and Stan just a few months earlier. All of us now fully fledged teenagers, much about us hinting at the men and women we would become – both physically and mentally.

Mally was the tallest of us all, his jet hair as unruly as ever, his arms and shoulders rippling with muscles from all the work he did in the fields. He was hardly ever at school now, but then we were all due to leave soon – to do what, we wondered? I was unsure, so was Flo, but Stan and Mally had started to make plans.

"I still want to travel and see other places," Flo would say to us sometimes, a wistful look in her eyes. "I haven't forgotten about that. Mally, you do too, don't you?"

Sometimes Mally would agree with her, sometimes he'd be downright evasive, blowing hot and cold as always, changing his mind. The plans he'd made with Stan, they suited him more, they excited him I think, but with Flo he kept up pretences.

I tend to think Stan's life was mapped out for him from the start – his parents ran an estate which, as their only son, they expected him to take over. "I want to paint, though," he'd say,

"I have to find time for that." For Stan, a life without art was unthinkable. His parents seemed to understand that and were taking it into account.

Stan had begun to fill out too, his sandy hair kept short and neat, his grey-green eyes as piercing as ever but in need of glasses – little round wire spectacles that he hated to wear and which Mally would tease him about, but which were necessary if he wanted to see the world in focus. I didn't mind them. I thought they made him look studious, something he laughed about when I told him. But he *was* studious, was Stan; he was cultured. Unlike Mally, and to an extent unlike Flo and me, he had the opportunity to be cultured, and he never squandered those opportunities. That's the thing with Stan. He made the most of each and every privilege bestowed on him. Not only that, he did his best to share his good fortune. He was a generous boy who grew to be a generous man. More generous than he ever gave himself credit for.

Regarding Flo and me, there were many who considered us pretty with our blonde hair, our blue eyes and our bodies no longer slim but curvaceous. I knew what Mally used to say to Stan sometimes about us (he was never as discreet as he liked to think he was): *The best thing about the girls is there are two of them to drool over!*

Stan would laugh when he said that. One thing I never heard him do, though, was agree.

Change was all around us, and not just in our close-knit group, but in my own family too. The man Mam had been chatting to on the day our village and the villages hereabouts had celebrated the end of the war, had, over a period of time, increased his visits to our house. And then suddenly it was official – Mam and this man – Robert – were in love and were going to get married.

Flo was thrilled. "We'll have a da again, Beth!"

I was furious. We *had* a da. We weren't in need of another. How could Mam betray him like this?

But Robert, a local farmhand, he'd beguiled Mam and he'd beguiled Flo too. As far as I was concerned, however, he'd wormed his way into our home, to sit beside our fire during the early evening; to eat our food. I would only speak to him when I had to; I'd barely even look at him. Flo, on the other hand, was like Mam around him. She'd clutch her sides laughing at the stories he'd tell; she'd itch to be the one to serve him a ladleful of broth or stew. When he returned to his own home for the night, she'd run to fetch his shoes and afterwards, her smile would continue, as would Mam's, both of them so happy at the prospect of having a man around again. Either one of them would catch my expression, my surliness, my resentment. If it was Flo, she'd simply roll her eyes en route to bed. If it was Mam, the brightness in her would dull a little, something I felt both happy and triumphant about.

Prior to the wedding, I was lying with Flo in the long grass one warmish day. Flo was excited about the outfits we were going to wear: white dresses with pink sashes.

"We're flower girls," she squealed.

"We're not, we're bridesmaids."

"Well, I prefer to be called a flower girl, because that's what we're going to do; strew rose petals in front of Mam and Robert as they walk down the aisle once they're man and wife. Isn't that lovely, Beth? Isn't that romantic?"

My response this time was noncommittal.

"When I get married," she continued undaunted, "I want flower girls. Oh and Beth, you can be my bridesmaid."

"Your bridesmaid?"

"Uh-huh, and I don't want my dress to be simple, I want it to be… what's the word, lavish. It's such a great word, isn't it? I want the bodice to be tight and the skirt to be full, and for my veil to trail five foot behind me. I'll wear flowers in my hair and my bouquet will have heather in it. It'll have to, because Mally loves the scent of it."

"Mally?" She'd captured my attention wholly now. "What do you mean, Mally?"

Flo turned to me then, and her blue eyes as she fixed them on me shone brighter than the sun. "Because, silly, it's Mally I'm going to marry."

I pushed myself up on to my elbows. "Has he asked you?"

"No, not yet, but he will."

"How?" My voice was louder than it should be. "How do you know he will?"

"Simple. Because Mally does whatever I want him to."

There's a look Flo gets when she's determined; her sweet lips set themselves into a thin white line and the nostrils of her upturned nose begin to flare slightly. *Mally does whatever I want him to.* She was right, he did. And yet… it was me he'd kissed first. Whether he had even kissed Flo I didn't know, she hadn't told me, but they were spending more and more time together so I guessed he had; and because he had, because she'd felt his desire as I had felt it on that hillside overlooking Loch Hourn, she knew what power she had and she was going to use it.

"Beth," her voice was tentative now. "Are you okay?"

"I'm fine."

Flo stared at me and I grew hot and uncomfortable and had to turn away.

There was silence and then she said. “Do you like Stan?”

“What?” Her question had taken me by surprise. “*Of course* I like Stan, he’s my best friend.”

“But do you really like him, I mean. The way that I like Mally.”

“I… Flo… What a thing to ask!”

Laughter creased her face. “Because wouldn’t it be something if you and Stan and me and Mally had a double wedding, right here in Glenelk? The two of us wearing matching dresses, walking down the aisle together. Mam won’t let us marry now, but once we’re eighteen she might. We’ll be adults then, our lives will be our own.”

This talk of weddings was incessant.

“I don’t want to marry Stan,” was my terse reply.

“Oh?” Flo had turned coquettish. “Who’d you want to marry then?”

“I don’t want to marry anyone!”

“What about Mally then, do you like him?”

Not wanting to listen to her anymore, I jumped to my feet. “I don’t know what game you’re playing, Flo, but I’ve had enough. I’m going home.”

She jumped to her feet too. “Because I’ve seen the way you look at him.”

Fear as well as anger turned my skin cold. “You’re mad,” I declared, turning my back on her and beginning to march away.

She ran to catch up with me, reaching out one hand to pull me round to face her again. “I’ve seen the way you look at him, and he’s noticed too. We laugh about it sometimes. We do!” Was it my imagination or was there unease in her eyes? She was! She was uneasy! I seized on that.

"You're a liar. You're also scared. Perhaps Mally doesn't like you as much as you think he does."

She actually bared her teeth at me. "He *loves* me. He's said it."

"He's said it? Liar!" I repeated.

"He's mine, Beth, and he always has been. Don't ruin it for us, and don't ruin it for Mam either. Mam needs a man and she won't find better than Robert. Don't ruin it because you're selfish, because you're jealous, because you always want things your way."

Her hand was still on my arm. "Let go of me," I demanded.

"Why can't you just be happy that we're happy? There's something wrong with you, I'm sure of it. You're my twin but sometimes I feel I don't know you at all."

"I said, let go of me."

"I know you kissed him."

"What?" He'd told her?

"You kissed him, years ago. *You,*" she emphasised, "kissed him."

"We were kids, not even eleven."

"But why'd you do it? Do you want to do it again?" If my eyes were capable of firing sparks, so were hers. In them, all lightness, all laughter had gone. I was angry too, but so what? There was a part of me that was forever angry. In Flo, however, anger never sat well.

"We were kids," I reiterated. "It meant nothing."

I was surprised at how easily I could say that, but obviously it convinced her.

"It's just… we've got plans, Mally and I."

"What plans?"

"To travel."

I shook my head, couldn't help it. "Mally doesn't want to travel, he loves it here."

Immediately she flared up again. "How do you know? How the hell do you know?"

"Because we're friends!" I shouted back. "And friends talk. He loves it here. You know it as well as I do. I think he and Stan are going to run the Comraich estate together. That's a job for life, Flo, a job that'll suit Mally down to the ground."

"It's… It's the edge of the world here, Beth, there's nothing but mountains and valleys and lochs."

"What's wrong with that?"

"I want to travel!" Her voice was panicked almost. "All the places Mrs McNeill's told us about, all that she's taught us, why wouldn't you want to see it for yourself?"

"Because…" I tore my gaze from her pinched little face and looked around me. "This is *our* land, Flo, this is Mally's – he won't leave here, it's in his blood."

Her voice had become low, brittle even. "I'll leave this place, and so will Mally, when we're old enough. I've told you, he'll do what I want. It's *me* that's in his blood."

She turned and flounced away, her blonde ponytail swishing behind her. I knew she was determined; I've already pointed that out.

But then again, so was I.

Chapter Nineteen

THE hustle and bustle of Maggie's Thursday night gathering was in stark contrast to how Jessamin had spent much of the day. As she took her seat in Maggie's living room, the chintz that Maggie so adored still very much in evidence despite Lenny living here now, and her prized cherubs covering practically every surface, those around her chattered excitedly about the forthcoming nuptials of two of their party. Rory was right to have been so confident; when he'd asked for Shona's hand in marriage she'd given him a resounding yes. Both she and Maggie were like the cats who'd got the cream, listening to the likes of Ina, Maidie, Ailsa, Eileen, Ally and Gracie asking them all about their plans; encouraging them; savouring every last detail.

Jessamin forced herself to listen too, trying to banish Beth's uncharitable words – *This talk of weddings was incessant* – from her mind. Also Flo's words: *Why can't you just be happy that we're happy?*

I am happy, for Maggie, for Shona, and for myself.

Even so, it was a relief to escape into her own thoughts; to stare at the bridal catalogues thrust under her nose, but not see them; to focus on another matter.

She'd found it. Duncan's headstone. That was how she'd

spent the day, in a Church of Scotland graveyard in the small village of Larnside, wandering diligently from marker to marker, trying to decipher so many wind-battered inscriptions. Many were illegible and this had filled her with fear – it was simply impossible to determine to whom some belonged to. But others had survived the elements well enough, and they made for harsh reading. So many had died so young in these parts, they'd: 'Fallen Asleep', 'Returned to God's Arms', 'Flown Free'. After poring over one such memorial, she'd straightened and looked around her, pulling the coat she was wearing tighter, trying to shield her bump not only from the persistent drizzle of the early November day, but from something else too – death, she supposed.

Maggie had a point. What was she doing, becoming so preoccupied with those who'd departed? Why couldn't she simply embrace the present rather than dwelling on the past? Because Beth wanted it – her's was a spirit that wouldn't rest, not until someone knew the truth. Only with a full confession might there be peace.

You want it too, Jessamin.

It was true, she did.

She empathised with Beth – her pain and her torment. It was as though she were the one related to her and not Finn. Finn was more like Mally, Jessamin's blood relation – dark and brooding. Tormented as well. *I'm Beth and he's Mally.* It was an interesting comparison. Unsettling. Intriguing.

Perhaps in Beth's story, she might find a way forward with her own.

While she continued to peruse, her feet had squelched deeper into the ground that covered the graves, which was more mud than grass. She'd promised herself a cup of tea afterwards at Millie's, the teashop in the village, and perhaps a slice of cake too. The cold, it had definitely seeped into her bones. *Where are you, Duncan?*

There were so many plots for such a modest churchyard, not just belonging to those from the village, but to those from all around, she guessed. *Coming home to roost.* Maybe even her great grandparents, Jack and Margaret, had given instruction that this be their final resting place rather than Glasgow; the pull of their roots strong despite everything. But Jack and Margaret Murray were nowhere to be found. Only Duncan.

His marker was simple, with no decoration at all. But on it, the inscription was mercifully easy to read, as if hewn recently rather than generations before.

Duncan Murray
Beloved Son and Brother
Into God's Care We Deliver You
1925 – 1936

She'd bent down to touch the stone, to run her hands over the words, to feel close to a great uncle – a *child* – she'd never known. As she did, the wind picked up speed. It groaned as it weaved its way through the trees. The rain hit harder too, as if mourning an untimely loss and its dreadful consequences – a family left in tatters.

Tears broke rank and chased the rain in rivulets down her cheeks. *Next time I visit, I'll bring flowers,* she promised Duncan. It was the least she could do.

"Jess, Jess, are you all right, love? What's wrong? Why are you crying?"

Confused, Jessamin lifted a hand to wipe at her cheek. It came away wet. She *was* crying. Not in the graveyard but here in Maggie's living room, the excited chatter now far more subdued as everyone turned to stare at her.

"Oh, gosh, sorry. I… didn't realise."

Maggie jumped to her feet. "Come away with me, into the kitchen."

Like a child herself now, Jessamin meekly obeyed, hearing someone whisper as she left the room. "Ach, pregnancy, it plays havoc wi' yee, so it does."

In the kitchen, Maggie indicated for Jessamin to sit whilst she ran the tap.

"I'm okay to stand," Jessamin insisted but Maggie was having none of it.

"Sit. Take the weight off your feet." Filling a glass with water, she handed it to her. "And don't guzzle it. Take your time."

Again, she obeyed. After a couple of minutes, she handed back the empty glass and apologised further.

Waving a dismissive hand in the air, Maggie sat too. "There's something the matter, Jess, and don't fob me off this time. There are only so many glasses of water I'm willing to hand out."

Jessamin managed a weak smile. "Honestly, I'm fine."

"I said you're not to fob me off."

"Maggie, really—"

"Is it all okay between you and Finn?"

"Yes, yes, of course it is."

"An unplanned bairn can put pressure on a relationship."

"It's not the baby."

"Then what is it, lass? I'm Finn's friend, but I'm yours too. If I can help, I want to."

"It's just… there's a lot going on." She lifted a hand and

tapped at her head. “In here. A lot to think about.”

“You’re getting the nursery sorted? Rory’s helping you?”

“He is, yes.”

“Beth’s old room, isn’t it?”

“Uh-huh,” Jessamin replied, more sombrely this time.

Maggie narrowed her eyes. “Is it something to do with Beth?”

Maggie’s sensitivity was clearly coming to the fore again. “Yes… and no… not really.”

“Jessamin, you’re confusing me.”

“I’m sorry… I…”

“Ach, stop it. I’m the one who’s sorry. I’ve been preoccupied lately.”

“Of course you have,” Jessamin declared. “Understandably.”

“Perhaps I’ve been a wee bit insensitive, though.”

“No! Not at all.”

“Jess…” Maggie prompted.

A dam burst inside her. “I don’t want to get married, Maggie! I just don’t!”

Maggie’s kind, lived-in face appeared startled. “Jess, I… Has Finn asked?”

Jessamin shook her head. “No. I think he’s afraid to.”

“Afraid?” Maggie rose from her chair and shut the kitchen door, which had been slightly ajar, before sitting back down again and taking Jessamin’s hands in her own. “What’s all this talk of being afraid?”

“I feel… as if I *should* get married. What with you and Shona—”

“What Shona and I are getting up to is nothing to do with you.”

"I know, but there's an expectation, around here I mean. I'm pregnant, people assume…"

"Ach, turn a blind eye to those stuck in the past, that's what I'd do."

"But it's everywhere I go. They assume and… it's awkward."

"Between you and Finn, you mean?"

Jessamin nodded before lowering her head. "I don't want to get married," she whispered again, hardly believing she'd admitted it, not just once but twice.

"Jess, you love Finn, don't you?"

"Yes! Yes, I do."

"Okay," Maggie replied, nodding. "And I know he loves you. I'm presuming here that you're presuming too."

"Huh?" said Jessamin, frowning. "What do you mean?"

"That he wants to marry you."

"I…" She was confident he wanted to marry her – very. Although there was no denying it, there'd been no actual proposal.

"You know, it might be that he's happy with the *status quo* too."

"But there are issues, Maggie. He's talking about a will—"

"Aye, very sensible."

"And adoption."

"Of his own child?" Letting go of Jessamin's hands, it was clear Maggie was as perplexed as she'd been when Finn had first mentioned it.

"We'd have to look into it; rules may have changed recently, as rules tend to do, but yes, if you're not married it's the mother who holds all the rights, not the father. It just… it seems crazy when you're in a loving relationship, unfair, you know, on him."

Before Maggie could answer there was a knock on the door and a head popped round it – Ina's. "Maggie love, I was just wondering if I could grab another bottle of the old vino collapso? Maidie's finished hers and she's on the warpath!"

"Sure." Maggie went to the fridge, retrieved a bottle and handed it to her.

Ina thanked her but her eyes were on Jessamin. "Are you going to be long?"

"Ina," Maggie's voice grew stern. "We'll be as long as we need to be."

"Och, aye, of course," Ina replied, beating a hasty retreat.

Maggie turned back to Jessamin with a smile on her face. "That Ina, she of all people should understand. She's had the 'kitchen treatment' more than once."

"The kitchen treatment?"

"Aye this, one of Maggie's homegrown pep talks."

Despite herself, Jessamin burst out laughing. "You give them in your shop too!"

"I do, you know that as well. To be honest I tend to give them as and where they're needed, even outside in the pouring rain if it befits the occasion. Ah, Jess, that's better, I'm glad you're smiling. That's what I want to see."

"I really didn't mean to burden you."

"I've said it before, I'm your friend and I want to help."

"Just being with you helps."

Maggie sighed. "This should be a sweet time for you, not bittersweet."

Bittersweet – it was certainly that, both her life and the life she was reading about.

"You've told me you don't want to get married, and I'm

certainly not saying you have to, believe me. But might it help to tell me why."

"To get it straight in my head, you mean?"

"Exactly that."

"My surname, Wade, it's all I've got left of James."

Maggie shrugged. "You don't have to change it."

No she didn't, but what surname would the child take? Both hers and Finn's, or rather James' and Finn's? Wade-Maccaillin. That was something to be decided too.

"It's also," Jessamin had to fight to keep her breath even, "the act of getting married, standing before a minister, or a priest, or whatever, and the memories it'll conjure. Call me an idealist, but I was so sure I was only going to do it the once."

The day she'd married James her heart had been so full, so innocent, so oblivious to even the possibility of tragedy. She was happy; she felt complete and then, ten years later, so *in*-complete. Finn had helped to piece her back together again and she'd done the same for him. Even so, to do that a second time, to utter vows similar in meaning; to forge a bond which wasn't sacred at all, which could easily be torn apart, what was the point? She wanted it to be sacred – what she and James had – and so she'd *make* it sacred, the only way she knew how: by not marrying again.

All these thoughts were swirling round in her head; some sentiments being expressed, but not all of them. Maggie though was focused; tuning in, and so she got the gist well enough. To Jessamin's relief, she didn't try to persuade her one way or the other, she simply let her try and make sense of the conflict.

Later, when she returned home, when she once more lay beside a sleeping Finn, feeling their baby twisting and turning in her stomach, hearing the house creaking and groaning, she realised that despite Maggie's efforts, she was still no closer to making sense of it at all.

Chapter Twenty

Beth

I was so angry with Mally. Why had he told my sister about what had happened between us so many years before? What was the point of it? I meant to have it out with him. It was already difficult enough at home with someone new entering the fold; I didn't want things to become worse – not between Flo and me. When there was upset between us, or anger, I couldn't rest, not properly, and it was the same for her. If one of us was out of kilter, the other was too.

It was too cold to go to the loch that day and in the sky rain clouds were threatening to burst. I knew where Mally would be though; on his way to ours, not to see me, but to see Flo. And so I set off on the path he'd take, ready to intercept him.

As I hurried to meet him, I realised the fire in my belly was tinged with something else. What was it? Excitement perhaps? He'd *remembered* that kiss, and although we'd never spoken of it since, *he'd* spoken of it, just to the wrong person.

There he was! Coming towards me, his clothes somewhat ill-fitting, just as they'd been when he was a child. But he was a child no longer; he was every inch the man.

"Beth!" He called, a grin on his face. "Or is it Flo? It's getting harder to tell you two apart."

I came to a standstill before him. "You know exactly who I am, Mally. Like Stan, you've always been able to tell."

His grin only widened. "Ach, Stan's better at it than me, I promise. You're the only one he has eyes for. He wears his heart on his sleeve, that one."

"Stan and I are just friends."

Mally shrugged. "Your loss. You could do worse."

"Like Flo, you mean?"

The derision in my voice shocked both of us. My mouth flew open; his grin slipped. I was angry with him, but I hadn't meant to hurt him. I *never* wanted to hurt Mally.

"I'm sorry, I…"

I reached out to him but he was having none of it. "That's the trouble with you," he said, as he pushed past and almost unbalanced me, "you're stuck up."

Stuck up? What did he mean?

"Mally," I called. "Mally, wait up."

"I'm going to see Flo."

"No."

He swung round, his eyebrows raised. "I can't go and see Flo, is that what you mean? You're trying to stop me?"

"Yes… No… I…" He could tie me up in knots so easily. "I want you to listen to me, just for a minute. Please… do that for me, will you?"

He didn't answer straightway; he made me wait, the seconds ticking by, each one of them gruelling. Eventually he nodded.

"I'm not stuck up," I began.

He rolled his eyes, as derisory as I had been. "You are, you're snooty."

"Snooty?"

"Aye, the things that you say..."

The type of things that Flo wouldn't say, that's what he meant.

"So you don't like me?"

"I do like you! You've just a way about you. You can be difficult."

I was the one who was supposed to be laying into him, but here he was, once more turning the tables. "In what way?" I demanded but then changed my mind, rushing to speak before he could answer. "Is that why you prefer her? Why you want to be with her all the time and not me or Stan, because she's easier?"

"Flo?"

"YES, OF COURSE, FLO!"

Again he stared at me, made me wait for an answer; a reaction.

"All I want is a simple life," he said at last, not looking at me anymore, looking beyond me, back towards his home.

Such words should have elicited at least a degree of sympathy from me, I *knew* how hard his home life was – the lack of warmth, the lack of love – but teenagers are selfish; often they can't see beyond themselves and their own burning issues.

"Why'd you tell her?"

Mally scowled. "Tell her what?"

"That I'd kissed you. When we were ten."

"Ten? We were older than that, weren't we?"

Vehemently, I shook my head. "No, Mally, we weren't."

"Ah well, no matter."

"No matter?" I repeated, incredulous.

"Why should it matter?" He looked me square in the eye as he asked me.

"All right, okay. If it meant nothing, how come you mentioned it to Flo, how come you even *remember* it?"

He reddened slightly at that. "Ach, Beth, you're making a fuss over nothing. It just... happened that I told her. She wasn't that bothered."

"She laughed?"

"Aye, she did."

"And you laughed too?"

"No... I—"

"She wasn't laughing when she told me; she warned me off you."

His dark eyes began to sparkle. "Did she now?"

"Aye, she did." A thought occurred to me. "Mally, are you enjoying this? Setting my own sister against me?"

"There you go," he said, turning to walk away. "Getting all difficult."

My hand shot out and grabbed him.

"You *are* enjoying this, aren't you? What's wrong with you, Mally?" Flo had asked me the same question. "In your head, I mean?"

Stoniness replaced the glitter. "You're a fine one to ask."

"Am I now? And why's that? Because I'm not always laughing and giggling like Flo? Because my feelings run a bit deeper perhaps? Because I *think* about things, I challenge them? And because of all that, in your eyes anyway, I'm cursed."

"Cursed?" he repeated, somewhat surprised I'd used such a word. But then he nodded as though in agreement. "We're too alike. Me and Flo aren't."

"And you knew that, did you, right from the start? From the very first day we met?"

"Perhaps I did."

"But, Mally—" There was a plea in my voice, one he fended off.

"Don't, Beth. It is what it is."

"It doesn't have to be!" Despite his efforts, that plea was still there.

"What about Flo? What about Stan?"

"Stan?" I queried.

Mally snorted. "Stop playing ignorant."

"We're just friends, how many times do I have to say it?"

"Aye, well me and Flo are more than just friends. We're meant to be together."

Lord knows I loved my sister, but in that moment I was not only cursed, I was bewitched. Not just in that moment, I had been for years and years. I banished Flo from my mind, Stan too, as I stepped closer to Mally, my breath mingling with his. At the same time my grip on his arm became something more; became a caress.

Sixteen, that's all we were, but I felt as old as the land I lived in; love, desire, and the craving in me had all combined to age me beyond my years. I was the darkness and Flo was the light. He wanted *her*, but as his arms tightened around me, he couldn't resist me either, because sometimes – just sometimes – like calls to like.

"Beth—"

I hushed him. I was done with words and the uselessness of them. I just wanted to feel – to *capture* him. Tilting my head upwards, I had to stand on tiptoe to reach his lips, but reach them I did – kissing him again, properly this time, deeply, our lips parting to allow our tongues the freedom to explore. Every nerve ending was tingling; every cell felt suffused with life; every sense was on red alert as every second was committed to the vaults of memory. Something else registered, a hardening – him against me, pressing into my abdomen – a way to take this further, to become whole.

"Mally," I groaned, having to part at last in order to draw breath.

His forehead was against mine, black and blonde hair mingling.

"This is wrong." His voice was barely above a whisper.

"Does it feel wrong?" When he didn't answer, I raised my voice slightly. "Does it?"

"I… I don't know."

I seized the moment. "Kiss me again."

There was a slight shake of the head.

"Kiss me!"

He gave in. So easily, he gave in.

These were kisses he'd never tell Flo about.

Chapter Twenty-One

"I, Shona Campbell, take you, Rory Stewart, to be my husband, to have and to hold from this day forward, for better or for worse, for richer, for poorer, in sickness and in health, to love and to cherish…"

Shona looked breathtaking as she stood at the altar, her bump barely showing and her classically styled white dress clingy but in all the right places. Rory looked very handsome too, in a blue suit, white shirt and matching blue tie; handsome and very nervous, his voice shaking as he in turn said his vows, although his eyes blazed with pride as they flitted between Shona's face and her stomach.

A few rows from the front, Jessamin sat with Finn, Maggie, Lenny, Gracie and Ina's lad, Dougie, whom Gracie was seeing and, who like Angus, had managed to bag some leave from the army. Around them the church was packed; no one in the village or those surrounding it missing out on an opportunity for a celebration.

As the service continued, Jessamin reached over to hold Finn's hand, partly needing his strength at this time to combat memories of when she'd stood at the altar too, and partly just wanting to offer some kind of reassurance. *I love you, Finn. We don't need this to prove it.* If only she could say it with as much conviction as she felt it.

Once the deed had been done and Shona and Rory were declared man and wife, an enormous cheer erupted to echo its way around the church. The pair of them sporting the widest grins Jessamin had ever seen, retraced their footsteps down the aisle, the congregation showering them in handfuls of confetti. It was such a wonderful scene to observe – the atmosphere was *alive* with happiness – not just the newly married couple's, but everyone's. The laughter and the congratulations continued outside the church as Rory struck a series of proud poses beside the woman he couldn't wait until Christmas Eve to marry – they'd gone ahead and snatched the first opportunity.

It was a special day; a happy day; a day that was far from over. Tradition in the village was to hold the reception at Comraich. Not just the Laird's house, it was also the biggest for miles; bigger than the pub and bigger than the church hall, which in actual fact was tiny. Not everyone took advantage of this tradition, especially in modern times, but, with Finn's permission, Jessamin had felt obliged to at least ask Rory and Shona and had to stop her smile from slipping when they'd eagerly agreed.

Since she'd received the news that their forthcoming nuptials were going to be so much sooner rather than later, Jessamin had gone into overdrive. She might be heavily pregnant, and she might have had help from many others in the village – Shona and Gracie's company doing the catering and Maggie putting up bunting and balloons – but getting Comraich ready to receive its merry guests was something she'd spent many long hours fussing over herself, striving to get every little detail right and only stopping when she'd found some blood in her knickers; just a few spots.

It was an anomaly; at least that's what she told herself, holding her stomach; cradling it as she'd done so often. *Hold on there, little one, we haven't got long to go now.* There was no need to tell anyone, to upset them, especially Finn.

As they all piled back into their respective cars to head to the house, she was confident that Shona and Rory would be thrilled with all the effort that had been made. The irony of preparing the hall for a wedding reception wasn't lost on her, nor perhaps Finn, who'd been courteous about lending their home for such an occasion, but also subdued by it. *Like salt being rubbed into a wound,* thought Jessamin. Once her pregnancy was over and they'd settled into their new roles as parents, she resolved then would be the ideal time to address the matter; to tell him what she'd told Maggie. But for now there were other things to focus on, the day in hand for one.

The last time she'd seen Comraich bursting with as many people as this had been at Stan's funeral. Then it had seemed that everyone within a one hundred mile radius had turned out. That had been the night she'd decided to leave Glenelk and return to the south. Things had not just been sensitive between her and Finn; they'd been disastrous – there was no way she could stay here, not when he held her accountable for Stan's death. Stan. She missed him, but how wonderful it was that Beth was keeping him 'alive' for her; keeping all four of them alive. Not that she'd had much time to continue reading lately, not even at night, when exhausted, she'd climb into bed and fall immediately into a deep sleep, barely even having the strength to dream. There wasn't a great deal of the letters left to read, which both dismayed and frightened her – dismayed because she didn't want to let go of Beth, the child and the young woman she'd come to know so intimately; frightened because she knew what was coming, at the loch; part of it anyway. What else there was to discover made her shiver.

"Jess, stop daydreaming, Rory and Shona are here!"

It was Maggie; forcing her from the reverie she fell so easily into nowadays, as if just like Beth, she was caught between two worlds.

"Oh, goodness, we'd better get on; start pouring the champagne."

"Jess," it was Finn this time, a concerned Finn, "Gracie and Ina are doing that. Everything's covered. Just... relax, will you?"

The plea in his voice was unmistakable, as if he knew that she'd spotted recently; as if he'd guessed.

Taking a glass of champagne, for appearances sake if nothing else, she held it aloft as the brand new Mr and Mrs Stewart alighted from their car for more pictures, the high grey walls of Comraich making a very imposing backdrop.

When everyone had gathered in the hall where the stagheads' expressions seemed more bemused than ever – Jessamin would swear by it – a toast was raised, after which another cheer resounded, the house soaking up the sound.

Just a drop of champagne, that wouldn't harm the baby; a sip or two. Raising the glass to her mouth, she noticed her hand was shaking somewhat and, despite being such a cold day, she could feel beads of perspiration breaking out on her forehead. Perhaps she'd have another sip. It was delicious, icy cold.

Weddings, funerals, gatherings of any sort, Comraich had been built for this; for families and friends; for sharing. And yet what was happening, here, today, it was making her feel uneasy rather than joyous. She remembered what Beth had said to Mally. *What's wrong with you? In your head, I mean?*

Talking to ghosts, *listening* to them; it wasn't the first time she'd done that.

When James had died, talking to him as if he were still in the room, standing or sitting right beside her, had preserved her sanity, although she had the sense to realise the irony. The night she'd been about to leave Glenelk, it was James who'd persuaded her to stay. Not just able to talk to him, she'd seen him that evening, actually *seen* him. He'd appeared by the fireplace in the living room of her cottage, Skye Croft, as real as her, as anyone here today. She was on her way back from the brink of despair, recovering, and that's why he had come: to say goodbye, to tell her to go to Finn. *It's time to move on.* She'd refused, but his next words had hit home. *I want you to start again. Try and understand. I need you to.* Maggie had said something similar to her, shortly after they'd first met. *Let him go… not just for your sake, but for his too.*

So she had – she'd moved on – with James's blessing. *Remember that, Jess, his blessing.* And it had all seemed so real…

"Jessamin," it was Shona, wrapping her in a big hug, "thank you so much for having the reception at Comraich. I'm so grateful, we both are, Rory and me." Lowering her voice to a whisper lest it should carry to Winn Greer, the proprietor of The Stag, who was imbibing as much here as he ever did on his own territory, his round face red with the effort, she continued, "I mean, the pub's great, but this… Oh, Jessamin, this is *grand!* I feel like a princess. I expect you feel like this every day."

Jessamin laughed. "Well… no, not really. But it is a lovely house and you are most welcome."

"What about Maggie and Lenny, will they have their

reception here?"

"We haven't discussed it yet, but I think Lenny's favouring the pub."

Shona looked appalled. "Get Maggie to put him straight, this is far better." Before Jessamin had a chance to reply, she rushed onwards. "And you, of course. What about you? You *must* have it here."

"Well… It's… erm…"

"It's what?"

If she was edgy before, Jessamin felt even more so now. "It's because…" Again she faltered.

"He has asked you, hasn't he?"

The perils of living in a small village, where everybody knew everyone else's business and made it *their* business too, were beginning to take their toll. As much as she loved it here, there were times when she missed the anonymity of a big city; the ability to just blend in. "Look, Shona, let's enjoy your wedding, rather than worry about—"

"Ah, there he is, the big man himself!"

What? Jessamin swung round. Finn was standing right behind her. *Oh no!*

"Mr Maccaillin," Shona began.

"Call me Finn, please. There's really no need for formality."

To her relief, Finn looked jovial enough, clearly not having heard their exchange.

"Finn…" Shona tested the name on her lips. "It's lovely to be here, in your home. Thank you."

"It's a pleasure," Finn beamed back at her, "it's good to respect an old tradition."

"If these walls could talk…" Shona breathed, glancing at them.

They sometimes do, thought Jessamin, or those that remained within them.

"I hope you'll be joining in the dancing later, Mr… Finn?"

Jessamin smiled. There was a time when she used to do that, mix the two addresses up and call him Mr Finn as well. Sometimes she still did, deliberately of course, when they were giggling together or teasing each other.

As their conversation continued, Jessamin relaxed at last, leaning into Finn, relishing the contact as his arm came round to rest across her shoulders.

The minute he did that, Shona took a step back. "Ach, you make a lovely couple."

Jessamin blushed and Finn mumbled a somewhat embarrassed 'thank you.'

"You just… you know… fit each other. Even with that bump in the way."

"It is quite sizeable," Jessamin agreed, "but not long to go now."

"And then afterwards, Finn, will you do it? Will you make an honest woman of her?"

No longer almost slumping against Finn, Jessamin stiffened. He did too, his arm dropping from her shoulders and returning to his side. Silently, Jessamin cursed. *For God's sake, not again!* Shona was every bit as bad as her brand new husband. She should have known this was coming; should have stayed more alert and steered Shona away from Finn, or vice versa. Yet it was out there again, the elephant in the room. How could she answer? How would *he* answer?

"Finn…"

"Jess?"

"My legs…" She wasn't making excuses, she genuinely

meant it; she wasn't sure if they'd support her a minute longer.

To her relief, Finn steered her away from the crowds and into the living room, which had been designated out of bounds to guests. Sitting her down on Stan's chair, he took the champagne glass from her. She realised it was now completely empty, the bubbles, after so long an abstinence, perhaps responsible for her wooziness. She closed her eyes briefly as she sighed.

"Finn, I know we need to talk."

"It's all right—"

"It isn't. There are things that have to be said."

"Honestly, it doesn't matt—"

"I just… I need a bit more time, that's all."

As he nodded, she reached out a hand and gently stroked his face. There was stubble there despite the fact he'd shaved that morning.

"You're like I imagine Mally, when he was young."

A puzzled expression replaced any trace of hurt. "What makes you say that?"

"Because…" Briefly she glanced at Beth's portrait. There really was so much to talk about. "We ought to go back, continue hosting."

"Sit for awhile, there's no rush."

"No rush," she repeated, leaning forward and brushing her lips against his, feeling a slight hesitancy from him at first, perhaps even fear and confusion, all the things she was feeling too. Despite what he'd said and her request for more time, a sense of urgency filled the air; so much was coming to fruition.

After a few more moments she stood and took his hand; led him back out of the sitting room to join the gathering once more. Gradually the hours passed. The food was eventually eaten, glass after glass of champagne was poured and dancing continued in the room where Stan, and more recently Finn, would stand and paint. The speeches prompted the inevitable tears but then there was laughter and love, with people constantly hugging and kissing each other, feeling the need to reach out and to touch, sharing the sentiment of the day. Finally it was over and an exhausted Jessamin and Finn climbed the stairs to bed, too tired to talk or even think. But read – she could do that. Not initially, only when Finn was asleep, after she'd dozed too; but then the baby had started to kick…

Tiptoeing from the room, she entered Beth's domain. As the bed had been removed to make way for the cot, which was arriving in a few days, she sat on the chair instead, not even turning on the side lamp, just noticing how different the house was at night to how it had been in the day. The shift. Holding Beth's notes in her hands she knew what was coming next – another wedding, that of Nancy to Robert. It was yet another contrast to behold. Another descent into darkness.

Chapter Twenty-Two

Beth

MAM couldn't believe it. Mr and Mrs McCabe had *offered* to have the reception at Comraich. It would only be a small affair, a drink to toast the happy couple and some light food, but they seemed keen for her to accept, so that the tradition be observed.

"And who are we to argue?" Robert said, as delighted as Mam. "It'll make it special, which is no more than you deserve."

She was so happy; it was hard not to be delighted for her. Flo certainly was. And yet, happiness continued to elude me. With no body recovered, Da hadn't had a proper burial, just a service held to appease us; to give us something when there was nothing left except, for me anyway, an imagination that continued to run riot; that conjured nightmares which dragged me flailing from the depths of sleep. What if he wasn't dead? What if he came back and found Mam married to another man? It would rip his heart to shreds. But Mam and Flo, they'd got beyond that – they'd *accepted*. In my brain, however, the thought wouldn't shift. *What if he came back?*

As much as I tried to avoid helping with the wedding preparations, Mam refused to let me. If I sulked, Flo would pinch me, hard. She'd glare at me. As we lay side by side in bed at night, she'd berate me. *Robert's a good man. We're lucky to have him.* That's as maybe, but no one could replace Da and I told her so.

"Da's dead," she'd whisper, her breath hot against my ear.

On the morning of their wedding I lay there with utter dread in my heart.

Mam was up early, so was Flo, whereas I had to be dragged out of bed, Flo's face as she tugged at my arm, tight with fury.

"There are times when I hate you, Beth, do you know that?"

And there are times when I hate you. I didn't say it out loud but Flo dropped my arm suddenly. There was something in her eyes too – shock? As if she *had* heard it; as if she realised the weight behind my words that was missing from hers.

Flower girls – the very term is frivolous; it's light-hearted, girlish, everything that Flo was and I wasn't. She looked beautiful in her cotton shift and pink sash, a small wicker basket filled with petals clutched in her hands as she waited with me for Mam to appear from her bedroom, where she too had been getting ready. I wore an identical outfit to Flo and held the same petal-filled wicker basket in my hands, but all I wanted to do was throw it from me; tear off the dress and find a place to hide; pretend none of this was happening; that Da wasn't in a watery grave, he was alive and well, and we were a family again, the way we used to be; the way we *should* be.

Oh the temptation to turn and run! I almost did and then… then a miracle happened. Mam stepped into the living room and if I thought Flo looked beautiful, she paled in comparison to the vision that was my mother. She was breathtaking, her hair still with so much blonde in it; her neat figure clad in a fitted cream dress; her eyes not icy, not that day, but cornflower blue. But it was more than how she looked physically, it was how happy she seemed, how relieved. She *glowed.* On realising this, something inside me changed, it melted. It's strange to think something as hard-edged as anger can do that, it can just dissolve.

"Mam!" Flo breathed. It was all she could say, which was one word more than me. I stood there speechless.

Mam smiled at Flo and then turned her gaze tentatively towards me. "Beth?"

"You look lovely." The words came out on a sob as I ran to her. She met me halfway, threw her arms around me, and held me tight as tears began to cascade down my cheeks. "Mam," I said, pulling away slightly, "your dress, it'll ruin."

"Don't worry about that," she chided, sobbing too, "I'm just… you are glad for me, aren't you? I need this, Beth. You girls are growing up, you'll find husbands, leave home and then… I *need* this."

"I am glad for you, Mam."

She pushed my hair away from my face. "Losing your da was terrible. I was sure the agony would never end. But it does, Beth, it changes; it becomes something you're able to manage better." I'd never seen her expression so intent. "I won't forget him. I used to lie in bed, hoping and praying… The nights I did that, there were so many. But sometimes, just sometimes, you have to admit defeat."

I swallowed, lifted one hand to dry my eyes and glanced quickly at Flo, who was staring at me just as intently as Mam. Defeat. That word lodged itself at the forefront of my mind. It was an ugly word. Terrifying. Before I could react, there was a knock at the door and Mam gave a sharp intake of breath.

"That'll be Robert. Flo, Beth, are you ready?"

Thank goodness it was a fine day. We walked to the church, Mam and Robert arm in arm in front of us. He was looking different too, so smart, as happy as Mam – two people who mirrored each other perfectly, who returned what the other felt.

Robert left Mam at the church entrance with Flo and me whilst he went to observe another tradition and wait for her at the altar. Inside we could hear the strains of *Gradh Geal Mo Chridh,* Ailsa Brody's high sweet voice lending this traditional Gaelic folk song a haunting quality.

I am sorrowful without your company.

The lyrics held such meaning for Mam. So much so, she began to shake.

"Mam," I said, as she stared blindly at the church door, "are you ready?"

Again, there were tears in her eyes, but this time they seemed to dull her. She just stood there, on that clement day, in her wedding finery and continued to stare at the church door. Admit defeat? She hadn't, not completely. There was a part of her that wouldn't let go, which refused to, that eternally hoped and prayed. That *clung.*

As I realised this, my throat constricted. In that moment, Mam was the perfect embodiment of her daughters, light and darkness trapped in one body rather than divided in two. She was torn, right down the middle. Should she? Shouldn't she? I could almost hear what she was thinking: *do I continue to wait?*

And then Flo reached out and gently nudged her.

"Mam, they're waiting, the people in the village, the McCabe's. They're all in there."

I wanted to say something too: *You don't have to do this.* I *was* going to say it, but when I opened my mouth a different set of words tumbled out.

“Mam, it’s all right, what you’re planning to do. Robert loves you.”

At last her head turned towards me and she nodded – a simple gesture that conveyed so much. *It’s all right.*

As Flo opened the church door, as I fell into step beside her, Mam followed, ready to let go of the past, to herald the start of a new chapter.

Chapter Twenty-Three

WITH the house back to normal, and Maggie promising Jessamin she was entirely happy for her reception to be held at The Stag rather than Comraich, the coast was clear to focus on a new chapter in her own life: becoming a mother. Whatever other issues were on her mind, this took precedence. Jessamin laughed. That was the understatement of the year. It *overwhelmed* everything.

Standing in Beth's room, the notes she'd just read still in her hand, she took a deep breath, felt the baby move from side to side. What complex creatures humans are, she thought, riddled with so many contradictory emotions – a melting pot in each and every one, even those who tried to hide it, who did their utmost to pretend it wasn't so. And here she was, breeding another of these magical beings. What would he or she face in life? What mountains would they have to climb in order to find happiness, and if not that, a degree of contentment? Hugging her stomach, Jessamin had an urge to keep the baby in there, safe from all that the world could throw at it – the heartache, the loss, the anger and sometimes, just sheer bloody bewilderment. *But there are good things too, Jess, don't lose sight of that.*

"Ah, Beth," she said, finally putting the notes back in the

bureau, which was standing against the wall. Walking over to the cot which had a bright mobile hanging above it, she ran her hands across its wooden frame as she gazed down at the soft mattress, on top of which cotton sheets and blankets were waiting to be made up. The enormity of what was happening hit her fully, perhaps for the first time. Her genes and Finn's had combined and their blood was running through someone soon to be another independent soul – a separate being. When it arrived she would stand here, as she was doing now, and hope and pray that they'd be granted a good life, knowing she'd move heaven and earth to ensure it.

Finn came up behind her, causing her to squeal.

"Christ! I didn't know you were home."

"Aye, business is finished for the day, so I'm all yours."

"Well, well, well. You're at my disposal, are you? What's a girl to do with you? Let me think..." Briefly she glanced at her watch. "It's Wednesday, it's the middle of the day, we could go over to Larnside, have some lunch at Millie's..."

"Lunch?" Finn murmured. "I'm not really hungry."

"Fair enough." Jessamin reached up to plant a kiss on his lips. "Neither am I. We could go for a walk?"

"It's raining."

"So? You're a Scotsman, you're not afraid of the rain!"

"I like a bit of warmth too on occasions," he replied, kissing her back, hard.

When he released her, she made a show of batting her eyelids. "It seems to me, Mr Maccaillin, that whatever suggestions I come up with, you're going to thwart."

"Or maybe," his hands were running up and down her spine, making her shiver, "you just need to come up with something a bit more interesting."

"Oh, right, I see." Enjoying this lightness between them, unexpected and so different to how it had been recently, she rested her hand flat against his stomach; relishing how taut it was; moving it downwards, inch by tantalising inch. Again looking up at him, she held his gaze, her own eyes at half-mast as she whispered, "Perhaps an activity such as this would be more to your liking?"

Without another word Finn clasped her to him, the bump a hindrance but neither of them prepared to let it stop them in their intentions. His lips bruising hers, his grip firm, the flame that he could so easily light within her burst into full brilliance. This was right, this was perfect; this was what they needed – a physical affirmation.

"Finn, Finn," she breathed, when she was able to. "There's no bed in here."

"Do we need a bed?"

The laughter that escaped her felt so good. "I can't do it standing up!"

He eyed her stomach. "I'd carry you to our room, but…"

"Yeah, yeah, you don't have to say it. At this stage of the pregnancy I'm likely to break your back! Come on," she said, taking his hand, pulling him out of Beth's room, across the landing and into their own room instead. As he undressed her, and she him, the past few months, the worry she'd felt, all the uncertainty, melted away. She marvelled, just as Beth had done, that it could so easily do that. This love, this light, she embraced it as she was embracing Finn – never wanting it to end, and determined that it wouldn't; not just their physical union, but their union as a whole. As they lay on the bed, his kisses growing more urgent, she gave up on thoughts, wanting only to feel. Love was so *powerful* – it could eat you alive, tear you limb from limb and then put you back together again. Whole, that's what you were when you joined with someone as she joined with Finn, his movements tentative at first, a natural fear of hurting the baby, and she assuring him it was all right; whispering in his ear, encouraging him.

When he climaxed, she did too – every nerve ending in her body pulsating with pleasure. This was how it was when it was just the two of them, how it used to be, how it *should* be.

Let no man put asunder.

Ironic those words should repeat on a loop in her mind.

Chapter Twenty-Four

Beth

HOW? How was it possible? It wasn't the way it should have been; the way I'd spent so long imagining, years, damn it. Years! And yet for Flo, it had been so different.

I can't… this is difficult, perhaps too difficult. All these words I've put down. Is it wrong of me? Should I forget? *Try* and forget. But how can I? It's all there; it's in my mind's eye, like a film, playing over and over – the horror of it.

And that's why I write. Because sometimes I'm afraid that all of this will burst from me, as it's doing right now; that my mouth will open and words will come spilling out – a stream of them, a river, an ocean, unintelligible, garbled, dripping with madness. Better perhaps that the madness is captured on paper; that I release it this way rather than self-combust. Stan will be so hurt. But that's all I could ever offer him, just a world of hurt. He knew that when he married me, when it was his turn to stand at the altar and wait, and my turn to stand and stare at the church door.

I'm trying to think; was I born mad or was it Mally that caused me to spiral out of control? Something happened; I changed inside, perhaps not the first time I saw him, but after, soon after. I was so young! And the years since have become so blurred. Does it help to blame him? In doing so, do I dare to hope that there's a chance for me, that I'll be absolved? No. Heaven wouldn't want me. Hell is where I belong.

Sorry, I'm rambling, I know I am. But tonight I can't seem to stop. My hand is trembling so much it's a wonder I can hold my pen. There's a rushing in my ear and blood is coursing through my veins. My hands… my hands… there's blood on them too. Not visible to the eye, but still I know it's there. I'm a monster, such a monster!

I have to stop this. This will get me nowhere. Stan's out, I don't know where; I never ask him although sometimes he makes a point of telling me. I'm at the window, peering outwards. Is that them, those two specks on the horizon, returning my gaze just as intently? When will they begin to draw closer? Flo, Mally, I'm sorry! Don't you know how sorry I am? I can't sleep at night, not anymore. I just lie there while it goes round in my head – everything that happened; every moment that led towards such catastrophe.

Breathe. I must breathe. Calm myself and turn away from the window; focus only on this sheet of paper. Write it all down whilst I still can.

There was a first time – *our* first time – mine and Mally's. And it wasn't something I instigated, not wholly. Since I'd intercepted him on that pathway, since we'd kissed again, Mally had started to take notice of me. Not openly, oh no, never that. He was Flo's and everyone knew it; *I* knew it. But surreptitiously he'd catch my eye; he'd hold my gaze for a fraction longer than he used to. When the four of us walked together, he'd hurry to my side and brush his hand against mine. One such time, when Flo and Stan were lagging far behind, looking at trees I think, Stan explaining to her about the different varieties, he grabbed me to him and kissed me – a quick kiss, snatched, that left my lips stinging but my heart filled with hope. So much damned hope.

Around that time – we were almost seventeen – Flo started to look at me too in a strange manner. Unlike Mally, however, she never held my gaze; she'd quickly turn away, pretend she wasn't looking at me at all. Sometimes there'd be a smile on her face, a smile that irked me; that suggested she knew something was happening between Mally and me, and that she found it oh so amusing. Other times, her mouth would be a thin white line again, and her eyes more navy in colour than ice blue.

I asked him once, who he wanted. *Really* wanted.

"You know who."

That's the only answer I got. And I didn't know. I honestly didn't.

The day all my dreams came true was more akin to a nightmare. I'd had a row with Mam. She said I was moping around the house, not helping her with the chores. There was washing to be done, the sewing of clothes and bed sheets – still a good source of income for my mother – and food to prepare.

"You have to make yourself useful," she insisted. "We've a house to run and a family to look after."

"What about Flo? Where's she?"

"Never mind Flo, she's gone to fetch some eggs. It's you I'm worried about."

"I don't want to spend my life sewing clothes," I declared, I fancy I even stamped my foot, but that could be imagination, guilty of embellishment.

"You'll do as you're told," Mam shouted back at me. "All the while you continue to live under our roof."

"*Our* roof?" I repeated. "Yours and Robert's, you mean."

Mam wiped a hand across her forehead. "Oh don't start," she said. And I noticed something, how tired she was. I noticed but I didn't care.

"It's like you don't want us here, not anymore. Not now you've got him."

"That's not true."

"You just want us to go."

"No."

"You'd probably throw us out to fend for ourselves if you could get away with it."

"NO!" This time she screamed the word. "All I'm asking is that you help!"

I shook my head, just as vehemently as she had done. "No. Not today. Ever since we left school, you've had us skivvying day and night. And Robert, he goes to work granted, but when he's at home, he doesn't lift a finger. You treat him like he's a king and we're his servants. *Fetch him this, fetch him that.* Why, Mam? You never treated Da that way. What are you afraid of, that he'll leave you if you don't run around after him, if you don't indulge him? Is that it? You don't want to end up old and alone?"

Her hand swung outwards, as quick as a viper, and slapped the side of my face.

I was stunned. Mam had never hit me before. We'd shouted at each other, had arguments, but it had never got that far.

Tears sprang to my eyes and hers too, I'm sure of it.

I wished I'd stayed and apologised, promised that I'd help out a bit more; asked her even if she was happy. I think she was, but for Mam life was never easy. She worked hard all her life, until the day that she dropped dead. There was never any let up. There isn't for ordinary folk, not here, not in the Highlands.

I didn't stay, however. I ran and I ran, all the way to Larnside, turning inwards, leaving the loch behind, climbing the hills and finally coming to a standstill on the ridge that overlooked Mally's house. Dare I do it, go down there? Encounter his parents again? It had been a long time since I'd done that. Years. But I was desperate to see him – my heart beating in my chest as hard as it's beating now.

Mally!

I willed him to hear me. If he was in the house, I begged for him to come out, to look upwards, to see me waving.

Mally! Mally, please…

"Beth?"

I heard him, I swear it even now, his voice in my head, answering me. And then I saw him. He was approaching the house from a side field and as he looked up I started waving frantically, shouting too, not caring if his parents should hear me.

"Mally! Mally!"

Whatever he had in his hands, farm tools I think, he dropped to the ground. He bounded up that ridgeside as if it were no more challenging than a hillock, reaching me at last, his breathing short in his throat just as mine was on seeing him.

"Oh, Mally," I said, throwing myself into his arms and closing my eyes as they encircled me. The scent of him, strong and peaty, was like the sweetest perfume.

All I wanted was the comfort he could offer, that day at least. Again, I swear this is true. But Mally – a young man with the fire of youth in his belly – wanted more.

His hands no longer around me but on my arms, he started

to pull me away from the ridge and into the shelter of the trees, backing me up against a towering Scots pine as his hand started to fumble with the dress I was wearing.

"Mally," I gasped. "What are you doing?"

He didn't answer, he just continued, tugging, pulling, both at himself and at me.

"Mally, please, listen…"

I stopped; *knew* what he was doing suddenly, what he wanted.

Surely I wanted it too?

The pain as he pushed his way inside me wiped all thought from my mind. He seemed to rage through me, tear me in half. As he started to writhe, to grunt, his breath hot with exertion, I started to moan too, but not with pleasure. This *wasn't* what I'd come for. It isn't what I'd spent so many nights dreaming about. I wanted him to stop but there was no stopping him. As he continued to thrust, I stopped moaning and was crying instead, but I said nothing. Not a word. I let him have his way and then, when it was over, whilst he laced up his breeches, whilst I pulled down my dress, I muttered something about having to go. He didn't stop me. That was the thing. He never stopped me. And he knew, just as I knew, that soon I'd be back for more.

Chapter Twenty-Five

JESSAMIN'S hand flew to her mouth. He'd raped her? Her grandfather had *raped* Beth? But was it that? Could it really be construed as such? She'd just written that she planned to return; that both she knew it and he did too. Jessamin exhaled, loud and heavy. This is where the lines blurred, no longer black and white but filled with grey after depthless grey. It was such a poisoned chalice that Mally and Beth drank from.

Another day was dawning. If she opened the window in Beth's room, she'd hear the call of birdsong, crystal clear, with no other sound to mask it. It was a peaceful time but because of what she'd just read, and Beth's obvious distress at the beginning of this particular section, she felt distressed herself. She wanted to hurry back to her bedroom, wake Finn and share what she'd learnt – just as Beth was sharing it, albeit from beyond the grave. But again she stopped herself. She was almost there – at the end. She had to hold on a little longer. The four of them were racing towards eighteen – towards tragedy too. The loch. She hadn't been there yet, not because of the weather – it was mid November and still fairly mild. It had rained of course, plenty of times, but there'd also been days when she could easily have driven out as far as she could and then walked the rest of the way. Why hadn't she?

Because you're waiting, that's why. For Beth to take you back.

Everything she'd written was leading up to that one event – and the terrible truth of it.

Leaning forward, she peered out of the window. It wasn't raining, not today, and the horizon was clear… or was it? Was there someone in the distance, just standing there, staring back at her? And not just one person but two – possibly even three?

Three? Surely there should be four?

"Christ, Jess, it's a bit early, isn't it, to be up and about?"

Jessamin swung round. "Oh my God, Finn! Will you stop doing that, creeping up on me."

"Sorry," he said, bridging the gap between them, "What are you looking at?"

"Nothing," she replied, averting her gaze, wishing she could tell him, trying her hardest not to. *What Mally did, the brutality of it…*

"Hey, hey," Finn cupped her chin with one hand so that she was looking at him again, "you seem a bit sad."

Sad *and* confused, but she denied it. "I'm fine."

There was a moment's silence and then he got that look on his face that she loved so much – that *determined* look. "Come on, let's go out for the day, head to Skye."

"Skye?"

"Aye, there's a lighthouse in the north-west corner, an abandoned lighthouse; we used to go there sometimes as kids, a bunch of us from the village; hitch a lift with one of the older lads; muck about there, you know, as kids do."

"Oh, right. You fancy a trip down memory lane?"

"I do, but it's not just that, it's a beautiful place to walk."

She inclined her head. "It's also because you think I spend too much time in the house, isn't it?"

"You do, Jess. In this room particularly."

"It *is* going to be the nursery."

"Aye, but it's decorated now, it's done. Yet early morning or late at night, I wake to find you're gone. And you're always here."

"Because… because… I'm looking forward to the baby, that's all."

The frown that had developed on his face, softened. "We both are. But a change of scene will do us good. C'mon. Let's grab some breakfast and then we can go."

His enthusiasm infectious, she agreed. It was certainly no hardship to disentangle herself from Comraich for the day and to go to such a magical place. From the moment she'd set foot on Skye she'd loved it – the sheer vastness of its unforgiving terrain which seemed to change in colour with the passing of every hour, and the ever imposing silhouette of the Cuillin mountains, at the foot of which were more faerie pools enticing you to play amongst their twinkling waters. They were not hidden as the pools at Stan's Loch were hidden, but a popular tourist attraction in warmer months. Finn had taken her there once, thankfully out of season and at Stan's behest, shortly after she'd moved to Glenelk. She'd swum whilst he'd sat on the bank and watched, and then the heavens had opened soaking them both. She remembered how invigorated she'd felt; how alive… for the first time in so long, and not just because of how cold it was, but because of the man she was visiting Skye with yet again. He'd revived her.

An hour or so later, sitting beside him in the Defender, so many memories came flooding back, but they weren't just hers, and weren't all sweet either, for mixed in amongst them were Beth's. Despite the distance Finn was putting between her and Comraich Jessamin couldn't shake her from her mind. Thinking again of how tortured Beth was, she inhaled. Finn reached out a hand, his concern obvious.

"Is it the baby?"

"It's not the baby."

"You'd tell me if it was."

"Yes. There's nothing to worry about." No more blood, no more sharp pains.

At last they reached their destination – Minch Point, Finn informed her. A real outpost, it had taken another hour's drive through wilderness even more barren than that which surrounded them at Glenelk to reach it. It was scenery so different to the rolling hills of the South Downs she'd grown up with, but how she loved the intensity of it. It fired the soul, her own and the souls of others too – for better and for worse.

"So, this is where you came as teenagers?" she said, easing herself out of the car and spying the lighthouse in the distance. "It's a bloody long drive, Finn!"

Finn looked around him, the wistfulness of nostalgia evident on his face. "As I said, it was just on occasion. It was far enough to escape the prying eyes of parents and guardians, to be free… be ourselves."

"To get off with each other, you mean."

He shrugged, a playful smile on his lips. "That too. Here, take my arm," he continued, nudging her, "the ground can get rough and I don't want you falling."

The closer they got to the lighthouse, the more she could hear the screech of birds. For a while it was deafening.

"Where are they all?" she queried. Certainly, a few were circling each other in the sky, but not enough to make such a racket.

"They nest by the side of the cliff. You have to get up close to see them; it's an amazing sight, as though the cliff itself is alive."

"Oh, I'd love to see that!"

Finn shook his head. "Another time, Jess. When I say get up close, I mean practically hanging over the side. Not a good idea for you at the moment."

Instead of arguing, she conceded, loving how protective he was being.

The lighthouse didn't stand on its own; there was a house to the side of it and a smaller structure right at the front, which looked to be some sort of cabin. Both it and the house were in a fairly dilapidated state, although the tower itself, long since decommissioned apparently, was surprisingly white against the azure of the sea that stretched out behind it. More islands were evident on the horizon – Lewis and Harris, Finn told her.

"When was it abandoned?" she asked.

"In the seventies apparently. And not just that, it was *suddenly* abandoned, by the family who lived here; they upped and left one day, and never came back."

"Why?" she breathed, amazed at how enchanting such a desolate place could be.

"Because of ghosts, that's why."

"Ghosts?" Coming to a standstill outside the cabin, she turned to face him, her sarcasm evident. "Really, Finn?"

"You of all people don't believe me?"

"I'm just wondering whether you're teasing again, that's all."

"I'm not – if ever the veil was thin, it's here. Don't you feel anything?"

"I'm not psychic!" she said laughing. "And besides, I've only just got here." Her laughter gave way to a frown. "Isn't it illegal to leave a lighthouse unmanned?"

"Probably. But if there are ghosts after you…"

She rolled her eyes. *Now* he was teasing.

"Can I go into the cabin?" she checked, coming to a standstill outside it and noting how rotten the door and window frames were.

"Best not to, it doesn't look that safe."

"Did you ever go in there? In the old days, I mean."

"Oh aye."

"Did you… erm…"

His grin matched hers. "I did not. Well… just a kiss perhaps."

"I believe you, Finn, thousands wouldn't."

Still smiling, he led her away from the cabin and towards the main house. "Come and look through the windows. I haven't been here for years but the last time I was the family's furniture was still here, as well as the books they were reading. There were cups and saucers on the table, plates and cutlery too. The people who discovered they'd fled found the TV was still on; it was blaring apparently, the volume turned up to screeching point."

"It could be aliens responsible," she suggested just before they reached it.

"Och, now you really are getting carried away!"

She was about to deliver a good-natured retort when his phone rang.

"Sorry, hang on, Jess."

As he walked on a few paces, one hand cupping his free ear so that he could hear the caller, Jessamin peered through the windows. There was still furniture *in situ*, in as bad a state as the four walls that contained them.

"Christ!" she exclaimed, lifting an arm to wipe at the window with her coat sleeve. The floor was covered in debris, including stuffing torn from a settee and an armchair, as well as pages that had been ripped from books, empty vodka bottles and crushed beer cans. Towards the back of the room, part of the ceiling had collapsed. Finn was right; it was best not to venture into these buildings, although she bet plenty did. They weren't cordoned off, and some of those empty bottles looked suspiciously like modern brands.

Unsafe. The word went through her mind as she turned from the house to the tower itself, its light forever extinguished, now replaced by an automated tower a little further down the coast, and she shuddered. As beautiful as it was here, as dramatic, she didn't want to linger.

"Finn?"

He'd wandered quite a way into the distance and was still speaking on the phone. Walking towards him, she was careful to avoid the stones that were so liberally scattered on the ground, her back to a sea that was calm for now, but which she'd bet was violent on occasion, dashing itself continuously against the rocks in a desperate attempt to wear them down, make them vanish too. So this was where he'd come as a teenager, just as Beth and her friends had gone to the loch; somewhere far removed – a bolthole; an escape. Despite its haunted reputation, or perhaps *in* spite of it, his memories were fond at least, ghosts probably part of the lure. He'd grinned when he recalled the mischief he and his friends had got up to here. And she was glad of that. Relieved. After all, teenagers could be more lethal than any spirit that refused to depart; something her current reading material confirmed.

When she reached Finn, she tapped him on the shoulder.

Just as he'd made her jump earlier, it was his turn to start now.

Abruptly he ended the call, as far as she could tell without even saying goodbye.

"Sorry, Finn, I didn't mean to inter—"

"You didn't, don't worry."

He had the look of a deer caught in headlights about him, prompting her to ask him, as he continually asked her, if he was all right.

"Aye, Jess, aye," he replied, still somewhat flustered.

"Who was that on the phone?"

"Erm…" He looked at the phone as if he'd never seen such a contraption before. "No one."

"No one? You were on the phone all this time to no one?"

"Well… no… It was *someone*, obviously. An old army friend."

"Angus?"

"Angus?" He shook his head. "Someone else."

"Oh right. What was it about? Anything important?"

"Nothing. It was about nothing." He made a show of shivering. "It's getting really cold, isn't it? I don't know about you, but I could do with warming up. Let's head to The Stein Inn. I'm not sure you've been there before; it's the oldest pub on Skye. You'll like it, it's really atmospheric. They do good food too."

"Okay, fine. If we're done here."

"We're done."

Without insisting she hold his arm this time, he started to head back to the car. As she trailed behind him, she realised the answer he'd given – *nothing* – had been the same as the one she'd given him in Beth's room this morning.

And she'd been lying too.

Chapter Twenty-Six

Beth

HOW did I know that my first time with Mally was so different to Flo's? Because she told me, that's how. She lay in bed beside me one night and described it in the greatest detail, even though I'd turned away from her, a gesture I hoped would make plain that I wanted her to stop. She simply ignored me and carried on. He'd taken his time, apparently; been gentle and considerate. All the things he hadn't been for me.

"He kept murmuring about how much he loved me, Beth; touching my skin and stroking my hair. It's funny to think, but he was as nervous as I was; I could feel how much he was trembling. But the first time – *our* first time – was perfect. He made sure of it."

"And this..." I swallowed. "This happened only today?"

"Early evening," she confirmed with a sigh, "just as the sun was setting."

"Where?"

"Guess!" Her laugh was like quicksilver.

"Oh, Flo, come on."

"The place he loves the most, of course; by the loch."

The loch? Whereas I'd been pushed up against a tree on the

ridge near his home.

Oh, how my insides twisted.

"How'd you know it was his first time; did he tell you that?"

She laughed. "Oh, Beth, he didn't have to, I know *everything* about Mally."

Inwardly I cursed her smugness. *You don't know everything. His first time was NOT with you, it was with me. Mally took my virginity and I took his.*

A sacred bond – or at least it should be.

As Flo continued to bask in the afterglow, I wondered if I should tell her how far it had gone between us; not just a stolen kiss, or the brush of a hand, but something else entirely. I opened my mouth, intent on doing so, but then I closed it again; clamped it shut. Of course I was afraid of the fall-out, of Flo's reaction; Mam and Mally's too. But would that alone stop me? No. It was the shame of *how* it had happened, with no words of love or tenderness at all. It was as though he'd been angry with me and he'd wanted to punish me.

If Flo and I had inhabited one body instead of being divided, he could have had us both and we could have had him. With the light and the dark balanced, it could have been perfect. But we'd been divided since the moment of conception, and that simple act of nature – that random act of nature – had complicated our worlds. *All I want is a simple life.* That's what Mally had said. But it was far from that.

Flo had fallen quiet, but she was still awake, perhaps returning to the moment of their union as I so often returned to ours.

Every now and then she let out another contented sigh and when she did, I wanted to scream; to shout; to be the one to push Mally up against that tree; to ask him, *demand*, that he choose; make the decision, once and for all. And if it was Flo, if it really was her, I'd be the one to leave this village; I'd run away. I'd have to. I wouldn't be able to stay. The thought of watching their relationship blossom; of seeing them exchange wedding vows in the village church, a garland of wild roses in Flo's hair as she smiled at him and he smiled at her – so *tenderly* – it would surely kill me. And then they'd have children; one bairn, perhaps two or three, and that... that would be intolerable. I'd have to disappear and they'd never be able to find me. Mally would have to be content with the light – not as easy as it sounds, not when his soul was as black as mine. Sometimes he needed the shadows to hide in.

A sob escaped me. Horrified, I clamped my hand to my mouth. If Flo knew I was crying she'd want to know the reason why; she'd drag it from me.

"Flo," I said, meaning to pre-empt her. "Flo?"

When there was no reply, I carefully turned over. She was asleep at last, a perfect little smile on her face – revisiting Mally in dreams no doubt.

My fists clenched.

Why does it have to be you?

Gone from my mind were all the times that twins inevitably shared; being born so close together; taking our first steps together; getting under our Mam's feet as we chased each other around the house; running down the path to our new school; laughing together. So much we'd done in tandem and yet there were things I'd done *before* her, important things, but still... still... he wanted her.

As I stared down at Flo, all I could see was an opponent. She wasn't just my sister, she was my rival. The darkness, the terrible darkness – it opens a door somehow and lets more come racing in. And my mind was ripe to receive.

I was so glad when dawn arrived; when light began to filter through the curtains to push the dark back into the four corners of the room, to reside there, sullenly, for the rest of the day.

I rose from bed, quietly so as not to disturb Flo; dressed and fled from the house, desperate to escape the torment I'd suffered during the night; the revelation of a side to me that was more fearful than even I'd imagined.

It was raining but not hard; it was a soft, light rain that I wanted to cleanse me both inside and out. I don't know how long I stood in it, my clothes and my hair becoming sodden, but if I'd stood there forever, it wouldn't have been long enough.

I started to walk away from the house. Aimlessly at first, with no real speed; not towards Larnside, not today; away from there. I walked past the other houses and cottages in the village, noticing signs of people stirring inside some of them; curtains being pulled back; a door being opened to let a cat or a dog out. I spent a while on the shore of Loch Hourn, staring over at Skye and at the water which simply carried on flowing out towards the sea, my father's burial ground. Eventually, I turned inwards, into fields that became woodland, that sheltered a well-trodden path, the one that led to Comraich. Suddenly it was there in front of me, as solid as ever; baronial in my mind – a castle rather than a country house. Sanctuary. That's what I wanted; to get away from everything; from a world I no longer understood.

I banged on the door. It was early still. Would his parents be cross with me for turning up unannounced?

Stan, Stan, come on!

The door took an age to open and when it did it was him standing there, rubbing at his eyes, his sandy hair tousled, his spectacles slightly crooked.

"Beth! What are you doing here? Och, look at you, you're soaking wet. What have you been doing? Come in. Come away in."

Unable to speak, I entered the walls of Comraich. There were tears on my face but maybe he wouldn't know; maybe the rain disguised them.

Stan took my coat from me and after turning his head, on the look out for his parents perhaps, he grabbed my hand and led me up the staircase to his room. There he sat me down on his bed then disappeared for a moment, coming back with a towel and gently rubbing at my hair and shoulders as I sat mute.

"There you are. You'll be all right, Beth. You're all right now."

Gradually I could feel my fingers, my toes and my limbs returning to life. It hadn't been that cold outside, but I'd frozen anyway. My breathing having been shallow, I took a big gulp of air and with it came release. I cried. Sitting there, on Stan's bed, I cried as if my heart would break. And Stan held me. He put his arms around me, clasped me to him and let me cry, all the while murmuring those same words: *You'll be all right. You're all right now.* Only when I think back on it, do I realise: he never once asked what was wrong. Either he guessed or he thought he was better off not knowing.

The tears may have subsided but my heart was as heavy as ever, like a thick slab of granite. Stan's grip loosened but I clung to him and he soon held me tight again. His arms, whilst not as powerful as Mally's – he was an artist not a farmworker – gave me the comfort I needed in that moment. They were as much a sanctuary as the house around me. It felt safe being this close to him, not dangerous. I knew he'd never harm me; that he'd always be gentle with me. That was his way. But my heart… my traitorous heart, it was a fool, wanting only what hurt it.

Finally, I let him go, apologising for disturbing him so early.

"I wanted to get up to do some painting anyway," he insisted. "The morning light, there's nothing like it."

That was an excuse, it had to be. "It's nothing but grey out there."

"Beth, even that has its beauty."

Frowning at his words, I checked with him if I could lie down for a while. I was exhausted, the lack of sleep and torrent of emotions having finally taken their toll. I slept for hours. When I woke up and realised the time, I couldn't believe it. Oblivion had claimed me; had given me some respite – another shelter to hide in.

I yawned and stretched; asked Stan what he'd been doing all the while.

"Sketching you," he said, adding rather bashfully, "I hope you don't mind."

I shrugged. "I don't mind." After all he'd sketched me many times before. "Let me see." When he hesitated, I cajoled him. "Ah, c'mon, let me see."

He picked up a bundle of sheets lying on the table to the side of him. I noticed a slight tremor in his hands as he gave them to me.

As I looked down, my eyes grew wider. He was a good artist, we all knew that, but he'd clearly improved since the last time he'd let me see any of his work. In a few pen strokes, he'd captured my likeness perfectly; my hair, the shape of my eyes, the curve of my mouth, but he'd captured something else too.

"I look so peaceful."

"You were peaceful."

A wry laugh escaped me. "Really?"

"Aye, and I was glad. That's why I didn't wake you, why I let you sleep."

Immediately I felt guilty. "Stan, you didn't have plans for today, did you?"

"I was going into Inverness with my parents, but they've gone now—"

"Oh, Stan, no! You should have said."

He shook his head, removed the spectacles he was wearing and held them in his hands. "I'd rather be with you."

In the ensuing silence we could barely look at each other; he lowered his gaze and I did the same, continuing to stare at those remarkable drawings.

"If you come downstairs, I'll show you some more of my recent work," he said eventually. "If you want to, that is."

I rose from his bed, intrigued.

Descending the stairs, the stagheads above us, he led me towards a room at the back of the house where he did the majority of his work. He opened the door and we walked inside, the house around us so silent with just the two of us in it. It was a lovely big room as all the rooms at Comraich are, with French windows that led into a small garden framed by the woodland. The air was rich with the smell of linseed oil. Stan had been busy. There were so many canvasses stacked up against the wall. Immediately I spotted several featuring the land around here, the mountains; the faerie pools, the waterfalls – mystical paintings, with a dreamy quality, and in contrast, amongst them, the starkness of Mally's picture of the loch.

"Are you ever going to give it to him?" I asked, walking over to it and touching it.

"Aye, it's his for the taking. When he can, that is."

I pulled a face. Not all the while he lived in his father's house then.

On his easel was a painting in progress – another landscape, this one with a stag in the forefront. Effortlessly, or at least that's what it looked like to me, Stan had captured the majesty of the beast; his strength and his defiance. Once again I thought of Mally and then quickly berated myself. Was he all I could think of?

"Beth, over here."

I swung round to face Stan. He had his glasses on again and was pushing them up against the bridge of his nose. Something about the act caused another conflict in me. Mally ribbed him for having to wear glasses and in that moment I *hated* Mally for doing that; for being so mean. What would any of us do without Stan? As humble as he was, even vulnerable, as he seemed at this moment, he was the lynchpin of our group – the most consistent, the sanest.

I smiled as I walked over to him, a new respect for my friend beginning to bloom. Such a strange feeling it was, but I welcomed it because it calmed me.

"Go on then," I encouraged. "Show me."

A blush lent colour to his pale skin, but he took a deep breath and led me to a group of paintings that had been turned inwards when stacked up. One by one, he revealed them to me. There was a figure in each and every one; a girl with blonde hair, sometimes tied in a ponytail, at other times left loose to hang in soft curls rather than ringlets around her shoulders. In various states of repose, she was either sitting, lying on the floor reading a book or simply standing, staring into your eyes, as the stag had stared. All were composed in pastel rather than the oils he favoured, bringing so much light to the subject. It was that which confused me.

"It's Flo," I said.

"It isn't, it's you."

"But… but…"

"It's how I see you."

Remembering the portrait he'd done of me once, I denied it. "Not always."

"I'm talking about now."

I continued to stare at them. "I'm not like that," I said at last.

"You could be."

"Impossible," I said again, starting to back away; turning from the paintings, from him; getting ready once more to take flight. "That's Flo; that has to be Flo."

He caught my arm, preventing me from fleeing. "Why say it *has* to be Flo?"

"Because that's what she's always been. And me, I'm something different."

"You are different. But, Beth, I *celebrate* those differences. I… I love them."

Them. He'd said 'them'. Perhaps it might have been different if he hadn't; if he'd said *I love you* instead. It might have changed the course of history.

I pulled my arm away. "I have to go. Mam will be wondering where I am."

I continued to retreat, out of the room and into the hallway where the stagheads remained defiant, even in death. Tugging at the oak door, I ran back out into the rain.

Stan might as well have been looking at me without the aid of his glasses, because the way he saw me was wrong, all wrong. I was worse now than I was then.

Far worse.

Chapter Twenty-Seven

"SO, that's what we're planning to do, go away mid December, just for a few days – a sort of pre-honeymoon if you like, and then we'll be back for the madness of the wedding. I don't want to go afterwards because it's too close to your due date. I want to be here in case you need me. Is that all right? Jess, hello, are you even listening?"

"Sorry, Maggie... You're going away mid December?"

"That's right, so I can be here after the wedding, whenever that little one," she nodded towards Jessamin's burgeoning midriff, "deigns to make an appearance."

"The baby... yeah, of course. I'm sorry, my head's elsewhere at the moment."

Maggie's smile was indulgent. "I can see that. What I want to know is *where* it's at?"

Jessamin lowered her eyes. "It's just baby stuff, you know."

"I don't actually, having no bairns of my own."

"Oh, I didn't mean—"

"Oh, Jess, I was joking with you. And on the subject of offspring, it doesn't mean to say I won't have any in the future. Like you, I might have an entire brood!"

Jessamin laughed along with Maggie whilst shaking her head from side to side. "Right now, the last thing I can imagine is going through this again."

Maggie grew serious. "Are you getting enough rest? You look tired?"

"I *am* tired," Jessamin confessed. "You can see why nature intended women younger than me to reproduce; it's damned hard work in your mid thirties."

"Doesn't leave much hope for me then," Maggie lamented.

"It's just… it takes it out of you."

"The decorating's all done at Comraich?"

"There's still quite a bit to do."

"But the nursery's ready?"

"Beth's room, yes."

Maggie tilted her head to the side. "You're still calling it that?"

Jessamin swallowed. "Well… maybe I won't when the baby's actually here." But right now, despite a change of wall colour and some furniture, that's what it felt like still: Beth's room – her presence still very much intact. Just a few more pages of notes were left, however. Would her presence dissipate after that, or remain as strong? She'd been reading the notes so slowly, eking them out – not just because the secrets, the lies, the sheer level of angst was more manageable that way, but perhaps because of something else too… the issues that were currently reflected in her own life? Not to the same degree, she didn't mean that, but they were there, like tiny buds beginning to flower. The slight distance that had been between herself and Finn, which she thought they'd got over, was back, ever since that day at the lighthouse and the phone call he'd received. He seemed preoccupied, worried even, but if that was the case, he wasn't offering any information as to why. Who'd been on the phone? Whoever it was, she was sure they'd been in touch again. On occasion, when he'd received a text, a shadow would creep across his face and darken it.

Each time she'd waited patiently to see if there'd be an explanation and each time there was nothing. Should she force the issue? Confront him? To do so didn't seem right. He never forced the issue regarding anything to do with her. She had to emulate that, respect it. But was it the right course? It was so damned hard to tell.

Maggie leaned over and took her hand. She'd clearly been tuning into at least some of what was running riot in Jessamin's head. "I agree, the business of others is just that: their business. There's many in this village that see fit to dabble in the lives of others, but I don't agree with it, I treasure my privacy and I appreciate it when others afford me the same courtesy, Lenny included. Having said that, Jess," she exhaled before continuing, "when you said there's a lot on your mind, you weren't joking, were you? Your thoughts are chasing each other round and round at about a hundred miles an hour. Sometimes… it's as if they're not even yours… as if they belong to someone else entirely; the line between them keeps blurring."

Jessamin looked at Maggie in amazement – her gift was astounding. And she would tell Maggie what she knew about Beth, once she herself knew the full story. Regarding Finn, however, was there really anything to tell? Or was she indeed allowing herself to be consumed by another, as Maggie suspected? She shook her head as if to rid her mind of such a notion. She'd trusted James implicitly; she should do the same with Finn. But then James had never given her reason to doubt.

For goodness sake, Jess, neither has Finn!

Drinking tea with Maggie, Jessamin drained her cup before bringing their conversation full circle. "Maggie, thank you so much for wanting to be around when the baby's due, for taking a holiday *pre*-wedding as opposed to afterwards." Tears of gratitude glistened in her eyes. "You don't have to, but… God, I'm not going to deny it, I'd love you to be there for the birth. You and Finn."

"At Comraich?" Maggie checked.

"It's definitely going to be at Comraich."

* * *

As she walked home from Maggie's, taking the short cut through fields and woodland, the wellington boots she was wearing kicking up the mud in front of her, Jessamin continued to chide herself. Suspicion was such an easy trap to fall into, and it was a dangerous one – its grip tenuous, but only at first.

Comraich reared into view – the grey of it set against the greens and browns of the woodland. This was how Beth approached it on that day, so early in the morning, although it had been raining then, soaking her to the skin. Jessamin stopped for a few moments and closed her eyes; she couldn't help herself as she drifted back towards Beth and the turmoil which had overwhelmed her. *And in the midst of that turmoil it was Stan she ran to; whom she knew she'd be safe with. Darling Stan, steadfast Stan, who never forced the issue either; never pressed for the truth.*

Only I will know the truth.

The sound of a bird cawing directly overhead caused her to release the breath she hadn't realised she'd been holding. Forcing one foot in front of the other, she continued walking. At the front of the house, she saw Finn's Defender. He was home and suddenly she couldn't wait to see him; to feel his arms around her; listen to the beat of his heart as she laid her head against his chest – her man mountain: he was her protector too, as much a haven as four walls could ever be.

Despite heavy legs, her pace quickened. She reached the door and turned the heavy handle to open it. No one locked doors around here and gradually she'd got used to that. *Everyone's so trusting.* As part of this world, that should include her.

He was home, he had to be, but to her cries of 'hello' there was no response. Coming to a standstill in the hallway, she decided to listen instead of calling out. All was quiet… initially. And then gradually a voice reached her… no, not a voice, not one that was raised anyway: a *whisper,* low and conspiratorial.

She'd heard the like before, several times – a murmur like a slow rumbling, sometimes laughter in it, sometimes not. They were the voices of those who'd gone before, that's what she'd always told herself, that thought – that *concept* – never frightening her but providing comfort. But this whisper, there was nothing quite so cosy about it; it chilled her to the bone, carrying with it a sense of foreboding. Who the hell did it belong to? Beth? She shook her head. No, Beth was still only accessible via words on paper. This had a masculine tone.

The living room door was slightly ajar. Reaching it, she poked her head around it; there was no one in there, the fire in the grate mere embers. She'd explore the kitchen next. That too was empty. Downstairs was the room that Finn occasionally used to paint in. It was slightly further than the living room and the kitchen, but in this house sounds sometimes carried; they tended to drift on the air. At other times, the house suppressed them, as if hugging them all to itself.

That door was ajar too and she had to push it slightly, hoping it wouldn't creak and give her away. Thankfully, it obliged. The room came into view, full of pictures, Finn's as well as Stan's, plenty of Beth hidden amongst them – painted the way that Stan had seen her, the *various* ways. There he was – Finn – with his back to her, staring out of the window, tall and broad, running one hand through his dark hair.

She ought to call out to him, let him know she was here. What she shouldn't do was stand and listen. Her mouth opened but words seemed to stick in her throat.

It seemed he was either placating someone or soothing them. "I know… sorry. I agree… yes. Difficult times… aye… wrong."

As he started to pace in front of the French windows, she shrunk back.

"Miss it… no." There was a sigh before he began again. "Miss you… yes."

Miss what and who? Only hearing one side of the conversation was frustrating but compelling – she couldn't walk away, not now. She was rooted to the spot.

"Yes… want to."

Jessamin's spine tingled. What was it he wanted to do?

"It's not easy. The situation…"

The situation? Again, what was he referring to? She'd never heard him sound so agitated before.

"Aye… Don't get upset. The last thing I want… upset."

She should walk into the room; see what happened and whether the conversation would continue. *Why shouldn't it continue? You need to trust him, Jess.* Despite such advice, her body refused to comply, even the baby lay quiet as if listening too.

"Okay… sort it out. No… it'll… fine. I… come up… an excuse."

Excuse?

There was wry laughter on his part and then another sigh. "Aye, it has… long time. Yes, yes… thought about you." There was another pause and then words that caused the blood to freeze in Jessamin's veins. "I still do, Suri… still do."

Suri. Where had she heard that name before? Because, as unusual as it was, she *had* heard it before, Suri was someone he'd mentioned, but only in passing. Her mind worked hard to follow the path that led back to the source of that memory. A woman, a fellow soldier, his lover – yes, yes, his lover; they'd had a relationship, but it had ended when he left the army; he hadn't stayed in contact. He'd just… cut ties.

And he hadn't spoken about her again, not to Jessamin anyway. She was American, African-American, so what was she doing here – in Scotland? She had to be here, because he was going to meet her; he was making some excuse so he could do just that. *Why'd you need an excuse? Why not just tell me?*

Pushing herself away from the wall which she'd been supporting herself against, she found the strength to move at last, back down the hallway and up the stairs, not towards their room, but Beth's. She gently closed the door and went to sit by the window, so many different emotions washing over her; a tidal wave that quickly proved relentless. *Yes, yes, I thought about you. I still do, Suri. I still do.*

This man she'd entrusted herself to, whom she was going to have a child with, did she know him, *really* know him? She thought she did, but, like her, he'd had a whole other life before they'd met; a *way* of life. Finn had lived and breathed the army for so many years. Was being back in Glenelk, a tiny Highland village, enough for him, when once he'd travelled the world? Was *she* enough? Could she compare to someone like Suri? When you fought with people, when you put your life in their hands and vice versa, it created a bond. What was it that Angus had said? *What we've gone through makes us more than friends, we're a family.* Something she was refusing to be, legally anyway. How could she even begin to compete?

From outside she heard an engine firing into life and the crunch of the Land Rover's tyres on gravel. He was going then, right now, rushing to Suri's side, because she'd asked him to; because she needed him. *For what?*

"Ow!"

The baby had started kicking again, the pain sharp, as if feeding off its mother's emotions. *Are these my emotions? All of them?*

Because if they were, they'd taken a distinctly black turn.

Chapter Twenty-Eight

Beth

"I hate you, do you know that? I hate you!"

I don't know what I expected when I said that, when I shouted it, when I screamed in his face, but what I got unnerved me. Mally's reaction – if you can call it that – was simply to stare back at me. His black eyes held untold depths, but they were guarded, refusing me access. His expression too was blank, *carefully* blank, just a hint of anger in the set of his mouth, pale lips whose edges were slightly white. *Don't push this. Leave well alone.* That's what he was telling me with those lips that had so recently been pressed against mine; that had left their mark, their taste.

"Damn you, Mally!"

Although I wanted to pummel his chest, scratch his face, tear his hair out, I turned away, grabbing my own hair instead, two bunches of it. How could he do this, treat Flo and me so differently? Or was he? Certainly, the end result was the same. *Two to drool over.* He'd said that once. He'd been laughing and joking with Stan. We were only thirteen or fourteen, but he'd said: *The best thing about the girls is there are two of them to drool over!* But one he loved and one he treated with such disdain. Despite that, he wanted me. He tried to resist me, but he never could.

We were now eighteen – just. We'd started having sex a year before, but it wasn't often; only a handful of times. Since Flo and he had consummated their relationship too, they'd become inseparable. But sometimes, just sometimes, Mam held Flo back instead of me; told me to go and get some fresh air whilst she and my sister sat and sewed. On such occasions, Flo's gaze would follow me as I got ready to leave the house; a look in her eye that wasn't as benevolent as the one in Mam's; that was more questioning. *Where are you going? Who are you seeing?* We're twins and deep down she knew it wasn't Stan who'd caused me to flush with excitement and garble my words even as I said goodbye and closed the door. *Come on, Beth, who is it?* I could almost hear her words form in my mind. *What are you keeping from me?*

"We can't keep doing this," I muttered, more to myself than Mally.

When there was silence, I repeated, "Did you hear what I just said?"

"Aye."

"We can't keep doing this."

"Then let's stop."

I was incredulous. Let's stop? Just like that?

At last I found my voice. "Would you find it that easy?"

He had the good grace to lower his eyes. "I'm just saying, perhaps you're right."

"But, Mally—"

"Don't, Beth. Don't go on."

Emboldened or incensed – I don't know which, perhaps both – I stepped closer. "You know *why* I'm doing this at least; because I love you. I'm not doing it to hurt my sister. Why are you doing it, Mally? You've never really said."

He swallowed – hard. "I have to go. My da, he'll be wonder—"

Closer still, I could feel the heat emanate off him despite it being a cold day – I could sense unease, fear even, denting his anger. "Why do you betray my sister with me?" I continued. "I want to know." When still he refused to answer, my hands shot out and grabbed the shirt he was wearing; wanting to tear it from him again, to feel not cloth beneath my hands – a barrier – but skin. "Why?"

"Because… because it doesn't feel like cheating, that's why."

"Mally, me and Flo are not one person, we're separate!"

"But you're so alike."

Stringently I denied it. "You can't have both of us."

He shrugged me off, turned away from me, but before he did, I saw what was in his eyes – a world of confusion. "I never wanted this. I never asked for this."

"And you think I did?"

"I love Flo!"

"So do I!" His cry became guttural. "It's you who seeks me out. I don't come to you."

"But you never turn me away. Whatever I've got to give, you take."

"Oh c'mon on, Beth, look at you. What man wouldn't?"

"An honourable man."

"You mean someone like Stan. He's honourable. Go to him instead."

"Leave Stan out of this." I hated him mentioning his name, *sullying* it.

"But why don't you, Beth?" The plea in his voice startled

me. "Because he wants you and he always has done."

"Because I want *you*! And despite Flo you want me too."

Vigorously he shook his head. "Flo's enough. She's definitely enough."

That did it. I flew at him, not holding back but doing as I'd wanted to earlier, to tear him apart physically as he was tearing me apart mentally. "If she was enough for you," I spat, clawing at him, hissing – a wildcat if ever there was one – "you'd turn me away when I come calling. I've seen you, Mally, when you've spotted me rushing towards you; there's a fire in your eyes – they light up; your whole body changes. Your back straightens, your shoulders. You spot me running to you and you come *striding* towards me; you catch me in your arms, you kiss me. You're not tender, not like you are with Flo, because believe me, she tells me how tender you are; how you take your time over her; how you kiss and stroke her, whispering all the while that you love her. I get none of that! Oh no. What I get is the real Mally, the animal that's in you, that won't be tethered or caged. No other woman can unleash that, not even Flo. You're *wild*, Mally, and you respond to the same thing in me. Don't shake your head. Don't say it isn't so. It *is*. With me you can be who you really are."

My fists continued to bang against his chest, drumming those words in, the truth of them, making him listen to me; forcing him to agree; *willing* it. Eventually he grabbed my wrists. I tensed. What was he going to do? Cast me aside; walk away? He did neither. He bent his head, found my lips, releasing one hand to grab the back of my neck, to draw me closer, all the way into him. Releasing my other hand, he pushed me down onto the woodland floor; another meeting place, *our* place, and I closed my arms around him, not wanting even skin to divide us, but our hearts to touch, our souls.

He entered me again, and I gasped because of it, triumph surging from some dark pit within. He wasn't like this with Flo – he couldn't be – Flo would be afraid of the savage within him; she wouldn't understand it like me; she wouldn't welcome it.

He thrust and he grunted; he kissed me, over and over, his hands in my hair, yanking my head back. If this was pain it was exquisite – if only we could die like this, in each other's arms; if only the world around us would fade away.

Finally he finished, collapsing on top of me, his weight something I was always glad to bear.

"She'll leave you, you know," I whispered into his ear, couldn't help myself.

His head jerked backwards. "You're not going to tell her…"

"About us? No. I don't mean that; I mean her desire to travel. She's going on about it more and more; she's obsessed with it. And you're not."

"She'll stay," he said, rolling off me and onto his back. "She'll never leave me."

Above us the branches of the trees swayed in the breeze. It was dark in those woods despite it being daytime, with storm clouds gathering, getting ready to burst.

If I was wrong and he was right; if she stayed, if we *all* stayed, then what?

Chapter Twenty-Nine

"OLD Mrs McConnell's heating's playing up, Jess, I'd best go and see to it."

"Really? It's on the blink again? Perhaps it's best if you get it replaced entirely."

"I did, three years ago," Finn shrugged as he answered Jessamin. "She's probably just pressed a button she shouldn't have; that was the case last time I went. It's a digital panel and she can't seem to get the hang of it."

"Can't get enough of you more like."

Finn made a show of laughing. "You think she's into toy boys?"

"I think you're a handsome man and probably few can resist you."

Although she was trying her best to sound jovial, she knew, that like him, she'd failed. Rather than a compliment it had sounded like an accusation. She bit her lip. *Why are we no longer honest with each other? When did it all start to go wrong?* When they'd found out about the baby? A precious moment that had somehow put pressure on them; that had changed them. *But it should be for the better!*

As he stood there, in the living room of Comraich, looking at her as she sat on the sofa, she decided to press for the truth on one matter at least.

"Are you really going to see Mrs McConnell, Finn?"

"Aye, Jess, I just said."

"You wouldn't lie to me?"

Was that a spot of colour in his cheeks? "Of course not!"

She closed her eyes, an attempt to stop any tears from being shed. Technically, it was possible to believe him. He hadn't lied to her about Suri. The day that she'd overheard him on the phone, he'd left the house and – she believed – driven over to see her. He'd said nothing about it because, of course, he hadn't realised she was in the house. But when he'd returned that same night, he'd said nothing then either. If it was a meeting, an *innocent* meeting, why hadn't he come through the door and said something like, 'Jess, you know I bumped into Angus the over day, home on leave from the army? Well guess what, Suri's on leave too and she's in Scotland. You remember Suri? I told you about her, she's an old flame of mine. Well, she's here and she fancied a bit of a catch-up. It was nice to see her actually; she's doing great.' Why hadn't he come in and said that? Laid it all to rest. Given her back her peace of mind. Instead, he'd kissed her hello, asked some general questions about her day and then gone upstairs for a long, hot shower. Later, he'd poured himself a good measure of whisky and set it down on the table beside him as he joined her in front of the fire. Whilst he watched the flames, she'd watched him – albeit surreptitiously. She noticed how often he picked up his glass and held it in his hands, swirling the amber contents round and round as he stared at the flames that pirouetted before him, lost in thoughts that remained stubbornly private.

Ever since that evening she'd continued to watch him, on the lookout for signs; waiting for more texts to come through, more phone calls. They didn't, not in her presence at least, and Finn was as attentive as ever, but the distance that was in her was now in him. There was a wall between them and it was getting higher.

"Jess," Finn brought her back to the moment. His colouring had returned to normal, but there was a frown on his face. "What's on your mind?"

Closing her eyes, she sighed. *What's on **my** mind?* Oh, the irony! *Go on say it, come right out with it.* "I'm feeling fat, that's all, and frumpy."

"Frumpy? Och, Jess, you could never be that. You're beautiful."

She was certainly beautiful – Suri. On a couple of occasions, when Finn had gone out, she'd rummaged through his wardrobe, not feeling great at resorting to such measures but unable to stop herself. He had some photos from his army days; photos she'd seen in the past, which, to be fair, he'd never tried to hide. She'd wanted to see them again, study them. Suri was in them more than she'd realised. She was a tall woman with dark hair in short braids. Wearing combat trousers, heavy boots and a tight black vest, she stood beside Finn and several other colleagues, one of her strong and muscular arms by her side, the other wrapped around his waist. This was Finn before the explosion; no eyepatch to hide the damage done, no long-sleeved shirt to cover the burns on his arm and chest. Even though it was just a photo, Jessamin could see that his eyes were sparkling, as were hers; they were comrades in arms, *lovers*.

In another photo, which included Angus, Finn was smoking, something she'd never known him to do – he'd given up after his accident apparently – and Suri was reaching across to take the cigarette from his lips. While Angus was looking at the camera along with several others, Finn and Suri only had eyes for each other.

In yet another, one Jessamin hadn't seen before, which perhaps *had* been kept from her, was a close-up of Suri, and that's how she knew she was beautiful. Her skin was clear, her eyes the deepest shade of brown, her full lips slightly parted. *I know that look*, Jessamin thought. *It's the look of a woman in love.*

Because Finn rarely asked about James, although if she freely talked about him he'd happily sit and listen, she hadn't asked him very much about Suri. She just knew the basics; that they'd been a couple; that he'd had the accident; that she'd wanted him to stay in the army, but he'd left. Apart from a few initial letters, they hadn't kept in further contact. That was nearly four years ago. She and Finn had been together for two of them. It seemed like such a short time now and yet she was due to have his child soon – very soon – the child of a man she loved but didn't know fully. It took more time than that to get to know someone. It could take a lifetime.

Finn was speaking again. "Why don't we go out and get some fresh air, a bit of lunch maybe?"

"What? Go out? I..." She wanted to make the effort and felt that she should, but she was tired; perpetually tired, and where food was concerned, her belly was full enough. God, their life was changing with every passing day and as Maggie had pointed out, it was frightening... If Suri was back on the scene, confusing him, as Beth had confused Mally, then it was more than that; it was downright terrifying. She could feel herself slump. "Why don't we just stay here? Although, old Mrs McConnell—"

"Don't worry about her, I can go there later. Aye, we can stay in. I'll rustle up something for us. I don't want you getting cabin fever, that's all."

"I'm not getting cabin fever and I'd like that, you and me together."

Just as Beth had wished, so she wished too: that it could stay that way – the outside world fading to leave just her, Finn, the baby and Comraich in existence.

Finn threw another log on the fire before he swapped the living room for the kitchen. "It's starting to get cold, Jess," he remarked.

He was right, temperatures befitting the season at last. It was early December and there'd been a smatter of snow in the last couple of weeks, but nothing that had forced Winn Greer to get his snowplough out. A month, not even that, that was all she had to go before the baby arrived and when it did, they'd both be spectacularly busy. 'You'll have no time to think, either of you,' Ina, the mother of Dougie and several other strapping lads, had warned. "Just finding time to brush your teeth, wash your face or feed yourself, that's a luxury that goes out the window, I can tell you."

If that was true, Jessamin would welcome it. If they were as busy as Ina and other seasoned mothers in the village kept insisting they'd be, then surely whatever was happening between Finn and Suri would peter out. She'd go back on duty or home to America and leave him to adjust to his new role. All she had to do was be patient.

When Finn returned with two plates of sandwiches stuffed with ham, cheese and lettuce, they ate and chatted, Jessamin simply enjoying the moment. After they'd finished eating, he settled himself back down beside her, putting his arm round her as she snuggled against him, breathing in his smell, finding comfort in the familiarity that they'd enjoyed so far. Two years, it was not nearly enough time. She wanted so much more from him – the rest of his life. And she'd give hers to him, willingly. Nobody could get in the way of that – they belonged together. Perhaps… perhaps if they made it official…

It was the clock on the mantelpiece chiming that woke her. Bleary-eyed, she looked at it – it was half past three in the afternoon, a full hour having disappeared since she last looked.

Christ, she thought, yawning, *I never even realised I'd gone to sleep!*

That was what one of Finn's hefty sandwiches and a roaring log fire could do to a girl – knock her for six.

Finn – where was he? No longer beside her. She was alone. Turning her head, all that met her was Beth's watchful gaze in her portrait, her persistent melancholy enveloping the entire room – *Winter Willow* not quite as soothing as promised.

"Finn?" she called out. About to rise to go to the window to check if his car was in the drive, she noticed a piece of paper under her cup. She picked it and read what was on it.

Hey, Sleeping Beauty, I dozed too for a while but woke up and decided to head over to see Old Mrs McConnell. You stay resting, I know you're tired and just lately you've been looking a bit pale. Not long to go, Jess, and then I can share the load with you. It's what I want, what I'm looking forward to – the two of us becoming three. I'll pick up some fresh fish for tonight's dinner. The Blair brothers should have docked with the day's catch by the time I reach the Kyle. I love you, Finn.

Reading the letter, not once but twice, Jessamin hugged it to her, feeling better than she had for days; more hopeful. They were about to embark on the biggest adventure of their lives and he wanted it as much as she did. He loved her, she had it in writing – and Suri; Suri was an old flame but she was also his friend; there needn't be anything more to it than that, despite the secrecy. Perhaps he was just worried that she might take her reappearance the wrong way and deemed it better to say nothing at all. As galling as it was that he might think that, it could all be innocent. And maybe, just maybe, this might be the evening he mentioned something.

"Milk, damn, we need milk."

Ignoring a slight twinge in her stomach as she rose – she'd clearly been lying in an awkward position and had got a bit of cramp – she went over to the sideboard where her phone was and rang his number, her heart sinking when she heard his ring tone answer hers, just a few feet away on the sofa. He normally checked that he had his phone on him before he left the house, but if like her he'd been dozing, he might not be vigilant on waking. Either that or he thought it was still in his back pocket. "That's annoying, Finn," she muttered. "*Really* annoying."

She could drive down to Maggie's shop, get the milk in herself, but that twinge in her stomach was getting sharper. Coming up with a plan, she called Maggie.

"If it's milk you need, I can drop some over as soon as the shop closes," Maggie offered.

"Thinking about it, I could do with a few other bits and pieces too," replied Jessamin. "It'd just be easier if I could speak to Finn. You don't know Mrs McConnell, do you, over in Kyle? That's where he's gone. Do you have her number at all?"

"Old Mrs McConnell, you mean?"

Jessamin laughed. "The very same."

"Aye, she's a bit of a character that one."

"Finn's told me."

"She's raised a fine brood though, dotted all around here, they are. Hang on, let me see if I can find it. Ach, here you go, here's her landline."

Jessamin jotted down the number, thanked Maggie and then redialled.

"Hello," a voice said, a slight quaver in it, when the line connected.

Quickly, Jessamin explained who she was.

"Ah, you're Finn's lass! Och, he's lovely is Finn! A fine lad and such a brave boy too, fighting for kin and country. One of ma grandsons is in the army, did he tell you? Well he's just joined to be fair, but I'm very proud of him. It's terrible what happened to Finn, though. It knocked his confidence for a while there. I'm glad he's got you to comfort him. He speaks about you, you know, and the bairn you're expecting."

"That's good to know," Jessamin replied. "We're both very excited."

"So you should be, children are such a gift. I was blessed in that respect, truly blessed."

"Erm… Mrs McConnell, is Finn there? I need to speak to him."

"Here, lass, at mine, you mean?"

"Yes."

"I'm afraid not. He pops in a lot, there's always something that needs doing. But he's no' here today."

Jessamin swallowed. "But your heating—"

"My heating's working just fine. Well, it is at the moment at any rate."

"I see. I must have got the wrong end of the stick. I'm sorry to disturb you."

"Och, not at all! It was lovely to speak to you. You must

pop in with Finn sometime so I can meet you, and soon enough the bairn too."

"Yes, yes, I'd love to meet you."

"I'll look forward to it."

"Goodbye, Mrs McConnell."

"Goodbye, hinny."

Ending the call, Jessamin glanced at the letter again and the words that Finn had written. *It's what I want, what I'm looking forward to – the two of us becoming three.*

They were words on paper – *just* words – with no meaning behind them at all.

Chapter Thirty

THE air was decidedly frosty, both inside and outside of Comraich. When Finn had returned that night, brandishing the salmon he'd bought from the Blair brothers, as promised, laughingly insisting that all the Omega 3 it contained was going to make his child the cleverest in the Highlands, Jessamin had merely stared at him before declaring that she was tired; she felt sick and couldn't face dinner after all.

Ignoring her guilt at his obvious disappointment, she rose and went to their bedroom, feigning sleep when finally he came upstairs to join her.

The next few days whilst he'd supposedly gone on his rounds, she'd spent time at home, shunning even a visit from Maggie; playing the sick card again, although not so much that Finn would summon Doctor Buchanan, but enough to give her time on her own; to contemplate how life had imploded again. Finn wasn't stupid, he knew something was up, but it was as though they were at stalemate – she refusing to be honest with him, and he clearly refusing to be honest with her. *Just say what's on your mind.* Perhaps it was because she hadn't, right from the start, that this had happened. By refusing to even broach the subject of marriage, had she alienated him? Made him feel second best, just as Beth had felt she was second best for Mally and as Stan had felt he was for Beth? Now she'd done it too, unwittingly. But Suri, she *hadn't* done it. She'd tracked Finn down, crossed oceans to be with him – the passing of time clearly having done nothing to diminish her feelings for him. *Once in love, always in love.*

How her head as well as her heart ached. *Do what Beth's doing with you; talk to him. Start from the beginning. Tell him everything.* As the thought formed in her mind, she doubled over again; it was another twinge in her tummy. *And tell him about that too, the pains.* She would. She'd pick a day and blurt everything out; deal with the situation; not hide from it any longer.

As another wintry day dawned, she left their bed and tiptoed to the bedroom window. Raising her hand to the glass, she felt how cold it was. Today was that day. It wouldn't be a confrontation, not as such. Her hormones might be raging, but she was no teenager: she'd deal with what was happening in as calm a manner as possible.

Rather than look behind her at Finn, who was still in bed sleeping, she tilted her head towards the sky. *James, where are you?* Somewhere far, far from there, where she could no longer hear him, only remember him and the love and security he'd provided. It was wrong to compare two such different men. Whereas James had been a city man, into fast cars, fancy foods, fine wines, film and theatre, Finn would jar with the neon of London; she didn't think even Brighton would suit him; it was still too much of a metropolis, compared to Glenelk. She'd once been like James, into all that a city could offer, but Finn's way was her way now; this house, this village and the history that defined it, that she was still so immersed in. It felt natural, ingrained. She didn't want to return to the south. She wanted to stay. And so, like Suri, she must become a fighter too, let no man – and no woman either – put asunder…

And commit, Jess. Fully.

Yes, no half measures anymore.

As she was about to turn, to wake Finn, another pain shot through her stomach, this one causing her mouth to open in a silent scream.

Get to a chair, sit down.

Taking her own advice, she did just that, resting at the dressing table, staring at her reflection whilst trying to regulate her breathing. As Finn had said, she was pale.

What's going on?

She only had a month to go; perhaps this sort of thing was normal. What had the midwife called it? Braxton Hicks – trial contractions in other words – her body preparing for the real thing. There were several of them, each one a wave she had to ride, but becoming less and less severe and eventually passing off.

Jessamin couldn't help but smile when they did. It's nothing but a storm in a teacup. Nonetheless, she continued sitting still for a while, breathing in, breathing out in a slow and purposeful manner, just as the midwife had suggested.

"Christ!"

Finn's raised voice caused her to flinch. Quickly, she turned to face him, "You're awake?"

"Aye, but look at the time! I've a meeting with the solicitor in Inverness this morning, do you remember me saying? I have to be there by 9.30 and it's 8.15 now."

She did recall him saying something, the previous night, but it was more in passing than to her specifically. Everything seemed to be in passing nowadays.

"I've got to hurry," he muttered, leaping from bed with an agility she could only envy, grabbing some clothes from a chest of drawers and hurriedly dressing.

"Shall I ring, say you're going to be late? I'm sure they'll be fine about it."

Immediately he dismissed her offer. "It's not just that... I've... I've other things to do today. I need to get to the solicitors, sign this new lease and then..."

"And then what?" Jessamin prompted when his voice died off. "What else do you have to do today, Finn, that's so important?"

He avoided her eyes as he answered, searching for his watch instead and making quite a show of it. "Where is it, where the hell is it? I really can't speak now; I'll tell you when I get back. Oh there it is, under the laundry. I thought I'd lost it then."

"Finn, it's just... this morning, I really wanted to speak to you."

"I can't," he reiterated, "but tonight, when I get back; we can speak as much as you like, I promise. Ah, this watch strap, it drives me mad sometimes."

The watch was an inheritance from Stan, a Rolex Datejust that had been left to him in turn by his father. The strap was temperamental and normally Jessamin would help Finn secure it if he was having problems, but this time she simply sat and looked at him – at how flustered he was, nervous even – so unlike the man she was used to.

"Finn..."

The watch dealt with, he tugged on his jumper, mussing his hair even more; thick hair, black hair, just like she imagined Mally's to be. Did he also share the same traitorous streak? Could she curb it if she gave him what he wanted?

She stood up.

"Finn, will you marry me?"

The look on his face surprised her – the *shock*. In all honesty she'd surprised herself that she'd asked him; that the words had finally left her mouth – the *first* time ever they'd left her mouth. With James, he'd been the one who'd done the asking.

"Jess, I… I…"

"… Don't know what to say. I understand that. I… well I've taken myself a bit by surprise too, to be honest. I've been thinking about it for a while though, you know, marriage; mulling it over, what with the baby on the way. People expect… " She shook her head, brought that trail of conversation to a halt. "It would just… It would be nice to get married again. I would, Finn, I'd like to marry you. We can be a proper family."

Instead of answering, he repeated her words. "People *expect*? A proper family?"

As her face flamed, her spine tingled. There was something in his voice, something wrong; a gravitas that perhaps shouldn't be there. When she analysed it further, she realised there was no joy in it. Consumed with nerves, she laughed, or at least tried to. What came out was actually a brittle sound, unpleasant on the ears. "Don't rush to answer or anything. It's not as if I'm standing here with baited breath."

"Jess…"

"Finn, what are you doing? You're just standing and staring at me, saying my name, repeating my words randomly. Normally, it's either a yes or no."

"This really isn't a good time."

Again his reaction stunned her.

"But I thought—"

"I told you I was late for an appointment; that I have to go."

"For God's sake, I'm not asking you to pick up some shopping here – a few loaves of bread, a pint of milk. I want you to marry me!"

She'd raised her voice and so did he. "What you want is to do what people expect of us."

"I thought you'd be happy!"

"No, Jess, you thought you'd appease me." He started to pace back and forth, running one hand through his hair. "This is really not a good time."

She stepped closer but didn't dare reach out and touch him. "Why's it not a good time? Any particular reason for that, beside the solicitors appointment, I mean?"

He stopped and regarded her, his gaze steady. If she had intended to embarrass him, she'd failed. "Yes, there is a particular reason. I'll talk to you about it tonight."

"So, you're going; you're leaving me here, alone at Comraich; you're not going to give me an answer, to anything?"

"Not now I'm not."

"I know about her."

Only after a moment's silence did he ask who.

"Suri. I know she's in Scotland."

It was infuriating how composed he was. Whilst she unravelled before him, inch by pitiful inch. "How long have you known?"

"A couple of weeks now."

"And you didn't think to say something about it beforehand?"

"No, I... I—"

"Wanted to wait and see if you could catch me out, and when you couldn't, you thought you'd back me into a corner; you'd force the issue by asking me to marry you of all things."

Vehemently, he shook his head. "No. There you are, that's your answer. You want to marry me but for all the wrong reasons. Actually, you know what, scrub that!" His breathing was becoming more ragged as he continued. "You *don't* want to marry me. I know that, full well. That's why I've never asked you. And I'm fine with it, with what I think is your reasoning. What I'm not fine with, what I'll *never* be fine with, is marriage as a trap—"

"A trap?"

"Aye, that's right."

"I'm not trying to—"

"Yes, you are, Jess. And as I've said, under those circumstances it's a no."

"But you're having an affair!"

When he looked at her, there wasn't just shock on his face, but something she didn't want to admit to, that made her cringe.

"I'm going now. Because if I stay—"

"If you stay what?" she challenged, aghast as he started to back away.

"Tonight, we'll talk. Just… wait 'til tonight."

Turning, he stormed from the room, leaving anger to consume her too.

* * *

How she navigated her way to Beth's room from her own, Jessamin didn't know. The last thing she remembered was staring open-mouthed at the door as Finn left her, actually *left* her, having accused her as she'd accused him. *You weren't supposed to accuse him, you said you wouldn't.* That's right, she had, but sometimes the heart and the head don't comply. She knew that and Beth knew that; a woman who would understand the depth of misery she was feeling right now; who'd *empathise* with her. And that's why she'd come here. It was the solace of a kindred spirit she sought – a woman who was not of her blood, but who in this moment she felt the closest to; someone who hadn't shut her out, as her grandson had just done; who'd welcomed her in, *all* the way in – right to the end. That's what was happening here – things were coming to an end, in ways both expected and unexpected. But first she'd see Beth's story through. She'd do that today; unveil what she'd kept hidden – secrets – more secrets. This house and its occupants were riddled with them.

Crossing over to the bureau, opening the drawer where Beth's notes were hidden, she took only what was needed – the last remnants. Because of Stan she knew what was coming, what had taken place at the loch, some of it anyway. And that's where she'd go; she'd wrap up warm, get out of Comraich. She wouldn't walk; there was no way she could walk that distance now. She'd take the car as far as she was able to.

She moved more with a sense of purpose, and was glad of the distraction. If she stayed here, if she continued mulling over what had just happened between herself and Finn, she'd go mad. Returning to her room, she dressed, grabbed her car keys and left Comraich. She paused only briefly outside its weather-beaten door, questioning the wisdom of what she was doing. Should she stay home, in the warm? Comraich was a haven, or at least it *used* to be. Would it be one again in the future? Would it ever feel the same?

It was never the same for you, was it, Beth?

Not after what happened at the loch; it became a prison,

albeit one in which she willingly incarcerated herself. Jessamin had wanted it to be so different for her and Finn; she'd tried to make it different, done her best, but perhaps all these walls understood was heartache and tragedy; perhaps that's what they perpetuated.

They're cursed as Beth was cursed, as I seem to be cursed.

Was happiness only ever to be fleeting?

That fearful thought caused a sob to escape her as she hurried over to her car. Climbing in she took a deep breath and fired up the engine, which rumbled slightly in protest at being woken from its sleep, and put it into *Drive*. The road that led to the loch could hardly be called that – it was more of a track littered with stones and rocks. It was such a cold day, but at least it wasn't raining. On a rainy winter's day this would be an impossible journey and the fact that it wasn't, that it was accessible, she took as a sign. *Let's get this over and done with. Meet it head on.*

Because she was driving at barely above walking pace, it took just under half an hour to reach the loch. She'd have to walk the remainder of the distance, turning inland and wading through tall grass, careful to avoid snagging her foot, lest she fall. Leaving the car behind, she pulled her coat tight around her, lowered her head and breathed in the sharp air. As she proceeded, her gait determined, it soon came into view; so many different pools of water, a light layer of mist hanging over them, lending an air of otherworldliness. It *had* been otherworldly – to Beth, Flo, Mally and Stan – their place; a happy place; a place where memories were forged and friendships had deepened. Once upon a time.

The breath left Jessamin's body.

She'd thought… she'd really thought… *that he was your soul mate,* ***another*** *soul mate? That's just greedy, Jess.* Lifting her hand to her temple, she rubbed at the skin there, her thoughts still churning. *Is that what I was? What I am? Greedy? Wanting another chance, when James got none? Do I deserve all that's happening to me?*

It was only when she took her hand away that she realised she was crying, the tips of her fingers slick with tears.

She'd been betrayed. Finn was having an affair. He hadn't confirmed it, but he hadn't denied it either. And she'd made a fool of herself by asking him to marry her, thinking that's what he wanted; that it was why he'd strayed in the first place, because she'd made him doubt her. *What a fool I am! What an utter fool!*

Out here in the wilderness, without another soul for miles, the sense of loneliness was crippling. It came out of nowhere and engulfed her. But she wasn't alone; she had to remind herself of that. She had the baby, she had Beth, and she had Flo, Mally and Stan too. She'd seen their shadows here once; the essence of them, replaying the scenes of their own betrayal, caught in the grip of it, as she was caught in the grip of hers. She was far from alone and their story wasn't done – in it she still hoped to find a way to deal with her own. Catching a slight movement in the mist, she looked up. Whatever she had seen was gone now, but it wasn't a wandering sheep or a deer. It had been taller than that, as tall as a man, or a woman. A shadow then, a wisp, one of the four. Digging in her coat pocket, she retrieved the notes, her teeth chattering slightly and not just because of the dip in temperature.

"The time has come," she said, beginning to read. "What really happened here that day, Beth?"

Chapter Thirty-One

Beth

MALLY was so damned sure of Flo. *She'll stay. She'll never leave me.* But as she grew into adulthood, the stronger that urge became in her – to break out, to be free. I'm not saying she would have left him, but I think, had she lived, they both would have travelled; seen the places she dreamt of; that she'd read about in the books Mrs McNeill had plied her with. This was the age of travel, that's what she used to say; the world was opening up, becoming accessible, so why stay here, so far from everything? For her, it was tantamount to being buried alive.

Mally had begun work for the Comraich estate, he and Stan carrying out their tasks under the careful tuition of Stan's father. There was still plenty of time for him to help his own father on his farm, and for Stan to paint, but they were enjoying learning the ropes as well as being together. They were such good friends, Mally and Stan, so at ease in each other's company. The difference in status between them never caused any complications. They were equals, in all the ways that counted.

But between Mally's happiness and Flo's dreams there was a rift that I at least could see coming, even if they pretended it wasn't happening; if Mally insisted on hiding from the truth in layers of self-belief and bluster. The Highland people are a determined people; they don't give up on their dreams easily. Flo certainly held onto hers, another way in which we were similar.

There'd been an argument. Mally and Flo had rowed. He'd stormed off in the midst of that row, left her, and had come to me; sought me out for once, just as I used to seek him out, although I hadn't so much lately. Not in recent weeks anyway.

As bold as brass he walked into the village pub. Whilst Flo continued to help Mam with her sewing, I had managed to pick up a few shifts at The Stag. I didn't earn much but when it came to finances every little bit helped, plus I was hoping it would lead to more work in the future. I was polishing some glasses when he strode in, not stopping until he was right in front of me, his eyes blazing as tremors coursed through him, causing him to pant slightly.

"Mally?" I enquired, puzzled.

"Can you get away?"

"I've another half hour to go."

"I need to speak to you."

I gestured around me. "The place is empty, speak to me here."

"No, I want to get out of the village, go somewhere private."

I knew where he meant. "The loch?"

"Aye, the loch."

"You'll have to wait—"

At that moment, Mrs Fairfax came in. She and her husband ran the pub, although as far as I could make out, she did the lion's share of the work. A woman just a few years older than Mam, she had none of her beauty; her back was stooped, her hair grey and wiry, often scraped into a severe bun, and her figure rotund. Sometimes I used to think she was in pain as she'd wince when she walked, or rather waddled, from side to side, but if she was, she was stoic enough never to let on. There was always a smile on her face, words of welcome on her lips and her pub was busy because of that, *usually*.

On seeing us, she smiled. "Is this your fella, Beth? The one that causes you to look so dewy-eyed at times."

"No!" My voice was harsher than I intended it to be. Quickly, I reined myself in. This was my boss I was talking to. "This is Mally, he's… erm… my sister's boyfriend."

"Oh?" She raised an eyebrow. "And yet here he is, come to see you?"

Mally answered before I could. "I need to talk to Beth. Can you spare her?"

"Can I spare her? It's urgent, is it?"

"Aye," replied Mally and something in his voice, his manner, stifled any objection she might have raised. She held his gaze for a second or two and then she nodded.

"Go on, lad; take her off for your urgent chat. If there's a sudden rush, I might regret it, mind. Beth, come in half an hour earlier tomorrow to make up for it."

"I will, Mrs Fairfax," I said, nonetheless taking the time to straighten the bar before I left, a part of me wishing she hadn't given her permission so readily; the other part, as always, anxious to hear anything that Mally had to say.

Once we were outside, he kept ahead of me, his hands in his pockets, his head down. Not bothering to catch up with him, I lagged behind, my gaze alternating between him and the birds in the air that swooped and circled.

I was breathless by the time we reached the loch, its often jewel-like waters much duller than normal, and not quite as still, a light breeze responsible for eddying them.

Curiosity got the better of me. "Mally, what have you brought me out here for? Do you want to end it between us? Is that your intention?"

When he turned to face me I was stunned. There were tears in his eyes, one or two starting to break rank. I'd never seen Mally cry before, never. Eventually he lifted a hand to wipe roughly at his cheek. "It's not you, it's Flo."

"Oh," was my somewhat deflated reply. Of course it was Flo. It was *always* Flo.

"What's happened with her?" I said, having to swallow hard.

"You think I'm wild, you've said it often enough, but Flo, she's untameable."

"Untameable? What do you mean?"

"She came over to see me and, Beth, she just went mad. She wants us to leave here, straightaway I mean. She says we *have* to; that there's a world out there and we need to be in it. Mrs McNeill's been lending her more books, encouraging her. I don't want to go away, not yet at any rate. This is my home; Stan's here, my work..."

"And me," I pointed out, my voice barely above a whisper. "I'm here too."

"Aye." Still his tears fell. "And that's maybe the only reason I *should* go."

I didn't think it was possible that he could hurt me anymore, but those words caused an already savaged heart to bleed further.

"I think Flo's right," I managed to respond, "you two should leave. Why not? Think about what's *really* here: a father who beats you, a woman who gave up being a mother years ago and me, the dark side of you that you hate."

"I don't hate you," he all but mumbled.

"You do. It's the opposite to what you feel for Flo."

His head came up abruptly, startling me. All tears had gone. Instead his eyes were fierce. "Aye, aye, you're right. Sometimes it is the opposite; I *do* hate you, with every bone in my body, just as much as you hate me on occasion. And don't bother to deny it. I know you do. God knows you've said it enough whilst beating at my chest. But sometimes…" He hung his head again but only briefly. "Ah, Beth, it's a fine line, that's what they say, don't they, between the two emotions. Perhaps Flo's right, perhaps *you're* right. But this place…" he stopped to look around him, his eyes resting briefly on the mountains that observed us, the water that was dull but ever flowing, the high grass that the four of us would lie in, laughing, joking and planning, "…it gets to you, you know? I can't imagine belonging anywhere else. It has everything," he turned back to me and his gaze was as intent as that time we'd sat on the hillside when we were kids, just before I'd made him kiss me; before he kissed me back – so hard. "But perhaps, in the end, there's too much of it."

"Mally…" above us those damned birds continued to circle, to caw, "…you're speaking in riddles. What is it you mean? What is it you want? To leave here because you think it's best; to leave me because what we have – this twisted thing that exists between us – it'll drag you deeper into the mire if you stay? Don't dress your words up in fancy clothing; I've not the patience for it. Speak plain. Tell me."

His hands flew up to cover his eyes as he sighed heavily. "I don't know what I want. Don't you see? I never have. Why… why does there have to be two of you? It's as though God's got it in for me, as if he's playing a cruel joke."

His words incensed me. "IT'S NOT ALL ABOUT YOU, MALLY!" For a moment, I had to pause, catch my breath. "I didn't ask for this either, to feel the way I do. But that's the thing, I have *always* loved you, from the moment I first set eyes on you. I've dreamt of you, I've prayed to a god I no longer believe in, that you'd be mine instead of hers. You've known how I've felt and you've taken advantage of it. And all you've ever been concerned for is yourself and Flo. It is *never* me."

Stricken by the truth of that, I turned to flee, desperate to escape what was essentially so rotten. He wasn't going to make it easy for me, however.

He grabbed me, swung me back round, his hands on my shoulders as he pushed me down, down, down, into the long grass – perhaps the same spot he'd first lain with Flo, the thought of which I found abhorrent; the sacredness of it.

"No, Mally. Not here. I don't want to do this here…"

"I do feel sorry for you, Beth, I do," he was saying, lying on top of me now, one knee pinning my body to the ground, the other pushing my legs wide apart. "I feel sorry that I've ever hurt you; that I can't stop hurting you."

As he pushed his way inside me, I sobbed louder.

"I'll tell you why I can't stop though, shall I?"

I turned my head to the side. "I don't want to hear it."

"You do."

"Mally, stop!"

His hand grabbed my chin, forcing me to look at him again.

"It's because, sometimes… just sometimes… I love you too."

At his words, my heart seemed to stop beating. He'd said it, what I'd been waiting to hear for so long. He loved me. *Sometimes.*

How can anyone love someone *sometimes*?

Once again, fury overwhelmed the desire that allowed him to treat me this way.

"Stop it, stop it, Mally, d'ya hear? Get off me!" With a strength that was almost preternatural, I heaved him off. Struggling to sit up, I felt my cheeks burning as I pulled my dress down as far as it would go. "No more. That's it. Enough. I want you to do as Flo says and leave here. This is a noble land. You've no place in it after all."

I think those words hurt him more than anything I'd ever said before. Reaching over, he tried to stop me as I struggled to my feet.

"No!" I said again, snatching my hand back. "I mean it. You can't stop this, so I'm going to. You talk about love but I don't think you know what love is. I don't even think you love Flo. You said to me once that you wanted a simple life, and she'll fit into that life; she'll be the one who makes it simple. Or so you thought. But as it turns out Flo's got more about her than that; she's not quite ready to settle down and play the meek and mild wife. Oh no, Flo's got far bigger ambitions than that. And you hate it. You hate being defied. You're more like your father than you think."

Mally had jumped to his feet too. "Don't say that."

"Why not? What are you going to do about it? Cry some more?"

The slap across my face caused me to lose my footing, to stumble. For a moment I couldn't think. Everything went dark, blessedly dark – a real sanctuary, one I could lose myself in. And then as the shock receded, the pain flared.

"You… you bastard, Mally!"

Before the words were out he was on me again, this time holding me tight, even as I tried to push him away, whispering how sorry he was; that he'd never hit a girl before; that this was why it would never work between us; because this was what I did – I pushed him to the edge, every time. "I'm not blaming you, because I know I do the same to you; we let each other do this. We cause each other so much pain, we'd destroy each other, but," he brought my face to his, not roughly this time, but with surprising tenderness, "there's joy in that pain; there's something about it that touches my soul. It does more than that, it *brands* it. I'm addicted to you; we're addicted to each other. I don't want to leave here; I don't want to leave you."

"But you love *her*."

"I love you both."

I swiped his hand away. "That's not possible."

"It is! Believe me, it is."

"You don't know what you want, you've just admitted it."

"I want you just as much."

"Impossible," I whispered again, but at that moment he straightened, his eyes not on me anymore, but looking beyond me, his mouth falling open in surprise.

"Mally? What is it?"

"It's them. It's Stan and Flo."

As I swung round I continued to pat my hair down, to smooth my dress. My breathing, already harsh, refused to be controlled. "God," I whispered.

Flo was storming towards us, Stan having to run to keep up with her. As she drew closer she was barely recognisable, it was as though she wore a mask, one carved in fury; nothing pretty about her now, nothing light. How much had she seen?

"Flo!" I said, at the same time as Mally did. He was standing rigid beside me, clearly wondering the same.

"What are you doing here…" she screamed, glaring first at me, then at Mally, "…together?"

"We came for a walk," I answered.

"I needed to talk to someone," Mally added.

I looked sideways at him – *someone*? *Just someone?*

Still I jumped to his defence. "Look, Flo, don't come here yelling at us. If Mally wants to talk to me, he can. You've been arguing again and he's upset."

She pushed her face – my mirror image – into mine. "If he's upset, it's my business, not yours."

"Flo, calm down," Mally begged. "What does it matter if I'm with Beth? You're with Stan!"

Flo dismissed that. If I'm honest, we all did. Stan was no threat – not to this unholy triangle. And we all knew it. Nonetheless, our friend spoke out.

"Beth, come away; let the two of them sort their problems."

It was such wise advice. I wish over and over I'd taken it. But I didn't. I *couldn't.* Mally loved me, he said he did; he loved us both, but he'd choose her; over and above me, he'd choose her. Did she know how *lucky* she was?

"You're such a selfish bitch, Flo! You've got a man, you've got Mally, and yet what do you do? You insist on tormenting him; putting your plans above his; insisting that he follows you halfway round the world when all he wants to do is stay here where he's got a career ahead of him; a *good* career, not just pipedreams." Despite everything I'd said to him earlier, I wanted him to stay, because maybe, just maybe, he might change his mind in the future.

My twin was having none of it. "If I'm selfish, *you're*

jealous, which is so much worse; you're eaten up by jealousy. You think I don't know; you think you're so clever at concealing how you feel, but you want my man and you always have."

She knew? How much of it, though?

Mally interjected again, desperate to change the subject. "Flo, Stan's right, we do need to talk, just the two of us. Come on, let's get away from here, leave Beth alone—"

"Leave Beth alone?" she screeched, tearing her eyes from me to rest on Mally. "Are you sticking up for her now?"

"Flo, what's got into you?" He looked like a little boy again; as vulnerable. "Why are you being like this?"

"Look at the state of you! Did you think I wouldn't notice? That I'm blind? Your clothes are rumpled. And, Beth, so are yours. What were you doing out here, *just* talking or something else? Were you fucking, is that it? Are you having an affair?"

My breath caught in my throat – never had I heard Flo swear before; somehow that was more shocking, more serious, than the accusation.

"Flo," Mally caught her by the arm, but with none of the force he used with me. He was always so damned gentle with her. "Let's just go, right now; you and me."

"Go?" she queried, a cold fire still burning in her eyes.

"Yes. We'll do what you want; we'll leave this place. Flo, I'd never betray you, never; you know that, and if you want to travel, then that's what we'll do; we'll travel."

My mouth fell open.

"What?" Not only had he lied, he'd *chosen* – there was no hope, none at all.

As the word slipped from my mouth, such incredulity

behind it, Mally looked at me, I think Stan did too. But more than that, Flo did; she stared at me. *Are you having an affair?* The answer was in my eyes and so easy for a twin to read.

As I'd flown at Mally, so many times, she now flew at me, her hands raised; her fingers like claws – a banshee, a fearsome creature. I raised my hands too, at first to protect myself, but quickly that turned to retaliation. *Damn you for having what I want, for being what I wanted to be.* If only we'd been one person, not two. How many times had I thought that? We should never have been divided, although, there and at that time, we *were* one – each as dark as the other – spitting and scratching, our teeth bared. Mally and Stan were shouting at us; pleading with us – *Stop, stop, you have to stop!*

But we'd gone too far, crossed the line. There was no stopping anyone, not that day. Or maybe… maybe Flo would have stopped. It's so hard to think of it, even now, to accept it; but there was a brief moment in which she seemed to wake up – come to – in which she looked at me not with hatred but in a quizzical manner, as if the devil had been riding her back, but finally she'd succeeded in throwing him off. I saw confusion cloud her eyes, perhaps even sorrow that it had come to this; two sisters, twins, best friends – trying to tear each other apart.

I saw that look and yet all I could think was: *that patch of light, it was you, but sometimes, on occasion, it was also me. If there was no you, if you didn't exist…*

Hope springs eternal, that's what they say.

She'd lowered her hands; she'd started to back down – but I kept mine raised.

If there was no you…

After drawing my hands back, I pushed them forward. I shoved her as hard as I could, summoning every ounce of strength I possessed, every nerve ending, every cell screaming at me to do it, *just do it.* She went flying backwards. She fell. There was a sound; it was such a terrible sound. A thud followed by a crack, and then, worst of all, there was silence. Utter silence. The breeze stilled. The birds disappeared. And in the distance the mountains were as watchful as ever.

How long the silence lasted I don't know, but eventually there was screaming. It took a while to realise who was responsible: me. My hands, my traitorous hands, were in my hair, pulling at it, tearing at it; that shrill sound pouring into the air like molten lava.

Mally fell to his knees; he was holding Flo, talking to her; telling her over and over how much he loved her; that *she* was the one; that they'd leave this place, this *hellhole*, that's what he called it, and never come back. He'd do everything she wanted; every little thing, if only she'd come back.

Stan ran to me, his hands wrestling with my hands, trying to calm me and hold me close, but before he managed to, I noted the look on his face. Both he and Mally had been close to us when we were fighting, each trying individually to intervene. Mally in particular had been close, close enough I realised, his hand reaching out… It was as if Stan saw the thoughts that were forming in my head, as if he watched them swirl then take shape. His eyes grew ever wider but he never said a word as I started screaming again, this time at Mally.

"*You* did that, you did it. You're to blame, Mally. For everything."

Pushing Stan away from me, I hurried to Flo's side. "Get your filthy hands off her," I said, grabbing her from him, watching as he rocked back on his knees, tears on his face again. He shook his head, but that's all he did; he offered no protest.

Finally Stan hauled Mally to his feet. "We have to go and get help. Come on, come with me, she needs help."

As they left me with my sister, her blood soaking my lap, I continued to cradle her, my tears mingling with Mally's tears on her cheeks, a waterfall, a torrent of them.

I knew Stan had seen that it was me who'd pushed her. When the police came, when it went to court, he maintained all the while that it was an accident, a horrendous accident, and looked at me not with scorn but with pity when I stood in the dock and swore just the opposite; when I told them that she and Mally had had an argument and she was leaving him; that he'd pushed her deliberately; he'd murdered her. I convinced them; I even convinced myself, and Mam, I convinced her too. The relief I felt at that. I'd lost a twin; I couldn't lose her as well – her love, her sympathy. Mam went to her grave blaming Mally; hating Mally, as did so many in the village, the memory of him lingering long after he'd been imprisoned for culpable homicide – a wild boy, violent, uncontrollable. Yes, he was all of those things at times, but he was also innocent. And only the three of us knew it, Mally, Stan and I – and as silent as the mountains, not one of us said otherwise again.

I'm sorry. I'm so sorry if there are stains on these sheets of paper; if the writing becomes smudged in some places, unreadable in others, I can hardly see for crying. I am an abomination, I fully accept that, and undeserving of sanctuary, which is what Stan rushed to offer me, so soon after Flo's death, asking for my hand in marriage and delivering me from a home I couldn't live in without her – this twin I'd been so jealous of all my life – the giggling Flo. Our marriage took place at Comraich and it was a solemn affair, even Stan could barely raise a smile for the photographer. We'd been torn apart, the four of us, and only two remained. He knew what I was; what I'd done, but I never saw blame in his eyes. A miracle, considering that he'd loved Flo too, and Mally – how he'd loved his best friend, Mally – both of whom I'd destroyed.

All the nights I cried; all the nights he held me.

Patient Stan, gentle Stan, Stan who eventually got what he wanted but at such a terrible price.

But the question still remains: would he have held me if he knew the other secrets I harboured? I think there's a limit to what most people will accept, Stan included. And so I never told him what I've written down. I've never told anyone, but at least my hand has succeeded where my lips have always failed.

When Mally and Stan left to seek help that day at the loch, Flo regained consciousness, but only for a short while – maybe not even as much as a minute.

One hand on her stomach, she raised the other to clutch at my arm.

"Oh, Flo," I said, on seeing this, "you're all right! You're going to be all right! The boys have gone to get help. They'll be back soon."

A moment of elation – *relief* – but that's all it was: a moment.

She continued to whisper, so I lowered my head.

"What is it, Flo? What are you saying?"

Her words were ragged, her breathing so harsh. "The baby."

"The baby? What do you mean, what baby?"

"The baby," she repeated.

"Flo, I don't under—"

"Mally's."

Mally's?

My eyes travelled to her stomach, her *flat* stomach. She was pregnant?

"Save… baby."

And then she closed her eyes, never to open them again, taking a breath in, never to expel it. I'd murdered not one person that day, but two.

Chapter Thirty-Two

JESSAMIN gasped. Flo had been pregnant with Mally's baby when she died? And he never knew – nobody did, until now.

Again, she and Beth were the only ones.

It didn't make sense, though. As a suspicious death, surely a post-mortem had been carried out on Flo, or weren't they so stringent in those days? She must have been very early on in her pregnancy. Beth had even pointed out how flat her stomach had been. Was that why she'd been so keen to leave Glenelk, why she'd told Mally they *had* to get away? Perhaps she only suspected she was pregnant. After all, in those days, initially at least, she would just have had instinct to go on. A girl could miss a period for any number of reasons. She could have been mistaken.

I'd murdered not one person that day, but two.

"Oh, Beth, what a mess, what a terrible mess."

There were no more pages, none that she knew of. But it was such an abrupt ending. As if… as if…

She peered into the mist.

"You can't leave it there, Beth! If there's more than that you should tell me; we should go all the way. I promise I won't judge you. You can tell me anything."

Supporting her certainty that this wasn't the end, was a

single pen stroke beneath that last dreadful sentence, as if Beth had started to write, but then changed her mind. She decided she should return to Comraich and search the bureau again, the wardrobe and all cupboards, just in case Beth had written something more and stored it elsewhere. Stuffing the notes she had back in her pocket, she quickly stood – *too* quickly. Temporarily, she'd forgotten her own pregnancy, her bulk, and the swift movement, the ungainliness of it, caused not just a kick but also another bolt of pain. As sharp as the others. Sharper, in fact. The worst yet, if she was honest.

"Oh, shit!"

In the same instance she realised how cold she'd become, sitting on a rock in the Highlands, in the middle of December. She was freezing, her breath forming plumes in the air; her joints stiffer than cardboard. And this time the pain wasn't receding...

She had to get to the car, reach Comraich and phone Finn.

Her phone, where was it? She dug around in her pocket, pulled it out, only just catching it as it almost dropped to the ground. She looked at it and a groan escaped her. It was as expected: no signal, there never was, not out here. *Get to the car!*

She started to retrace her footsteps. The car was visible but at the same time seemed an impossible distance away. How could she reach it when she could barely even stand up straight? Should she crawl to it on her hands and knees?

Hold on, baby. Please, hold on.

Whatever was happening – Braxton Hicks, a trial run or whatever they called it – this was too soon. The baby wasn't due for another three weeks – three weeks and four days to be exact – and even then she'd been told on numerous occasions, not just by the midwife but other mothers, not to be surprised if it was late; first babies were notorious for that.

Why are you so eager? This isn't the time.

Her feet sinking into the mud, she continued to stagger, reminding herself to breathe; to ride the wave of each contraction, as tall as any mountain that happened to be surrounding her, reaching the summit, and then sliding down the other side, only a small amount of respite before beginning the ascent yet again. If she could just reach the damned car…

Because she was staring at the ground rather than straight ahead; because her eyes were screwed shut some of the time; because she was so scared, it took a moment to register what else was happening. Around her the landscape was changing, myriad shades of green and brown becoming another colour – white.

Coming to a standstill, she threw her head back. The lowering clouds had finally burst, shedding their load, but not of rain; it was too cold for rain.

"Oh, Christ, no, not snow."

Was it snowing in Inverness too? Would Finn look up and realise he had to hurry if he was going to make it back home over the mountain pass before it got too heavy? Was Winn Greer on standby with his snowplough? *But they wouldn't panic, why would they? The baby's not due yet.*

When she got a signal, she should call Maggie. Maggie was closer.

She's not here, remember, she's gone away with Lenny for a few days, she wanted a pre-wedding moon, so she could be present for the birth. The birth? Jessamin inhaled. If this wasn't a trial run, if this was the real thing, there'd be no one present. She'd be alone. *Oh God, I need to get to Comraich!*

Finally reaching her car, she slumped against it, tears of relief cascading down her face that she'd made it thus far.

Digging in her pocket a second time, she extracted the car key, unlocked the door and hauled herself into the driver's seat, more aware than ever just how confined the space was, how she barely fitted it. Her hands shaking, it took several attempts to slide the key into the ignition but when she did and the familiar roar of the engine filled the air, more tears erupted.

Never, ever had she been this frightened.

Stan had died soon after she'd brought him out here. If the baby died too…

Two murders.

Not murders, Jess! Accidents. All of them were accidents!

Her baby couldn't suffer the same fate.

I'm not cursed. Please don't let me be cursed.

She had to let go of the past and focus on the present. The first task was to turn the car round, to face the right direction. Damn it, that she hadn't done this before. She tugged at the steering wheel. It felt so heavy, and the sweat poured off her brow despite the cold, ignoring the pains that threatened to cripple her.

"Come on, come on!"

Shunting back and forth, twisting the steering wheel all the way to the right and then all the way to the left, she was finally pointing towards Comraich. She had to drive carefully, not floor it, as she'd done when trying to get help for Stan. *Look what happened then – you almost crashed.* That wasn't an option this time. She had to remain calm. That word almost causing her to laugh hysterically. *How can I remain calm when I'm about to give birth, not even at Comraich, but in a bloody Land Rover on the way to Comraich!*

Alone.

With no one to help her.

The first time she'd ever given birth. Not knowing what to

expect, not really, despite what she'd been told; all the books and magazines that she'd read. Birth was like death, you knew it was coming but nothing could prepare you for the real thing.

"Oh shit, I'm alone, all alone."

The words gushed from her in a sob.

"I can't do this alone. Finn, where are you? And Maggie, I need you too."

Her tears threatened to blind her but they refused to stop.

How long was this going to take? Where was the house?

"Who's going to help me?"

Just drive.

"Yes, yes, I am."

You're almost there.

"Comraich. Sanctuary."

Almost… Almost.

The windscreen wipers were frantic now, trying to combat what had turned into a deluge, but Jessamin could just about make out where the gate was; the barrier that divided this wilderness and the land that belonged to Comraich. She'd left it open so there'd be no barrier, so that the two lands, the two *worlds* could collide.

We're here.

Comraich. It stood tall. Brave somehow. Unafraid of the elements.

You have to be brave too.

"I will. I'll try."

Stopping as close as possible to the house, she swung open the driver's door and half clambered, half fell from the car, her feet sliding initially and forcing her to grab and hold onto the car door. Not just a deluge, this was a blizzard, coming out of nowhere – as fierce as Flo had been, as relentless as Beth. She should have checked the forecast before heading out to the loch; it was something you should always do in the Highlands; leave nothing to chance. But that's exactly what she'd done, left everything to chance. And now she – *they,* her and the baby – were paying the price. This was no trial run. Instinct was not just telling her that, it was screaming it in her face. As she continued to stagger to the front door, as she pushed against it, gaining entry, a gush of fluid between her legs was the final confirmation.

On the other side of the door, she rested for a moment against the hardwood, breathing, panting, crying, her mind working frantically, trying to come up with solutions; things she should do, but failing in every respect. It was as though she was watching herself – a character in a play with Comraich the stage set, preparing itself to welcome its next victim, not with glee, but with ever-persistent melancholy.

The sound of a door banging startled her. It came from upstairs. Was Finn home?

Hope flared. She pushed herself forwards and, calling out his name, managed to make it to the bottom of the stairwell before having to lean against the balustrade.

"Who's there? Finn, is it you?"

He'd made it home after all!

Dropping her sodden coat to the floor, the weight of it agitating her further, she left it there as she began to climb, using the carved staircase spindles like handholds, hauling herself upwards. No longer cold, she was feeling hot and feverish, almost begging for the feel of snow on her face again and its icy caress.

Extremes. It's all about extremes. An extreme land breeds extreme emotions.

At the top of the stairs she continued to call for Finn, but her voice was becoming weaker. "If you're there, help me, you have to help me."

There were five doors around her – all of them shut. But one she'd left open. She knew she had: Beth's door, the nursery. So why was it closed now?

"Finn?" she called again, having to summon the energy to once more heave herself forwards. Her hand on the brass handle, she turned it, pushed the door open. He wasn't there. The room was empty. Of course it was. If she'd been thinking straight instead of panicking, she would have registered that only her car was on the forecourt; there was no sign of his. And yet just as Beth had done, she'd continued to hope against all the odds.

I'll phone him. I can get a signal here.

She reached down then realised she'd left her coat with the mobile phone in the pocket at the bottom of the stairs. The landline phone was also downstairs. *Shit!* She couldn't face those stairs again. A hideous vision of falling down them to land in a bloodied heap beneath the stagheads seemed to plague her. She was up here. Stuck. She couldn't even call Rory, or Shona, Ina; not one of them. Oh the irony of it! She'd wanted a home birth, had insisted on it. But not like this, far from this.

We shouldn't tempt fate. Isn't that what Finn had said, or words to that effect?

As more pain ripped through her, she fell to her knees. Right there, in Beth's room, not the nursery; it might *never* be the nursery.

I'm alone, all alone.

Only silence greeted her – the silence of Comraich.

And then slowly, gradually, the voices started up. Those she had sometimes heard, ever since she'd set foot in this house;

echoes of the past.

You are not alone.

Chapter Thirty-Three

JESSAMIN was lying on a bed, a *comfortable* bed. How could that be? There was no bed in Beth's room any longer; it had made way for the cot. But this was definitely a bed. Her eyes at half-mast, she forced them to open more fully and looked down at her legs; they were bare, no longer clad in jeans, or thick socks and boots. Again, it was a mystery. She had no recollection of removing any item of clothing. She squinted. What was that running down the inside of her thigh? It was red, as warm as the fluid had been, *blood* red. Although panic tried to fight its way through the fog that had enveloped her, so did relief. If it was blood, it was just a trickle.

There were voices all around her – familiar voices. *Finn? Maggie? Are you here?* They weren't, they couldn't be; these were more like echoes, although one had more substance to it than the others – a female voice – the voice that had been in her head ever since she left the loch. *Just drive. You're almost there. Almost.*

She'd thought it was her own voice at the time, but it was something quite separate – and still it was encouraging her, guiding her; insistent. *You're not alone.*

There might be blood but the pain had largely subsided – for now. Whether this was a good thing or not, Jessamin had no idea. But she was grateful. God, she was grateful. If the pain continued she felt sure it would kill her. *If that has to happen, then so be it. Just don't let the baby die.* It could though, depending on how long Finn took to get back over the mountain pass, if it was left alone for too long, on this bed in Comraich, lying between her legs, cold, naked and hungry.

Oh, Beth, don't let that happen to my baby. You've got to help me!

A hand. Was that a hand stroking her forehead? It was such a light touch.

"Beth," she called out this time. "Will my baby be all right?"

Still the hand stroked her.

"Did something else happen at the loch?"

The hand stilled and Jessamin reached up only to grab at thin air.

"Or did it happen after Flo had died? Was it something to do with the baby?"

She didn't want to know and yet she did. Everything was coming full circle, one story merging with another. She'd left the gate open; she'd let everyone through. And it wasn't just Beth, it was all four of them – Flo, Mally and Stan were in the room too, hovering. And Beth had never told them; she'd never told anyone, never even written it down.

It was far from a full confession.

"Tell us now," Jessamin whispered, her hand falling back to her side to lie there, limp. "While you can. You have to be honest, Beth. We all do."

There were no more whispers, and there was no more pain either. It was as though she were suspended in some kind of hinterland, as white as the snow, and just as stark. Was this Beth's realm, this limbo that she alone inhabited, not fully at peace? How could she be, when she still harboured secrets?

Beginning to float upwards, weightless when she'd been heavy for so long, she found herself walking alongside Beth; not a Beth she could see or touch, but there nonetheless – keeping perfect pace, matching each other step for step.

Look, a voice as soft as gossamer whispered in her ear.

She did as she was told and peered at the horizon – it was pure white, but slowly, gradually, it started to change. Images began to flicker, grey and grainy at first, like on a television screen, one of those old fashioned ones; the figures jagged and distorted; the sound weaving in and out, loud one moment, barely audible the next. Gradually the images became more substantial and any fuzziness surrounding them disappeared. Not only was she standing beside Beth; she was *looking at* Beth. It was Beth as a teenager, cradling Flo's head in her hands by the side of the loch. There was no sign of Stan and Mally; they must have gone to get help. Beth's mouth was open as if she was screaming, but there was still no sound, shock seemed to have absorbed it, or internalised it, shoving it back down; caging it.

Then the boys were back. There was someone with them, Jessamin didn't know who; possibly Mr McCabe. He knelt beside Flo and there was a struggle, a wrestle as Stan put his arms around Beth and prised her firmly, but not roughly, away from Flo. The man then held Flo, examined her, and finally looked up at the three of them, shaking his head.

Beth was mute no longer,

"He did it! It was his fault, Mally's. He pushed her. They'd been arguing."

Mally turned to her, his eyes wide, his mouth open. But he didn't deny it, he never said a word. But Stan did, Stan *tried*.

"It was an accident. Just an accident."

Too late – blame had been apportioned; the seed sown.

The image seemed to fold in on itself, to crumble, only to be swiftly replaced by another. Comraich, where Flo's lifeless body had been brought back and laid on a bed, just as Jessamin was on a bed, even though she was standing, she was staring at the scenes unfolding.

This bedroom was the fifth bedroom, the soon to be nursery, that had also been Beth's room during the years after Kristin – a room which had witnessed so much misery, so much grief. *An accident*, Jessamin wanted to shout, *whatever Beth said, it was still just an accident.*

There came a series of flashes, one sliding into the other, of those who'd visited Flo, who'd wept and screamed. Nancy, their mother, was too terrible to watch.

"Please, Beth, no."

A mother should never have to bury her child. It went against the order of things. It was unnatural. But then so was sororicide – the killing of one's sister.

Jessamin gasped. She didn't know that word; it had been put in her head. She turned to the space beside her, empty but also far from it.

"Beth, you did wrong. I won't deny it. You blamed Mally and because of that, he served time for something he didn't do. But, Beth, Mally wasn't blame*less* either. He played you and Flo off against each other; he always did, right from the start. The truth is Mally wanted it all and in the end he was left with nothing, not even his homeland. It was wrong, all of it, but none of you were evil. Through your own handwriting, I've got to know you, and the others too, including my own grandfather whom I knew nothing about before. What you were was young, and hand in hand with youth comes recklessness. Sometimes that recklessness, that *hot headedness,* leads to tragedy. I said I wouldn't judge you and I don't. I don't blame you for what happened to Flo, I don't think Flo does either or she wouldn't be here; none of them would. You were *not* a bad person."

If Jessamin thought her words might be met with some relief, some gratitude even, she was wrong. The white horizon around her seemed to eddy and swirl as if a storm had suddenly reared – the weather in this hinterland like the weather in Scotland, able to change in an instant. It changed colour too, and became so much darker, dull and muted; dust in the air that threatened to choke her.

"Beth, what is it? What are you doing?"

She had to close her eyes, bring her hands up to shield her face, all the while feeling the pain start up again in her stomach – but that was dull too. Standing in this world between worlds, she was removed from it. There was a whoosh, a roar, and then there was a shriek, which forced her to open her eyes again; to stare at the change of scene, and to inhale the different smells – not that of death and grief, but the smell of the woods; the Scots pine that scented the air only slightly tainted by something else; something as acrid as the smell which had been in Flo's room.

Is there death here too?

A girl, a young girl, no more than a teenager, was squatting in the woods, her dress pulled up around her waist, her face so twisted it was hard to recognise her.

At first.

As realisation dawned, Jessamin inhaled. "Beth, is that you?"

Turning, she was stunned to see the space next to her didn't appear empty anymore; a woman was by her side, a woman she recognised from Stan's portraits, but not looking back at her; she was staring at the girl she used to be.

"Beth," Jessamin repeated, this time in wonder. "The girl in the woods… that's here, isn't it, the woods behind Comraich?"

There was a slight nod of the head.

"What are you doing? Why are you squatting like that?"

No answer this time causing Jessamin to stare again at the vision – to analyse it.

"Oh my God," she breathed. "You were pregnant too!"

That's why she'd kept away from Mally in those last weeks, because she also suspected. What a terrible situation, an *impossible* situation, especially if Flo had indeed been pregnant, if she'd lived. The woman by her side had closed her eyes – an instruction? In case it was, Jessamin did the same and that's when she saw it. Not the woodland but the stairs at Comraich, a blonde girl at the top of them, her blue eyes red because of the amount of tears she'd shed; the smoothness of her skin contradicting the ravages of guilt, which would erase soon enough any sign of youth. She was staggering, beside herself, unable to see properly… And then she was falling. All the way down to lie at the bottom, the stagheads silent.

Not dead. Not Beth. Not yet.

"But something died, didn't it?" How she knew all this, how any of this was happening, baffled Jessamin. Perhaps it *wasn't* happening. Perhaps this hinterland was the result of a fevered brain, a hallucination. Perhaps Beth wasn't with her at all, she was simply a conjured figure dressed in Beth's clothing, Jessamin's own mind being responsible for creating, for fleshing out, what had never been known; never been said; never even been written. She was on the verge of accepting this when the woman grasped her hand and nothing – *nothing* – had ever felt so real.

Initially, Beth wouldn't move from Flo's side, no matter what anyone said and who tried to persuade her, even if it was Stan, who for the most part remained with her in the fifth room; with the pair of them: three when there used to be four, but Mally had been taken away and there would never be four again.

Finally, in the early hours, just before they came to take Flo away for good too, when Stan had eventually succumbed to sleep, Beth *had* left her sister. She'd risen from her chair, gently opened the door and stumbled over to the stairway to teeter at the top. Around her the house creaked and groaned, settling into itself or lamenting.

Afterwards, her body had taken the place of Flo's on the bed – two girls who looked the same but were so different – one who'd been dead, the other who looked to follow suit, whose breathing was now dangerously shallow. Again Stan had kept close, soothed her brow, whispering soft words in her ear. *I'll never tell about Mally, I promise. I love you, if only you knew how much. I won't say a word.*

When Stan slept once more, Beth knew it was time to rise again – her stomach was cramping and she could feel stickiness between her legs.

She'd risen when Flo hadn't been able to, and she'd drifted, like the ghost she saw in dreams drifted; the one that hovered over her with such a look on her face – *We were going to leave,* she'd say to Beth. *Why didn't you just let us leave?*

I'm sorry, so sorry. I'm trying to make amends.

Beth's apology had died in her throat. Who could she possibly make amends to?

She wanted to go to the loch, but couldn't make it that far – not initially – the pain in her stomach worsening with each step. The trees then, they'd offer her the shelter she needed, they'd hide her, provide her with sanctuary – Comraich always did that, the grounds as well as the house. It threw a cloak around those who needed to hide. Hunkering down, what was in her – she refused to give it a name – was expelled, in blood, in tears, in sweat and urine; the soft mud below offering a burial place, one she tore at with sodden fingers, digging, digging, and then covering with leaves; such soft leaves, summer leaves, that when autumn came, would crumble.

She had to wash herself – she could neither return home nor to Comraich, like this – she needed water, to immerse herself in it.

She made it to the loch at last, she found herself waist deep in it, alone where once she'd swam with others; where love had been forged, in all its guises.

The thought occurred: she could sink deep into these waters, let them wash right over her and never emerge. She walked further and further in, over sharp stones at the bottom which she didn't try to avoid. It didn't matter, they didn't hurt – *nothing* seemed to hurt anymore. Where once it had revived her, the coldness now only numbed her. She could do this. She could close her eyes and let it be. Soon flames would replace the water, and she'd burn; the sins she'd committed, all of them, each and every one, unforgiveable; *unspeakable*.

Jessamin spluttered as Beth spluttered when she emerged from the waters in a brilliant arc of droplets, no longer numb, but so very afraid.

She wasn't ready to burn, not in the fires of hell.

On the shore she lay sobbing, wet from head to toe, cursing

the desires that ran deep in her. She wanted to live so badly, despite stealing life from her sister; despite what else she'd destroyed… No she wouldn't think of it – she *couldn't.*

And that's how Stan had found her. Stan who'd woken to see she was missing; who'd rushed straight to the loch; who'd held her; who'd told her again and again, that he'd keep her secret – the only one he knew; that he'd look after her; he'd *marry* her. She could stay at Comraich. She need never leave. She could hide. Always.

Love made monsters of us all. In the first letter she wrote Beth had said that and Jessamin had shaken her head. Stan was no monster: he was the kindest, most gracious human being she had ever known. But he was also guilty. He'd let Mally go to prison because he could endure that. What he couldn't endure was losing Beth. He loved her, and he'd seen an opportunity to possess her, even if it was just the shadow of Beth. That was better than nothing; better than the alternative.

But if he'd known the full truth, about the babies too, perhaps he would have chosen the alternative. That's what Beth feared. And that's why she never told him, why she couldn't write it down; why she couldn't even admit it to herself, because there was only one person between heaven and earth who wanted her and that person might change his mind.

"Oh, Beth." Jessamin stared at the woman in front of her, the woman who'd spent a lifetime burning. "They say if it's love it shouldn't hurt, but it's not true. Love *does* hurt. It's cruel. It doesn't lighten your life, not all the time; it can cause heartache and suffering; it can change you, twist you, snuff out any trace of lightness to leave you howling in the dark. In this world, even in the world that you inhabit now, it can simply be too big. Love is cruel," she repeated, "but you're not. This broke you, Beth, and you remained broken. You didn't escape lightly. None of you did. And you're wrong about Stan; he would have loved you regardless – he would have understood, because he's like his grandson, he understands everything. He wasn't as beautiful as Mally to look at; he was pale and skinny," she tried to laugh. "He wore those funny round spectacles. He wasn't as exciting or dramatic and his passion… well, it was a quiet passion, but still it was passion. He was content to be second best, do you realise that, Beth, *content.* That takes guts. That takes a hero. In many ways you were heroic too, because you came to love him, didn't you, in the end? Mally never loved again; he married my grandmother, but she always felt she couldn't reach him; she could never break down his defences, sturdier than any prison walls, than even the grey walls of Comraich. My mother didn't think he even loved his own children. I disagreed. Every parent loves their own child, surely? How naïve I was. She was right and I was wrong. He didn't *dare*, that's why. When he'd loved before there'd been terrible consequences and he was simply too afraid. But you *did* dare. Stan was right to bide his time, to seize his chance, because it was you two who were destined to be together, and his faith in that was unwavering. Look behind you: Flo and Mally are together now. Stan's there too, as patient as ever. If *I* know what happened, so do they. They know and still they wait, no trace of hatred on their faces. What's done is done and it can't be changed. It may not have been written on paper, not all of it, but it was written in the stars. Beth, it was just the way your story played out – forces so much bigger than we can understand at work; that we're not meant to understand, not yet. Perhaps we will when the time is right; we won't always be at their mercy. You've done your time, Beth.

Go. You deserve peace, all of you. What's wrong is to keep the three of them waiting any longer."

There was such a need to believe on Beth's face that Jessamin smiled to see it: smiled before opening her mouth wider to scream. Oh the pain! It was no longer distant; it was engulfing her, worse than before – far worse. This was it. There were to be no more lulls in the proceedings, no more trial runs.

She was back on the bed – she'd never actually left it – her white-knuckled hands tearing at the sheets. Where was Beth? Where was she?

"I can't do this on my own!"

Again the voice insisted. *You are **not** alone.*

Chapter Thirty-Four

"JESS, Jess, it's okay, you're not alone. We're here, we made it."

Who was here? Who was it even talking? It wasn't Beth – not this time; it was a male voice, filled with such urgency.

"Jess, open your eyes and look at me, please. You're not alone. Oh, Jess, what was I thinking? I'm sorry that you ever were."

It was Finn talking to her. He'd made it back over the mountain pass! He was home at last. Desperate to see him, to believe it was true and not just wishful thinking, she forced her eyes to open. He materialised in front of her, and not only him; there were others in the room too, mere shades except for one. He'd said, '*We're* here.' Again she wondered: who was he with?

Clutching at his arms as another contraction started to peak, grateful to feel solid flesh and bone beneath her fingertips, all she could do was whisper, "The baby."

"I know, it's come early, it's on its way. Christ! Why didn't you answer your phone, Jess? As soon as the snow started we left Inverness; we raced back, but that mountain pass, that bloody mountain pass… Why didn't you answer your phone?"

"Finn, quit interrogating her! Who cares about the damned

phone right now? Put these towels beneath her. Like you say, the baby's coming, there's not much time."

The second voice was deep and velvety; it had an accent, a definite accent – one that Jessamin couldn't quite place. What the hell… she couldn't think any more or catch her breath. All she'd been told by Jenny Campbell, the midwife, about inhaling slowly for a count of four and then exhaling for a count of four, that it would help, was clearly nothing but a lie – this pain stole your breath clean away. She couldn't cope with it. It was impossible to cope. She *had* to though, the life within her depended on it and she'd do anything to see it safely into the world, anything.

That was a mother's instinct, to preserve the life of her child.

Wasn't it?

Her head turned sharply to the right, to where the shadows lingered. *In the woods, Beth, you didn't show me everything.*

"Honey, look at me. You're gonna be ready to push soon and when you are, you're gonna wanna scream the house down, but that's a waste of energy. Push that scream back down, deep into the centre of you, and use it to get the baby out."

Suri – it had to be Suri who was speaking – a beautiful woman, tall and majestic, her thick black hair in braids and eyes as bright as onyx. Finn had brought her to Comraich – the woman he was having an affair with. And she was helping Jessamin; she was taking control – *delivering* the baby.

"Finn," she gasped, "I don't understand. What's going on?"

"There's no time to explain," he replied, clutching her hand, allowing her to clutch back, not just that; to squeeze the life from it.

Her gaze shifting between him and Suri as well as Beth, she growled. "You damn well explain!"

"Jess—"

Suri interrupted. "Do it, tell her."

"But—"

"Finn," Suri continued, "you deny a woman in labour nothing."

Finn swallowed. "Suri… Suri came over to Scotland to find me. Angus is a friend of hers… ours, and she's been staying with him. When we bumped into him in the restaurant, when we exchanged numbers… that's how she managed to get in touch with me."

On the brink of another contraction, her stomach squeezing like a vice, Jessamin gritted her teeth. "But I was with you then. I was pregnant, he could see that!"

Unlike hers, Finn's voice was filled with panic, not anger, "This isn't the time!"

"No more secrets, no more dishonesty," Jessamin screamed as she climbed yet another peak. "Are you having an affair?"

"No! No, I'm not."

"But you thought about it, didn't you?"

"No!"

"You did."

"Jess, it wasn't like that."

"You're like Mally, so like him."

"Your grandfather? Jess, what's he got to do—"

"He's here, so is Stan, and Beth and Flo."

"What?" Finn looked around him, abject confusion on his face. "Jess, there's just me and Suri. Winn's still busy clearing the mountain path. We had to wait at the top for him. We couldn't make the descent in the Defender; climbing up one side was treacherous enough, so we had to wait." Fervently, he shook his head. "He'd lost the key to the blasted thing. Can you believe it? Probably mislaid it one night whilst drunk again. I was furious; I was going to hike down the pass because I knew something was wrong when you wouldn't pick up the phone. I just… I knew it. It was Suri who stopped me. 'You're no good to her injured,' she kept saying. All the while Winn was looking for the key and then… suddenly he found it. It was there on the floor in front of him, just lying on the carpet when it hadn't been before. He'll fetch Doctor Buchanan and the midwife and bring them back. I don't know how long they'll be. Not too long. They can't be, we need them. Suri has some experience, but—"

Suri stepped in. "Finn, you do not need to be panicking the lady any further. Get yourself under control."

Her words did nothing to calm Finn. There were beads of sweat on his forehead and his breath was coming in short, sharp pants, almost rivalling Jessamin's. The shades too, they seemed to shake; to quiver as if agitated. Only Suri looked remotely calm and Jessamin was glad of her – she *needed* her, this woman that Finn shared a secret with. Again her attention was drawn towards the shadows. *Beth?* A snippet of Finn's story surged to the forefront of her mind.

"You said the key was on the floor?"

"Yes, yes," replied Finn, both his hands gripping hers now and a frown on his face that despite everything caused Jessamin to laugh.

"Oh, Finn! You really are like Mally. Look at you both; you've got the same eyes, the same colour hair," she paused for a moment, "the same scowl."

Rather than question her again, his attention, hers too, was caught by Suri. She was on the phone, talking to someone. "I know you can't fly a 'copter in these conditions, but have one on standby. And get on the road to meet Greer too with all the medical supplies you can muster; bring it all… just in case…"

As her voice trailed off, Jessamin closed her eyes, guessed what she was doing; utilising the might of the army to help a former colleague's woman in need. But an army up against the Scottish weather? It was a formidable foe indeed.

Although her strength was continuing to drain, she wasn't done with questions – she was craving honesty now, even if it hurt worse than the contractions.

After another one subsided, she gazed at Finn. "There's something going on between you both, you can't deny it."

"But it isn't what you think."

"Then for God's sake, tell me!"

He hung his head but only briefly, raising it to look her in the eye. "There was no ending between Suri and I, no *proper* ending. I left, because of the accident. There were no real goodbyes. At the time…" again he paused, seeming to be in as much agony as she was, "…all that concerned me were my own thoughts, my own feelings. There didn't seem to be any room in my mind or heart for anyone else. It was cruel what I did to her… It was wrong. And I always felt sorry for it. Suri was good to me. She didn't deserve to be discarded. I *do* love her and I always will. She's part of my history. But it's you I'm *in* love with, Jess. She and I, we've spent a lot of time talking and finally, we've lain to rest what happened between us, and more to the point, what *didn't* happen. We just had to end it properly, that's all."

Jessamin laid her head back against the pillow, processed his words, let them sink in. He wasn't lying. He was telling the truth. And she agreed, he *did* owe Suri. The photos she'd seen of them, how close they'd been, flashed into her mind, one by one, as though on a movie reel, one in particular stood out, the close up of her. *A woman in love.* Theirs had been a moment in time, held in suspension. It had needed resolution so that they could both let go, not just one of them; move on with their lives. It was so easy to get stuck in a moment, to become trapped…

Although it took effort, she raised her head. "You should have just said."

"You're fragile at the moment, what with the pregnancy."

Fragile? Like Beth? "I'm not."

"I was just scared of upsetting you when sometimes you seemed so upset anyway. You're right, though, I should have said something. I'm an idiot."

She shook her head. "I guess we're still getting to know each other."

"Jess, Jess, look at me, it's you I love; only you."

Jessamin did indeed gaze at him. "I asked you to marry me."

"Ach, don't worry about that, please. We don't have to be like all the others. We're not. We're different. I understand why you don't want to get married. Who cares? We've got a baby trying to be born; we're as committed as it gets."

"The reason why… it's not because you're second best."

"Even if I am, it's okay. I'm just happy to have you at all."

"Like Stan then," she could feel her voice drifting, her body too, the shadows becoming more substantial – what did that mean? "You're a mix of them both, but the good things, only the good things. There was so much good…"

"Jess!"

Suri spoke too, no longer sounding calm and collected, but as panicked as Finn. "Jess, honey, you have got to get ready to push. Come on now, listen to me, this is all that's important right now – you *have* to push."

No, Suri was wrong, something else was important too. She'd made Finn explain and she wanted an explanation from Beth too.

Come closer, come a little closer.

Beth duly obliged – a young woman but with eyes that belonged to a dying Beth.

What else happened in the woods?

Oh the pain – it was so hard to bear – for both of them.

Show me, Beth, show us.

As the walls around her faded, she could smell the scent of pine again – such a heady smell, clean and fresh. She could see the trees rising upwards, the leaves that adorned them as well as the woodland floor; a *carpet* of leaves and in amongst it all was Beth. Not just bleeding, or screaming – a victim of another accident – she was hitting her stomach, over and over again, with small but lethal fists; going against a woman's greatest instinct and beating, beating, beating. The look on her face, the grim determination, it was horrible to witness. It was such a contrast to the look on her face now. There was pain still, but overriding everything was shame. "So it wasn't an accident after all, was it, falling down the stairs? You weren't simply unsteady on your feet, you *threw* yourself down and then you bided your time."

Sororicide *and* infanticide, she'd been guilty of both.

"And yet your friends are still here. They won't leave without you. *I'm* still here, listening. Beth, no one was innocent and no one was a monster. And finally, *finally*, you're bigger than all of it. All your life you've been stuck at eighteen. Not anymore. You've grown up; you've been honest at last, admitted everything, and there's no blame, because blame belongs in the past. That moment by the loch, that moment in the woods, and all the moments that led up to them – the glorious moments, the ones that were bathed in sunshine, and the inglorious ones, so dark and deep, let them all go. No one could punish you more than you've punished yourself."

"Jess, Jess, who are you talking to, what is it that you're saying? Come on, Jess, please, come back. I don't want to lose you. I *can't*."

Oh, Finn.

She continued to gaze at the faces of those who once were, and they gazed back at her. *Love is cruel. Love is beautiful.* She was losing love – again.

"No more death, not here, not at Comraich. Listen to me. Listen! Start pushing. This baby *will* be born. Start pushing now."

The command forced her from the moment she was drifting in. *No more death?* Who was saying that? It seemed so many voices had melded into one; had become a chorus – both male and female, as deafening at the birds at Minch Point.

No more death! No more.

"Beth, oh Beth. You found the key, you made amends. You saved me!"

"Jess, never mind the damned key!" It was Finn speaking, grabbing her by the shoulders. "Look at me. Focus."

"You saved me too, Finn. You and Suri."

"Jess, please." Finn's voice was choked, as if he was crying.

"You saved me," she said again, marvelling at it. And if she was being saved, it was for a greater reason: it was so that this baby wouldn't grow up motherless, as Finn had had to grow up motherless. At Comraich, tragedy was done with. This was their time, their moment – the three of them – no more living with ghosts. Taking a deep breath, working with her body instead of fighting against it, she began to push.

"That's it, honey, that's it. You can do this. I just heard some noises from outside, I think it's Greer with the snowplough, or it's Angus with all the supplies. No don't go and see, Finn, this is no time to abandon your post. They'll find us soon enough, all they have to do is follow the screams. That's it, that's better. Continue to encourage her. You can do this, all three of you. Jeez, this baby sure is impatient! So come on… let's get the job done. We're talking about new life here, people. And *only* life."

In reply Jessamin managed a hoarse 'Yes, ma'am', which caused Suri's face to light up, and miraculously, Finn's too.

No wonder Finn loved her, right now **I** *love her, and she's right, we can do this. It's a girl; I think it's a girl. If it is, I'll call her after you, Beth. And not just you, but Flo too. She'll be Elizabeth Florence or maybe Florence Elizabeth. Yes, that's it, Florence should come first, it'll help to further right the wrongdoing. She'll be one person. A balance of light and dark, free to make her own decisions; to find love; to experience its good side and its bad side, as we all must during the course of our lifetimes, but hopefully – oh, I do hope, I do pray that it'll err on the side of the good. It will be what it will be. I have to accept that, because it's her life, her path to tread. Whatever happens, we have to learn, we have to evolve and everything's so much simpler if we're honest. Oh God, I'm babbling. What I'm trying to say, Beth, the point I want to get across, that I want to reiterate, is that she's one person, and one person only; and if she's like her great grandmother and her great aunt, she's going to be perfect.*

As Beth stepped away from her, her three friends flanking her in death just as they'd done in life – the four of them inseparable, ever since their first day at school – she nodded. There was no more suffering, not for her; but for Jessamin it wasn't yet over. Even so, she'd never have guessed that pain could be so positive, and that at the end of it, something wonderful waited; something akin to heaven.

"Perfect," she whispered, holding onto Finn's hand, holding onto Suri's too, and listening with such excitement for that first cry.

Chapter Thirty-Five

In memory of Larnside residents,
Jack Murray, Margaret Murray
and their two beloved sons,
Duncan and Ben (Mally) –
cherished members of our community
and true Highlanders.

WHEN the minister at the church in Larnside agreed to place a plaque alongside other more ancient plaques that adorned the walls of his church, Jessamin was thrilled. She was also surprised. A gruff man, he'd seemed untouched by the story she'd told him, but Finn had stayed behind, had had a quiet word, and suddenly he'd obliged. However Finn had swung it; whatever strings he'd pulled or funds he'd suddenly made available, she didn't care. It might not mean much to anyone else, but it meant a lot to her that her grandfather, her great uncle and her great grandparents had a memorial in the village they'd once belonged to, with all their names on it, rather than separate headstones scattered across the country – a family torn apart, *her* family. She was pleased that in some small way she'd helped to unite them too, and perhaps, just perhaps, that might offer a degree of solace to her great grandparents should they happen to be looking over her shoulder – and they could be, she knew that well enough. Even so, she felt no shiver racing up and down her spine, just a satisfying sense of completeness.

She'd better go; stop staring at the plaque. Finn was waiting outside with Florence, who'd grown into a 'bonny wee thing' as everyone in the locality insisted on calling her, especially her surrogate aunt and uncle, Maggie and Lenny, who frequently declared they wanted one just like her, once they'd enjoyed a bit of time to themselves as newlyweds that is. Aged eleven months, she was almost walking, determined, as all Highlanders seemed to be; refusing to give up. She was probably practising right now, and giggling too no doubt, as she always was. Not always actually. That was maternal bliss talking. If she didn't get her way… well, then there'd be hell to pay. Jessamin shook her head. *Florence, you're both a trial and a joy!*

Outside, Finn swooped their child up in his arms and walked towards her. Low in the sky, the autumn sun encased them both in a shimmering haze that caused Jessamin to slow her pace; to come to a standstill. What did they look like together – father and daughter? Ethereal. That was it. As dazzling as angels.

Finn put his arm around her, kissing her on the cheek. "You pleased with it?"

"I'm ecstatic."

"Good. More ghosts laid to rest, eh?"

"I hope so, Finn, I really do. I don't condone what my great grandfather did. He should never have caused pain because of his own, but having to leave his farm behind, his land; feeling *forced* to, well perhaps that was punishment enough."

"Aye, they're together now, if not in spirit, in name. That's something."

"It is. I really think it is. And last week, at the house itself, or rather the ruin, I planted some forget-me-nots. They should be in full bloom by springtime."

He smiled. "We'll go and see them when they are."

They would, they'd take Florence to run as her kin had once ran. She'd play in the woods at Comraich too, build shelters there out of long lengths of stick; admire the trees as they changed with the seasons, gather armfuls of bluebells so that they could be dotted around the house – creating good memories to supplant the bad.

"Right," she said, clapping her hands together, "now all that's seen to, on to more pressing matters. Millie's tearoom beckons, and a slice of her infamous cake."

Florence's eyes – as dark as Finn's – lit up.

"Do you see that, Jess? She knows the word 'cake'. That's your influence that is."

"Don't blame me, Mr Maccaillin, you're rather partial to it yourself."

"Me?"

"Yes you."

"Only since we've met."

"See how good I am for you?"

"For me yes, but not my waistline."

"There's nothing wrong with your waistline," she said, reaching out and pinching slightly more than an inch. "Well, not *much* wrong anyway."

Despite her teasing, Finn managed to devour a whole slab of chocolate fudge cake, while Jessamin and Florence tucked into theirs with just as much enthusiasm. As they left for home, Florence instantly fell asleep in her car seat.

"That's a sugar coma, that is," Finn pointed out, nodding back at her.

"I think it's affecting me too," Jessamin replied, yawning. "Or it could be…"

Finn took his eyes off the road to glance at her. "It could be what?"

"Another reason." Instead of looking at him, Jessamin stared out the window.

"Another reason? What do you mean?"

She kept her gaze averted. "Okay, not a reason, a *suspicion*."

"A suspicion?" As realisation dawned, he brought the car to such a grinding halt, Jessamin was thankful there were no cars behind them. "You can't be!"

Finally gracing him with a look, she raised an eyebrow. "And why can't I?"

"It's so soon."

"So you're not pleased?" This time she was only part teasing.

"Pleased? You think I'm not pleased?" He grabbed her by the shoulders, bringing her lips to his and kissing her.

She still had her eyes closed as he pulled away, but finally opened them, slowly, languidly. "Finn, I do believe you're sending me mixed messages here."

He laughed, just as she'd wanted him to do. "I'm thrilled. Truly. Another one can't come soon enough. It's what we wanted, wasn't it, to fill Comraich."

"And we're doing just that. Fast workers, that's us. There are those in the village that'll be shocked, you know. They'll continue to think us indecent."

"Let them. They may even have a point—"

"Hey!" Playfully, she hit his arm. "There's nothing indecent about us."

Unexpectedly his expression grew serious.

"Finn, are you okay?" she asked, perplexed.

"Aye," he answered, but still there was no trace of a smile left on his face.

She winced. Unmarried, with one child and another on the way, in a tiny Highland village where the old ways still prevailed, the old *values* – perhaps it *did* concern him. Should she do it, bite the bullet and propose again? Was now the right time?

"Finn—"

"No, Jess, no."

She frowned. "Hang on, you don't know what I'm going to say yet!"

"Aye, I do, you're going to ask me to marry you, and the answer is still no."

"But… How did you know?"

"It's that look you get in your eyes, that guilty look."

"Guilty?"

"Aye, and there's no need. Some people might think we don't have everything, but we know better. We've more than enough and God, Jess, I'm grateful for it."

A gratefulness that for a moment had overwhelmed him.

"How come you're so good at reading expressions anyway?" she asked, remembering what he'd said to Maggie; when he knew she'd been lying about Jessamin climbing ladders.

He shrugged, back to his normal self. "Perhaps I'm as fey as you are, deep down."

"I rather suspect you are." A sigh escaped her, one of pure contentedness as she ran her hands up and down her stomach.

"I wonder if it'll be a boy this time."

"If it is, do you want to call him after Stan or Mally?"

"No." She shook her head. "But I would like to name him after someone; his middle name I mean."

"James?" he said without the slightest hesitation.

"No, Finn. I want to call him after you; his father, the man that I live for."

Mulling that over for a second, he revved up the engine again, that smile of his – that grin – firmly back in place as they continued towards Comraich.

Epilogue

IT was raining again. Beth watched as rain slashed down from the skies in vertical sheets to saturate the ground below. She extended a hand to touch the window. It was dry inside at least, and in the confines of Stan's bedroom at Comraich, it was warm too. Despite this, her shoulders slumped as her hand fell. They shouldn't be inside. This wasn't the winter; it was the height of summer. They should be outside by the loch – that lovely, magical loch Mally had shown them, that no one else in the world seemed to know about. *Their* loch – Mally and Flo's, Stan and Beth's.

The bright blue of her eyes – like ice Mally sometimes said – scanned the clouds that hung so low over the moor. It was a sudden rain and just as suddenly it might peter out. She hoped so, offering up a silent prayer that something could be salvaged from the day. Not that she didn't love being at Comraich; she did – the big house in the woods that belonged to Stan's family, the McCabes, a house that was comforting; that was familiar, but at the same time had an air about it – a kind of atmosphere. Sullen. Comraich could be accused of being that on occasion. Then again, if she was honest with herself, so could she.

"Beth, come away from the window, we're playing a game."

It was Stan, cajoling her.

Sullen – no, she wouldn't be that today, despite how disappointing she found the weather.

Beth swung round. It wasn't just Stan looking at her hopefully; Mally and Flo were as well. "Okay, as long as it's not hide and seek," she smiled as she said it.

"It isn't," replied Flo, with an answering smile, "we know you don't like that game anymore. It's a card game; Gin Rummy, that's right, isn't it, Stan? His da taught him to play it and now he wants to teach us."

"His *far-ther* you mean," Mally stretched the word out, making a meal of it. "The McCabes don't use words such as 'da', don't you know?"

The ribbing was affectionate and Stan laughed, as Mally knew he would. All of them did, before Beth settled herself down beside her friends to start learning the rules of this new game. Stan was his usual patient self throughout, not getting irritated when Flo slipped up yet again or Mally tried to cheat his way to victory, simply accepting it all in good humour, albeit exchanging a wry smile with Beth every now and again. Not everyone was perfect; Stan accepted that and Beth's heart swelled with admiration for him because of it. She wished she could be the same, but she wasn't. Flo was irritating her slightly, Mally was exasperating her, but still she loved them just as they loved her when she was being annoying.

There was a knock on the door and Mrs McCabe entered.

"Is that lemonade you have for us there, Mother?"

Mally started sniggering again. To those who came from lesser backgrounds such formality did sound funny.

"Aye, it is," replied Mrs McCabe, oblivious to what was causing amusement. "Must keep the troops going, mustn't we?

There's a wee scone for you each too."

Climbing to their feet, all four hurried across to the tray. Mrs McCabe made the best lemonade as far as her grateful recipients were concerned and her scones were delicious too.

"You've got crumbs round your mouth," Beth mentioned to Flo, when she'd finished devouring hers.

"So have you," Flo responded, reaching out a hand at exactly the same time as her sister, not to wipe their own mouths, but each other's.

Mally stared at this perfect synchronicity with wonder – he always did. The girls being twins was an unending source of fascination. 'It's like you're the same soul,' he'd say. 'They're not,' Stan would answer, saving them the trouble of having to. Beth could understand his confusion, though. It must be odd being friends with two girls who shared the same hair, eyes and build. Sometimes, when night had kicked in, and she and Flo were at home in their cosy little cottage on the edge of Glenelk, they would stare at their reflections in the windowpane and marvel too. The same soul? It was so easy to believe.

"Look at that, will you?" Mrs McCabe broke Beth's reverie. "The rain's stopped, just like that."

Beth looked to where she was pointing. Her prayers had been answered.

"Come on!" she yelled.

Mrs McCabe's hand flew to her neck. "What is it? Where are you going? It might have stopped raining, but it'll still be wet underfoot."

Mally, needing no further instruction from Beth, shrugged as he rushed by Mrs McCabe. "It doesn't matter," he declared, "we're going to get wet anyway."

"Stan?" His mother beseeched, but he was halfway down

the stairs too by then, following the rest of them on feet that seemed to have grown wings.

Mrs McCabe was right, though: the ground *was* wet. Their feet sank deep into the mud as they continued to plough through it, prompting them to turn it into a game, kicking soft brown earth at each other; the boys roaring, the girls squealing in protest.

"Our clothes," Flo shrieked. "Mam will kill us!"

But Beth knew that Mam would do no such thing – since their da had died, she was glad whenever she knew her children were having fun. She was relieved.

The loch soon reared into view. Situated alone, surrounded by mountains, it was a series of pools in which gem-coloured waters sparkled. Oh, how Beth loved it; how glad she was that Mally had found it and shared it with them.

Despite the atrociousness of the weather that morning, the sun had come out of hiding and the rest of the day promised to be a reasonable one. As they tore off their outer clothing and plunged into the freezing cold waters in just their vests and pants, the boys still roaring, the girls still shrieking, Beth had never felt so alive. She felt invincible, as if what had happened to Da – to other people in the village – death – could never happen to them. On the contrary, with youth came immortality; surely it was so? They'd be together forever, she, Flo, Stan and Mally, again she hoped so; she prayed, because a life without them? She couldn't contemplate it.

"Beth! Beth! Come on, get your head under!"

It was Stan shouting at her, noticing that she'd come to a standstill as these thoughts filled her mind.

"Aye, aye, I will," she assured him.

Satisfied with this response, Stan continued to duck and

dive as Mally grabbed Flo and dragged her under for a few seconds, both of them giggling and spluttering when they eventually resurfaced.

A game of tag broke out: a difficult game to play on land when Mally was involved – no one could outrun Mally, he was faster than the stag – but if you played the game in water, as awkward as it was, everyone stood an equal chance.

"You're it!" Mally had tagged Flo, who subsequently came wading through the water with Stan in her sights. Stan turned, slipped and temporarily went under, surfacing, much like Mally and Flo had done earlier, full of laughter. Lunging for Beth, he caught her, his arms circling her waist, holding her tight, and his breath hot against her ear as he whispered, "You're it."

As the games continued, the sun broke into full splendour and even the mountains seemed to brood less.

Their energy finally spent, all four clambered ashore to lie amongst the tall grass – four of them in a row with either fingertips or arms touching – Stan with his grey-green eyes and smattering of orange freckles; Mally with his pale skin and shock of jet hair, and Beth and Flo, two girls who looked alike and who weren't so different underneath it all either. Not anymore. Not now they'd found sanctuary.

The End

Also by the author

Jessa*mine*

"The dead of night, Jess, I wish they'd leave me alone."

essamin Wade's husband is dead - a death she feels wholly esponsible for. As a way of coping with her grief, she keeps im 'alive' in her imagination - talking to him every day, aughing with him, remembering the good times they had together. She thinks she will 'hear' him better if she goes somewhere quieter, away from the hustle and bustle of her ometown, Brighton. Her destination is Glenelk in the Highands of Scotland, a region her grandfather hailed from and the ubject of a much-loved painting from her childhood.

Arriving in the village late at night, it is a bleak and forbidling place. However, the house she is renting - Skye Croft - is varm and welcoming. Quickly she meets the locals. Her landord, Fionnlagh Maccaillin, is an ex-army man with obvious nd not so obvious injuries. Maggie, who runs the village shop, s also an enigma, startling her with her strange 'insights'. But t is Stan she instantly connects with. Maccaillin's grandfather nd a frail, old man, he is grief-stricken from the recent loss of is beloved Beth.

All four are caught in the past. All four are unable to let go. heir lives entwining in mysterious ways, can they help each ther to move on or will they always belong to the ghosts that aunt them?

Eve: A Christmas Ghost Story
(Psychic Surveys Prequel)

What do you do when a whole town is haunted?

In 1899, in the North Yorkshire market town of Thorpe Morton, a tragedy occurred; 59 people died at the market hall whilst celebrating Christmas Eve, many of them children. One hundred years on and the spirits of the deceased are restless still, 'haunting' the community, refusing to let them forget.

In 1999, psychic investigators Theo Lawson and Ness Patterson are called in to help, sensing immediately on arrival how weighed down the town is. Quickly they discover there's no safe haven. The past taints everything.

Hurtling towards the anniversary as well as a new millennium, their aim is to move the spirits on, to cleanse the atmosphere so everyone – the living and the dead – can start again. But the spirits prove resistant and soon Theo and Ness are caught up in battle, fighting against something that knows their deepest fears and can twist them in the most dangerous of ways.

They'll need all their courage to succeed and the help of a little girl too – a spirit who didn't die at the hall, who shouldn't even be there…

Psychic Surveys Book One:
The Haunting of Highdown Hall

"Good morning, Psychic Surveys. How can I help?"

The latest in a long line of psychically-gifted females, Ruby Davis can see through the veil that separates this world and the next, helping grounded souls to move towards the light - or 'home' as Ruby calls it. Not just a job for Ruby, it's a crusade and one she wants to bring to the High Street. Psychic Surveys is born.

Based in Lewes, East Sussex, Ruby and her team of freelance psychics have been kept busy of late. Specialising in domestic cases, their solid reputation is spreading - it's not just the dead that can rest in peace but the living too. All is threatened when Ruby receives a call from the irate new owner of Highdown Hall. Film star Cynthia Hart is still in residence, despite having died in 1958.

Winter deepens and so does the mystery surrounding Cynthia. She insists the devil is blocking her path to the light long after Psychic Surveys have 'disproved' it. Investigating her apparently unblemished background, Ruby is pulled further and further into Cynthia's world and the darkness that now inhabits it.

For the first time in her career, Ruby's deepest beliefs are challenged. Does evil truly exist? And if so, is it the most relentless force of all?

Psychic Surveys Book Two:
Rise to Me

"This isn't a ghost we're dealing with. If only it were that simple..."

Eighteen years ago, when psychic Ruby Davis was a child, her mother – also a psychic – suffered a nervous breakdown. Ruby was never told why. "It won't help you to know," the only answer ever given. Fast forward to the present and Ruby is earning a living from her gift, running a high street consultancy – Psychic Surveys – specialising in domestic spiritual clearance.

Boasting a strong track record, business is booming. Dealing with spirits has become routine but there is more to the paranormal than even Ruby can imagine. Someone – something – stalks her, terrifying but also strangely familiar. Hiding in the shadows, it is fast becoming bolder and the only way to fight it is for the past to be revealed – no matter what the danger.

When you can see the light, you can see the darkness too.

And sometimes the darkness can see you.

Psychic Surveys Book Three:
44 Gilmore Street

"We all have to face our demons at some point."

Psychic Surveys – specialists in domestic spiritual clearance – have never been busier. Although exhausted, Ruby is pleased. Her track record as well as her down-to-earth, no-nonsense approach inspires faith in the haunted, who willingly call on her high street consultancy when the supernatural takes hold.

But that's all about to change.

Two cases prove trying: 44 Gilmore Street, home to a particularly violent spirit, and the reincarnation case of Elisha Grey. When Gilmore Street attracts press attention, matters quickly deteriorate. Dubbed the 'New Enfield', the 'Ghost of Gilmore Street' inflames public imagination, but as Ruby and the team fail repeatedly to evict the entity, faith in them wavers.

Dealing with negative press, the strangeness surrounding Elisha, and a spirit that's becoming increasingly territorial, Ruby's at breaking point. So much is pushing her towards the abyss, not least her own past. It seems some demons just won't let go...

Psychic Surveys Book Four:
Old Cross Cottage

It's not wise to linger at the crossroads...

In a quiet Dorset Village, Old Cross Cottage has stood for centuries, overlooking the place where four roads meet. Marred by tragedy, it's had a series of residents, none of whom have stayed for long. Pink and pretty, with a thatched roof, it should be an ideal retreat, but as new owners Rachel and Mark Bell discover, it's anything but.

Ruby Davis hasn't quite told her partner the truth. She's promised Cash a holiday in the country but she's also promised the Bells that she'll investigate the unrest that haunts this ancient dwelling. Hoping to combine work and pleasure, she soon realises this is a far more complex case than she had ever imagined.

As events take a sinister turn, lives are in jeopardy. If the terrible secrets of Old Cross Cottage are ever to be unearthed, an entire village must dig up its past.

Psychic Surveys Book Five:
Descension

"This is what we're dealing with here, the institutionalised..."

Brookbridge housing estate has long been a source of work for Psychic Surveys. Formerly the site of a notorious mental hospital, Ruby and her team have had to deal with spirits manifesting in people's homes, still trapped in the cold grey walls of the asylum they once inhabited. There've been plenty of traumatic cases but never a mass case - until now.

The last remaining hospital block is due to be pulled down, a building teeming with spirits of the most resistant kind, the institutionalised. With the help of a newfound friend, as well as Cash and her colleagues, Ruby attempts to tackle this mammoth task. At the same time her private life is demanding attention, unravelling in ways she could never imagine.

About to delve deep into madness, will she ever find her way back?

Blakemort:
A Psychic Surveys Companion Novel
(Book One)

"That house, that damned house. Will it ever stop haunting me?"

After her parents' divorce, five-year old Corinna Greer moves into Blakemort with her mother and brother. Set on the edge of the village of Whitesmith, the only thing attractive about it is the rent. A 'sensitive', Corinna is aware from the start that something is wrong with the house. Very wrong.

Christmas is coming but at Blakemort that's not something to get excited about. A house that sits and broods, that calculates and considers, it's then that it lashes out - the attacks endured over five years becoming worse. There are also the spirits, some willing residents, others not. Amongst them a boy, a beautiful, spiteful boy...

Who are they? What do they want? And is Corinna right when she suspects it's not just the dead the house traps but the living too?

Thirteen:
A Psychic Surveys Companion Novel
(Book Two)

Don't leave me alone in the dark...

In **1977**, Minch Point Lighthouse on Skye's most westerly tip was suddenly abandoned by the keeper and his family – no reason ever found. In the decade that followed, it became a haunt for teenagers on the hunt for thrills. Playing Thirteen Ghost Stories, they'd light thirteen candles, blowing one out after every story told until only the darkness remained.

In **1987**, following her success working on a case with Sussex Police, twenty-five year old psychic, Ness Patterson, is asked to investigate recent happenings at the lighthouse. Local teen, Ally Dunn, has suffered a breakdown following time spent there and is refusing to speak to anyone. Arriving at her destination on a stormy night, Ness gets a terrifying insight into what the girl experienced.

The case growing ever more sinister, Ness realises: some games should never be played.

This Haunted World Book One:
The Venetian

Welcome to the asylum…

2015

Their troubled past behind them, married couple, Rob and Louise, visit Venice for the first time together, looking forward to a relaxing weekend. Not just a romantic destination, it's also the 'most haunted city in the world' and soon, Louise finds herself the focus of an entity she can't quite get to grips with – a 'veiled lady' who stalks her.

1938

After marrying young Venetian doctor, Enrico Sanuto, Charlotte moves from England to Venice, full of hope for the future. Home though is not in the city; it's on Poveglia, in the Venetian lagoon, where she is set to work in an asylum, tending to those that society shuns. As the true horror of her surroundings reveals itself, hope turns to dust.

From the labyrinthine alleys of Venice to the twisting, turning corridors of Poveglia, their fates intertwine. Vengeance only waits for so long…

This Haunted World Book Two:
The Eleventh Floor

A snowstorm, a highway, a lonely hotel…

Devastated by the deaths of her parents and disillusioned with life, Caroline Daynes is in America trying to connect with their memory. Travelling to her mother's hometown of Williamsfield in Pennsylvania, she is caught in a snowstorm and forced to stop at The Egress hotel – somewhere she'd planned to visit as her parents honeymooned there.

From the moment she sets foot inside the lobby and meets the surly receptionist, she realises this is a hotel like no other. Charming and unique, it seems lost in time with a whole cast of compelling characters sheltering behind closed doors.

As the storm deepens, so does the mystery of The Egress. Who are these people she's stranded with and what secrets do they hide? In a situation that's becoming increasingly nightmarish, is it possible to find solace?

A note from the author

As much as I love writing, building a relationship with readers is even more exciting! I occasionally send newsletters with details on new releases, special offers and other bits of news relating to the Psychic Surveys series as well as all my other books.

Simply go to my website – www.shanistruthers.com – and sign up!